Praise for the Food Lovers' Village Mysteries

"A pleasing read with a thoughtful heroine, a plethora of red herrings, and some foodie tips."

—*Kirkus Reviews*

"A lighthearted and amusing story with the added bonus of several yummy recipes."

—*Mystery Scene*

"*Treble at the Jam Fest* has all the necessary elements to satisfy cozy mystery lovers: likeable, believable characters, a fast-moving plot, and a logical ending. Great fun!"

—*Suspense Magazine*

"A delicious mystery as richly constructed as the layers of a buttery pastry. Wine, enchiladas, and song make for a gourmet treat in the coziest town in Montana!"

—Krista Davis, *New York Times* bestselling author of the
Domestic Diva Mysteries

"Leslie is a fellow foodie who loves a good mystery and it shows in this delightful tale!"

—Cleo Coyle, *New York Times* bestselling author of the
Coffeehouse Mysteries

"Music, food, scenery and a cast of appealing characters weave together in perfect harmony in Leslie Budewitz's latest book."

—Sheila Connolly, *New York Times* bestselling author of the
Orchard Mysteries and the County Cork Mysteries

Books by Leslie Budewitz

Food Lovers' Village Mysteries

Death al Dente
Crime Rib
Butter Off Dead
Treble at the Jam Fest
As the Christmas Cookie Crumbles
Carried to the Grave and Other Stories

Spice Shop Mysteries

Assault and Pepper
Guilty as Cinnamon
Killing Thyme
Chai Another Day
The Solace of Bay Leaves

Nonfiction and Cookbooks

*Books, Crooks and Counselors: How to Write Accurately About
Criminal Law and Courtroom Procedure*

Contributor

*The Cozy Cookbook: More than 100 Recipes
from Today's Bestselling Mystery Authors*
The Mystery Writers of America Cookbook
Writes of Passage: Adventures on the Writer's Journey
How to Write a Mystery: A Handbook by Mystery Writers of America

Writing as Alicia Beckman

Bitterroot Lake

CARRIED
TO THE
GRAVE
AND OTHER STORIES

A FOOD LOVERS' VILLAGE MYSTERY

LESLIE BUDEWITZ

Contents

Carried to the Grave

"Many of us came to know our sister in Christ, Gwendolyn, through her extended family, and her generosity to our friends and neighbors."

The Reverend Anne Christopherson opened her arms, the sleeves of her gold-trimmed white robe reminding me of the wings of a bird. The effect was highlighted by a ray of early afternoon sun streaming through the wide clerestory window above the altar as the good reverend beamed down at that extended family.

It was easy to tell the relatives from the friends packing the pews of Jewel Bay United Methodist. The Gottfried-Taylor bloodline bore dark eyes and strong brows, and dark hair gone pure white in the older generation. Granny G—everyone called Gwendolyn Gottfried Taylor that, related or not—had kept a full shimmery white crown until her death last week at ninety.

My seat, near the back on the outer aisle, gave me a decent view of the front row, where my village neighbors, Wendy Taylor Fontaine and her husband, Max, sat with her parents, her two older brothers, and their wives and kids. Behind them, on both sides of the aisle, sat Granny G's brothers and sisters and their families, three and four generations deep.

"I remember well," Reverend Anne said, "as a classmate of her granddaughter, Wendy, how Gwendolyn taught the entire third-grade class how to use frosting and plastic bags to make bunny ears on our Easter cupcakes. Some of us learned those lessons better than others."

The smile she aimed at Wendy, the village baker, spread through the gathering. Thinking of Granny G made my eyelids hot and my throat swell. No matter how expected, death always hits us like a surprise.

"Granny G attended every school and church event for her children, grandchildren, and great-grandchildren. The choir counted on her clear soprano to lead them through the most challenging hymns. And the rest of us counted on her cakes and pies at church socials." Another smile, another ripple of amusement. "She epitomized the volunteer spirit that makes this community such a gem, treating each and every one of us like family, in the truest sense."

Near the front of the church, someone let out a muffled cry, followed by the soft and not-so-soft murmurs of those whose peace and comfort was being disturbed. I craned my neck to see a thin, older woman push her way out of the pew and into the side aisle. Corinna Gottfried, Granny G's youngest sister. A teacher in Spokane, two hundred miles way, recently retired. Corinna didn't spend much time in Jewel Bay, and I barely knew her. Unlike the rest of the family, she had soft red hair that appeared natural, though she had to be nearly seventy, a smattering of freckles on her pale cheeks.

Those cheeks were drawn now as she marched down the aisle, her pale eyes not moist with grief, but flashing. In anger? Or something else?

Did I hear actual whispers, or just the tiny movements of the multitudes as we turned to watch? Impossible to say. Church mice might be quiet, but churches themselves are not.

From her spot between my sister and me, my mother squeezed my hand and I gave my attention back to the Reverend Anne.

"The Lord knows our hearts, and our histories," Anne said, "and commands us not to judge, but to love one another, in heart, thought, and deed. Let us pray."

The mourners rose with the shuffling of feet, the whispering of fabric, and more than one muttered groan that I chose to attribute to creaky knees rather than a reluctance to follow ministerial instruction. Anne had been two years ahead of me in high school, in the same class as Wendy and my sister, Chiara. Her great-grandmother had been a sort of foster child to our Murphy great-grandparents, after her father, a local minister, was murdered. Our families had been close ever since. Family lore also said our great-grandmother had solved the crime, but no one knew for certain. Anne had returned to Jewel Bay only a year ago, but I was sure that like me, and every kid who'd left and come back, she drew on her hometown knowledge every day.

And that made me wonder, as the sturdy preacher raised her face and arms to the heavens and called for the Lord's blessing on Gwendolyn Gottfried Taylor and those gathered here, whether the caution against judgment was one she shared at every funeral, or whether she had reason to remind this particular crowd of that most basic principle.

"I still can't imagine the girl I used to sneak out of study hall with for a smoke presiding on the altar," my sister said a few minutes later as we stood on the church's broad steps, blinking against the sunlight. Her name is said with a hard C, and rhymes with tiara, but she was no princess.

Neither was I, for that matter. "Senior year, I went to homecoming with her brother, Lonnie. He's a theoretical physicist. For NASA. The kid voted 'most likely to be jailed' is a rocket scientist."

"Erin, hush," my mother, Fresca, short for Francesca, said. One of the many challenges of running the family business has been learning to call my mother by her first name, at least when we were in the shop. "The Christopherson kids were late bloomers."

"I'll say. Lonnie showed up wearing the jacket and shirt to a rented tux, with board shorts and orange Chuck Taylors. My corsage was silk flowers he cut from the wreath on the front door with his pocketknife."

"Ohmygosh. I never heard that." Chiara had already left home for art school in San Francisco by then. "Mom didn't kill him? And Dad didn't send him home to change?"

"They didn't know until we showed up at the dance—they were chaperones. But the flowers matched my dress, so it was all good. Plus, he was a great dancer and an even better kisser."

"You girls are not helping me polish my glowing memories of your childhood," Mom said, but while the set of her jaw was stern, her dark eyes twinkled.

You would not have guessed we'd just left a funeral from all the laughter around us. Granny G's family were not a reserved bunch—siblings and cousins teasing each other, greeting friends with squeals of joy and slaps on the back.

Even Wendy, who'd swapped her chef's jacket and cherry-red rubber clogs for a sky-blue linen tunic and loose-fitting black pants, seemed to light up among them.

Actually, I knew her glow came from another source. I'd popped into the bakery one morning a few weeks ago and found her in the bathroom, retching. After ten years of marriage and two adoptions that fell through at the last minute, she was pregnant. Thrilled and terrified, she'd made me promise to keep quiet, under penalty of refusing to sell me another chocolate-filled croissant. Ever.

My sister says if you have a secret you need to keep, but you're itching to tell someone, tell Wendy. She'll carry it to the grave.

Along with her secret to perfect croissants.

A few feet away, Uncle Frank, Granny G's twin brother, told a story, hands rising and falling. Wendy smiled, saying nothing. Max grinned, his arm around her waist.

A gaggle of older women clustered around Frank's brother Al, the family flirt. Among Granny G's extended family were dairy farmers and teachers. The building supply manager, Wendy's oldest brother. And theater people—Wendy's parents had founded the Jewel Bay Playhouse and Summer Theater, now run by her middle brother.

No sign of Corinna.

But I did spot Kim Caldwell, my childhood BFF, on the far side of the crowd, and waved. After a long breach, we'd tentatively renewed our friendship. She'd taken a leave of absence from her job as a sheriff's detective to wrangle horses in California for a few months, and was home for a visit. If she'd made up her mind about her future, she hadn't told me.

"Chiara," Mom said, "you're going to the Taylors' house with me? And Erin, you're coming out later?"

We nodded. Taking food to the Taylors was a bit like that coals-to-Newcastle thing—Wendy and French-born Max run the bakery and bistro next door to the Merc, the hundred-plus-year-old brick building where my family has run some version of a grocery since 1910. Max had been running both kitchens while Wendy helped her mother keep vigil at Granny G's bedside. She hadn't so much as kneaded a loaf of bread in days.

But you can never have too much funeral food. Taking dishes to the family is a community ritual. A human ritual. When my father died, February of my senior year, bowls and platters covered the tables in the high school cafeteria after the service. He'd been a popular coach and history teacher and the Catholic church had been too small, so we'd held the funeral in the gym. Wendy and Anne had been away at college. But I remembered Lonnie Christopherson giving me a long, hard hug. One of the few kids who'd dared look me in the eye, let alone touch me. Like losing my father was contagious.

"Gotta get back to the Merc," I said. I blew them each a kiss. Wendy and Max had joined the circle around Uncle Al. No point interrupting to take my leave; I'd see them in a few hours.

I rounded the east corner of the church, heading for the WPA steps that link the residential area to the village, the original town site, now home to art, food, and all things mercantile and *touriste.*

"What were you thinking, stomping out of there like that?"

Startled, I looked around, but saw no one. I've been called the village snoop, as well as the unofficial village PI, and I admit to enjoying the role. I stopped and cocked an ear.

The man spoke again, hidden by the forsythia, a few of its yellow, star-like blossoms littering the cracked concrete sidewalk. "Disrespecting your sister, after all she did to hold this family together."

"Don't you be telling me what to do, Frank," a woman answered. "Gwen did that my whole life. She didn't die and leave that role to you."

Family feuds, I thought, as I hurried away. Another part of the human ritual.

"Erin, would you take these truffles to the Taylors' house?" Tracy, my shop assistant, held out a box of dark chocolate beauties. "Wendy loves my huckleberry chocolates."

"Everyone loves your huckleberry chocolates. If they don't, they need their pulse checked. Why don't you come with me and deliver them yourself?"

"No. I should stay here," she said, voice trembling, eyes downcast.

I'd have happily closed the Merc for an hour to let Tracy attend Granny G's service, but she'd refused. Midday, midweek, well before tourist season, a brief closure would not have touched our bottom line. But I hadn't pushed her. Funerals aren't everyone's cup of tea.

Neither, it seems, are the gatherings afterwards.

Fifteen minutes later, I parked my Subaru on the long dirt lane serving both the Taylors' house and Uncle Frank's. More than a century ago, two brothers had homesteaded next to each other, and their farmhouses, still in the family, stood a few hundred feet apart. The farms had long since been combined. Passersby often stop to photograph the twin dairy barns, one red and one white, standing out against the willows and cottonwoods and the glacier-topped mountains beyond.

No sign of my mother's car—I'd missed her and Chiara. Granny G and Frank had six living brothers and sisters, all younger, and judging by the long line of cars and trucks, every relative had descended on the home place.

Despite my family's earlier offerings, I'd felt my own tug of obligation. I reached into the backseat and grabbed Tracy's box of truffles and a tote bag with my contribution.

The soles of my Mary Jane clogs crunched the gravel. After she'd been widowed, Granny G had moved into a small house in town, not far from the school. She'd given this place to her eldest, Wendy's father, and Wendy grew up here. As I neared the white farmhouse, I slowed, drinking in the scent of old-fashioned lilacs with undertones of cow pie, and marveled at the massive clumps of tulips. Most of us have to fence our tulips or go without, but Frank's sons and grandsons run dairy cattle, and that keeps the pesky deer away.

On the spring-green lawn, Max, Wendy's brothers, and a swarm of twelve-and-unders played soccer. I'd tagged behind Chiara often enough when we were kids to know my way around the place, and bypassed the wide steps leading to the front porch and headed for the kitchen door.

Granny G had created a lovely flower garden along this side of the house, where heat from the brick path gave the early bloomers a boost. The tall purple iris seemed to have an edge over the white buds, but in the race for garden glory, never bet against a yellow flower.

I stopped to admire a bumblebee hopping between the bluets, one of the bravest blossoms in these mountain valleys.

"Don't you be telling her," a man said, his stern voice coming through an open window framed by a clematis heavy with buds. "Gwen carried that secret to the grave, and we damn well better do the same."

"If she knew," a woman answered, "it might help her understand a few things about the family. About her place in it."

Frank again, speaking not to Corinna, but to a different woman. His wife? I couldn't tell. Village snoop or not, their tone made me decidedly uncomfortable.

"I told you before, woman. She don't need to know."

I lingered in the garden, and by the time I opened the back door, the big kitchen was empty. The original farm kitchen had been thoroughly remodeled, but the homestead spirit remained in the painted cabinets, pine floors, and a butcher block counter, where I set my load. I opened two bags of Jewel Bay Critter Crunch and poured the nut-and-chocolate caramel corn into a spatterware bowl.

I carried my bowl into the dining room and set it on the long, lace-covered dining table. Chatter filtered in from the living room. I picked up a nearly-empty bowl of potato salad and a tray holding one lonely Caprese salad kabob—my mother's creation, skewers of cherry tomatoes, seasoned balls of mozzarella, and basil leaves, grilled and dressed with a thick blackberry balsamic vinegar.

Grief makes some people hungry.

It wasn't my home, but after a funeral, it felt natural to refresh the salads and the chips and dip. I ate the last kabob, then arranged tiny French tarts and *palmiers*, the French sugar cookies made of puff pastry, on a plate.

I was cutting a rhubarb crisp I found on the kitchen counter, with a note from a neighbor, when footsteps sounded behind me.

"Oh. I didn't know anyone was in here." The speaker's tone made me feel like a kid caught with the cookie jar.

I wiped my hand on my gray denim skirt and held it out. "Corinna, you probably don't remember me. I'm Erin Murphy, Tom and Francesca's younger daughter."

"Oh, yes. I'd have known you from your face. No recessive genes there." She ignored my hand, scanning me tip to toe with that "I know all about you, and I don't like it" look some teachers give cheeky students. She'd once been attractive, I could see, though not with the same dark-eyed intensity as the rest of the Taylor clan.

"Your mother and sister were here earlier," she continued. "Being the perfect family, unlike ours."

"I'm a friend of Wendy's," I said, trying to reclaim firmer ground. "I thought I'd refill the plates and trays before the kids come in. Unless you'd rather?"

Corinna's blue eyes flashed again, her brow darkening. She tugged her thigh-length cream cardigan across her chest. Her gaze swept from me to the bounty on the counters and back. Not bothering to reply, she stalked out of the kitchen and through the dining room. A minute later, I heard her footsteps pounding up the stairs to the second floor.

∞

"He went flying through the barn like a bat out of hell." Frank's hand went flying through the air, punctuating his story.

I stood in the doorway with the box of truffles. I'd never known whether Frank or Granny G was the elder of the twins, but it hardly mattered. He was presiding from the burgundy leather chair, enjoying the full house and the audience.

He wiped a tear of laughter from the corner of his dark brown eye. "Jumped out the hayloft and kept on running. Didn't come back till the supper bell rang."

The Frank I knew, the family raconteur, had replaced the harsher version of the man I'd overheard in the kitchen, chiding his wife. And earlier, lecturing Corinna outside the church.

"How was I supposed to know the shotgun wasn't loaded?" Uncle Al said from the matching armchair, but he was laughing, too. Two older women and Wendy's father, George, sat on one of two matching couches.

"Anybody comes after you with a shotgun, assume it's loaded," George Taylor said. "Especially if it's Frank. Those huckleberry truffles, Erin? Bring 'em right here."

His rich tones swung octaves, much like Granny G's had when she taught us girls how to roll out pie dough. His hands waved me over with the same broad, graceful gestures as his storytelling uncles. The family traits had served him well in the theater. George plucked two chocolates from the box, then I moved to the other couch, where Wendy sat with her mother, Lynn.

"Thank you, Erin," Lynn said. "Your family's taken good care of us today."

"As you did for us. The buffet is ready for the next go-round."

When I'd finished the truffle circuit and followed up with the coffeepot,

Lynn called to me. "Come sit. You'll love these marvelous pictures Corinna found, from when Granny G was a girl."

It's hard to imagine someone you've only known as an old lady having once been young. Not that she'd been old when I first knew her—just past sixty—but to a small child, everyone seems old.

A thick, black leather-bound album lay on the coffee table, open to two pages filled with shots of smiling men in uniform. Lynn picked up the album and flipped back to the beginning. I recognized this house, and Frank's. She paused at a photo of an unfamiliar barn, a shiny car with a long hood parked in front.

"'The 1937 Buick.'" I read the thick white script written across the bottom of the black-and-white snapshot.

"Destroyed when the barn burned," George said. "They couldn't get another car until after the war ended, though they rebuilt the barn right away."

"Priorities," Frank said, his voice booming. "That was 1941. I'd already enlisted. This loser waited to be drafted, after Pearl Harbor."

I glanced at Uncle Al, for once not laughing, not responding to the jibe. The great-aunts were silent, too.

Next came a family portrait. Seven kids, all sporting minor variations of the same face, all dark-haired, with intense brown eyes that managed to dance despite the army uniforms Frank and Al wore. The girls' classic 1940s dresses would make any vintage shop owner swoon.

The next shot showed Frank and Al, again in uniform, with a third soldier, light-haired and pale-eyed, his arm draped not-so-casually over a woman's shoulders. Behind them stood the new barn, framed and roofed but not yet sided.

"Is that your father-in-law with Granny G?" I asked Lynn. "I never knew him."

"No, George's parents didn't meet until after the war," Lynn said. "I don't know who that is."

"Oh, just some bloke who sniffed the scent of girls and followed us home on leave." Frank had ambled over and stood behind the couch. "Move on, move on."

Next came a collage of smaller shots. The two dark-haired soldiers and their fair-haired friend, in regular pants and white undershirts, tossing bales of hay. The same three men mugging for the camera. Then the friend, milking a cow, a grin on his handsome face.

"What happened to him?" I asked.

Out of the corner of my eye, I saw Frank stiffen. Across the room, Al's lips tightened and he bowed his head.

And I knew the fair-haired man hadn't returned, and his death had left a gap.

Lynn flipped to a shot of seven kids, ranging from Gwen and Frank on one end to the youngest on the other. The three boys wore dark pants and white shirts, the girls in dark skirts and white blouses with Peter Pan collars, but even without the matching outfits, anyone would have known they were siblings. Each stood beside a steer or a heifer, a 4-H banner hanging above them. The white ink across the bottom read "We Are Cattle Champions— 1936."

"That's my favorite," Wendy said, her voice softer than the others', but carrying the same expressive quality. She pointed to the middle girl, bent over a sweet-faced calf while her brothers and sisters aimed forward. "I love Aunt Louise. More interested in her calf than the camera."

"That didn't last," Al said. "She sang and danced with the USO in Seattle. She probably had her picture taken with more soldiers and sailors than anyone short of Betty Grable."

"What about Corinna?" I asked. "I don't see her in any of these pictures."

"She came along later," George said. "A caboose."

Frank dropped a half-eaten palmier on his saucer. "Enough of this fancy French food. Did you say there's pie?" He shuffled toward the dining room, and I spotted his wife, her brow furrowed, giving him a slight shake of the head. She hadn't spoken since I'd come in, but I was sure she'd been talking with Frank in the kitchen. *What had she said?*

Something about knowing something, and how it might help "her" understand her place in the family. Who had they been referring to?

"There's something underneath this one." Wendy slipped the Cattle Champions photo out of the black paper corners that held it to the page.

Above us, feet descended the stairs. A moment later, a screen door banged shut.

Beneath the Cattle Champions was another black-and-white, smaller, worn around the edges, not held by the framing corners. As if it had been tucked in hastily.

Gwen and the fair-haired soldier, embracing. Across the decades, I could see the longing in their eyes.

The three of us stared at the picture. Finally, Wendy turned it over. I squinted to read the faded penciled handwriting.

"Gwen Gottfried and Ira Cory. Once in a lifetime."

I stood in the kitchen, slicing ham. On the other side of the island, Wendy arranged miniature sweet peppers and tomatoes stuffed with herbed goat cheese on a blue-and-white platter.

"Your Uncle Frank might give you guff about the fancy French food, but I notice he eats his share," I said.

She sighed. "Is every family a rat's nest of contradictions?"

I spooned spicy mustard into a small white bowl. "Yep."

The backyard soccer game had ended, with Max's team declared the winner, the kids on the losing side grousing that they'd have won if the last goal had been counted.

Win or lose, they were all hungry. And as if hunger were infectious, the older crowd decided it was time for a little something. Then the gang of cousins who'd gone for a drive and the crew who'd taken the kayaks out on the river slough returned.

For the next half hour, Wendy and I fed the hordes. She mixed up lemonade and brewed iced tea. One of her brothers came in search of a beer, and I sent him to the dining room with another plate of ham and mustard and a basket of French rolls. Wendy added more buffalo meatballs to the Crock-Pot. We found bags of cut-up carrots and celery in the fridge and laid them out, with ranch dressing.

Half the family wandered through as we refilled bowls of four bean salad and tabbouleh. We sliced up quiche and pie, and made sure there were plenty of plates, forks, and napkins.

But there was no sign of Frank or Corinna.

"Zis is wonderful, all zis food, all zis family." Max sauntered in, for once not in chef's garb. He kissed Wendy on the mouth and patted her rear end.

"Make yourself useful," she said, and he gave me a wink on his way back to the dining room with a plate of iced cookies.

Then we were alone in the kitchen. Wendy's eyes welled with emotion, and I wrapped an arm around her.

"He's going to be a great dad," I said. "You're both going to be great parents."

Nothing like a family gathering to trigger all one's doubts and insecurities, along with the love and gratitude. Conversation continued in the living room and on the front porch, but muted, sandwiched between bites.

"We should wash the dishes." Wendy pulled away. "Pack up the leftovers."

"Leave them," I said. "Your mother will want something to do later." I darted into the dining room and grabbed two carrot cupcakes with cream cheese frosting. "Let's take a walk."

We headed out the side door and through the garden. In another week, the iris would be a marvel.

"Granny G planted these," Wendy said. "When she moved into town, she dug up some of her favorites, but she kept on collecting new ones. There's a nursery in Oregon that specializes in iris. Every January, she sat at her kitchen table, poring over their catalogs."

"I remember that garden. After school once, she punished you and Chiara by making you weed."

"Anne Christopherson was there, too. We'd soaped the windows on another girl's house, and Granny G was furious. But you—" She let out a soft sound, almost a cackle.

"Yeah, me. Stupid little sister who wanted to be part of the gang so badly, I ended up weeding most of the bed myself."

"We bribed you into not telling your parents by giving you a cupcake."

"Which Granny G would have given me anyway. I never did tell, by the way." As a rule, I don't like secrets. But I love cupcakes.

We circled to the front of the house, wandering onto the path that led past the duck pond. I finished my cupcake and stuffed the paper wrapper in my skirt pocket. Wendy hadn't touched hers.

"Which barn is where your dad's uncles chased each other?" I pointed at the two barns facing each other across an invisible property line.

"The white one," Wendy said. "The original barn. The tack room is filled with all kinds of junk. Tools, milk cans, broken chairs—you name it. That's where I found the blue canning jars Chiara made into the chandelier for the bakery."

"You know, I always knew Corinna was younger than the rest of Granny G's brothers and sisters, but I didn't realize she isn't much older than your dad."

Wendy broke off a bite of cupcake and ate it slowly.

"No husband, no kids?" I continued.

"She was married. They moved to Spokane ages ago," Wendy said. "Divorced. Granny G said it was because she didn't want kids."

"She always seemed different from the rest of the family," I said. "That strawberry-blond hair, the pale skin, but more than that."

Wendy lowered her eyes and tightened her jaw, her throat working.

Working on figuring out what to say, or how to tell me to hush up?

"Granny G taught me how to bake," Wendy said. "How to sift flour, cream butter and sugar, plump the raisins for Sunday morning scones. She knew about the baby"—Wendy's free hand went instinctively to her belly—"and it breaks my heart that she won't be here to get to know him. Or her."

A mallard emerged from the reeds at the edge of the pond and waddled toward us.

I had to ask. I wasn't the village snoop for nothing. "Wendy, in all those hours you spent by her bedside in those last few weeks, did she talk?"

Wendy's dark eyes darted toward me as she fed the duck a chunk of cupcake. "You mean, did she tell me her secrets?"

"Did she tell you about Corinna?" The duck stood in the middle of the path, its webbed feet spread wide, head raised. Wendy gave him another morsel and he squawked for more. In moments, we were surrounded—three ducks, four, five.

Beside me, Wendy stood still, hands raised, eyes about to pop. I felt myself stiffen as the ducks pressed in on us. The fun of feeding them turned ugly as their bills opened and shut, as they squawked and shoved. It felt like they could gobble us up if we didn't give them what they wanted.

"Aunt Wendy!"

A child's frightened cry broke the moment and we spun toward the white barn. Wendy's ten-year-old nephew ran toward us, the ducks scattering.

"Aunt Wendy, you have to come. It's Uncle Frank and Aunt Corinna."

The boy skidded to a stop in front of us and wiped his nose with the back of his hand. "She's got the shotgun."

∞

"You knew," Corinna said. Her tone was high and airy, as if not quite of this world.

Wendy and I stood in the shadows just inside the barn. We'd sent the boy to get his father and make sure someone called the sheriff.

"You always knew," she continued, "that I wasn't who I thought I was. Don't you move."

Seated in an old ladder-back chair, Frank froze, the shotgun Corinna held aimed at his chest.

"Gwendolyn," she said, her tone a sneer though I couldn't see her face. "Everyone praised her family values. Her generosity. She sure welcomed your friend Ira Cory, didn't she? But she didn't welcome me."

The soldier in the photos. The one who didn't come back.

The one Gwendolyn named her daughter—his daughter—for, and who'd inspired her love of iris.

"Everyone called me the caboose. The surprise." Her words darkened and she gripped the gun with both hands. It couldn't be the shotgun from Frank's story—or could it? Wendy had said the tack room was crammed with junk. If she'd found ammo, too, Corinna would know how to load the gun. She was a farm girl. "They all knew, didn't they? And I was the fool, always feeling different, not having a clue why until today. Until those photos."

"Corinna," Frank said, his voice shaking. "If he'd survived the war, they would have gotten married. She did what she thought was best, letting our parents raise you as if you were their own—"

"Shut up." She raised the gun, her hands tight on the stock. Her stretched-out sweater had fallen off one shoulder, the loose fabric bunched above her elbow. "She told you to keep your mouth shut and you did. But I had a right to know."

"You didn't see how Ira's death devastated her. She did her best in a bad situation."

"I didn't see because no one told me. Because you were all ashamed of me. Of the secret." Her fingers inched dangerously close to the trigger. Late afternoon sun streamed in through an upper window and picked her out like a spotlight, the dust motes all that moved.

"No, Corinna." Frank tried for a soothing tone. "We were never ashamed of you. We all loved you, prickly as you were. Seeing you, knowing she couldn't tell you, nearly broke Gwen's heart."

I glanced at Wendy, finger to my lips, and slipped into the shadows. The smells of hay and manure clung to the air, and I prayed I wouldn't sneeze as I crept up behind Corinna.

"But times were different. We were protecting you from the gossip, the hurtful things people said back then." Frank was still talking. With the sun in his eyes, he couldn't see me, but Wendy could.

"Keep your mouth shut now, you stinking old man," Corinna said. "You're not my brother. And I don't want to claim you as my uncle. I'm the oldest grandchild, not George. Precious George who got all the attention, while quiet, mousy Corinna got shoved aside. 'Be quiet, Corinna. Be a good girl, Corinna.'"

The cavalry would arrive any minute. I had to get to Corinna first, so we wouldn't be burying anyone else.

"You were my favorite aunt," Wendy said from the doorway, her voice low but assured. Corinna swiveled toward her, the gun barrel wavering. "You gave me my first Barbie doll, with the skating outfit and the little white rubber figure skates."

"You!" Corinna said. "How much did you hear?"

Wendy held out a hand. "I guessed ages ago, Aunt Corinna, when I took a genetics class in college. Last week, Granny G and I looked through the old albums, and that's when she told me the rest. She loved Grandpa, but not like she loved Ira."

"What about me?" Corinna let out a sob. "She never loved me like she loved your father and her other children."

"I think she loved you the most," Wendy said, as I moved carefully, quietly behind the mad woman. "You were all she had left of him."

"I don't believe you." Corinna raised the shotgun, aiming first at Frank, then Wendy.

"I'd never seen the picture of her with your father until today," Wendy said. "You look just like him. Anyone could see how much they loved each other. It was a different time, like Uncle Frank says. They did their best in a terrible time."

Corinna lowered the gun and I took the final step. I jammed my hands onto her shoulders. Pulled the sweater down, pulled her arms down, knocked the gun to the ground, away from the old man and my pregnant friend.

Shouts and footsteps filled the air as Wendy's husband and brothers surged into the barn. Max led Wendy away, while one brother took charge of Corinna and the other helped the old man out of the chair.

My hands shook as I broke open the shotgun. Empty.

I took a deep breath and crossed the barn to the tack room. Hung the gun on a hook on the wall and closed the door tightly before walking out into the sunshine.

I used my hip to open the screen door and one foot to keep it from banging shut. I handed Kim Caldwell a glass of lemonade and sat beside her on the top porch step.

"You're not going to tell me what really happened?" she asked. Kim had arrived moments behind the uniformed deputies. Despite being officially on leave, she'd responded when she heard the call. We'd all insisted nothing had happened, apologizing for the unnecessary summons.

"Just a little argument," I said. Max had taken Wendy home. Lynn Taylor was sitting upstairs with Corinna, in her old bedroom. "You know how tempers can flare at reunions. A little talk, a little time, and everything will be fine."

A dark green Toyota pulled up, the blond minister at the wheel.

"Then why," Kim said, "is Reverend Anne here?"

My hand tightened on the icy glass, then relaxed, and I took a sip.

"Some stories are better left untold," I replied.

Carried to the grave.

Pot Luck

ront Street looked like a giant potluck.

This was Autumn Fest. All summer long, Jewel Bay, Montana, the Food Lovers' Village, is about other people. The tourists, astonished to find a town bursting with art galleries, live theater, and great food high in the Northern Rockies. The summer people, often with deep roots, who nestle into the valley's embrace for a few weeks every year.

But this was the festival we'd created for ourselves, the hometown folks. On the second Saturday in October, we turn Front Street into a buffet, selling tickets to raise money for a scholarship program. All week, I'd been crossing my fingers and rubbing my lucky stars for good weather. We locals pride ourselves on our rugged nature and proclaim our love for winter, but it's a lot easier to eat finger food and swap stories over casseroles if you can actually feel your fingers.

And I was in charge of those casseroles, grateful that was all that was on my plate today. That and running the Merc. If I get involved in something, I tend to wind up running it. It's a family trait. Call the Murphy women "take charge" or reframe our bossiness as leadership skills; I don't care. Just don't call me the morning of the Big Event to say you won't be able to bring your stuffed cabbage rolls or help staff the tables because you have to take your dog to the groomer when you knew that days, even weeks, ago.

Volunteers. They're the lifeblood of a small town and the bane of every organizer's existence.

"All set," Tracy, my shop assistant, said as she surveyed her work. I can organize just about anything, but she makes it look good. Front Street, our main drag, was closed off for the day so booths could be set up without blocking sidewalks and shop entrances.

Tracy and Lou Mary, sales clerk extraordinaire, had covered the long plastic tables with leaf-print cloths. They'd made holders out of twigs for the matching paper napkins. Surgically altered pine cones held place cards identifying each dish and its creator. Lou Mary, who is even bossier than I am, directed Adam, my fiancé, as he ran a heavy extension cord out the shop's door to a power strip, well-secured with duct tape to prevent tripping. Giant bouquets of sunflowers, teasel, and wheat stalks beckoned. A canning jar tied with ribbon held this year's prizes, wooden spoons hand-carved of cherry from my family's orchard.

And it all echoed the display in the front windows of Murphy's Mercantile, the grocery my great-grandfather built more than a century ago out of pale gray bricks made from clay dug at the foot of the mountains. These days, it's a thriving local foods market.

"Erin! I'm here!" a voice called. I turned to see Nan Crawford, cradling what looked like a baby bundled in too many blankets. Her white-haired husband, Joe, trailed behind her, pulling a cooler on wheels.

Adam dashed forward to take the bundle.

"Careful," I said. "Don't drop the front-runner." Every year since the festival began, Nan's elk medallions with mustard-thyme cream sauce had taken home the prize for best casserole. Except the year a prankster sneaked psychedelic mushrooms into the chicken and biscuits with gravy.

The Crawfords lived in a waterfront condo complex just across the bridge at the south end of town, so walking made more sense than driving and trying to park. Despite the exercise, Nan looked perky and stylish in a fringed suede jacket, a stack of bracelets on her wrist.

"It wouldn't be fall without Autumn Fest," Nan said. "I got carried away. Made too much to fit in the cooler. The warmer, I should call it. This is not a dish that can be served cold."

"And it wouldn't be Autumn Fest without you. We'll tuck these inside until it's time to serve." Though the skies were clear, the air did have a nip to it. I reached for the handle of the cooler and Joe gave me a big smile, but there was something vacant in his expression, as though he knew he should know me but couldn't place me. As though he didn't quite understand what I was doing.

"I'll take that," I said, and only then did he release his grip. Nan held the door and I boosted the cooler over the threshold.

Inside, Adam set Nan's bundle on the steel counter that separates our commercial kitchen from the shop floor. I unwrapped it, the steamy aroma tickling my nose, and opened the cooler, then slid the red-and-white baking dishes into the warm oven. Heidi at Kitchenalia, the kitchen shop across the street, had started selling the dishes this past summer. I'd bought several myself. Then I checked on my rigatoni, making sure it didn't dry out.

"Any chance you kept some of that for us?" Adam said. "Only problem with all these food events is that by the time we get the chance to eat, the good stuff's gone."

I pointed to a square baking dish, covered in foil, on the back of the stove. "After town clears out, we'll have our own little feast in the courtyard."

"See why I love you?"

When Adam smiles at me, I feel like the luckiest woman alive. We met in college fifteen years ago, but truth be told, I'd barely noticed him, despite his gorgeous black-coffee eyes and dark curls, his broad shoulders and long legs. How could I possibly have overlooked that smile? Because I was wrapped up tight in my own life, in the grief over my father's unexpected death a few months earlier. After graduation, I'd moved out to Seattle, working my way up the grocery side of SavClub, the international warehouse chain. It was a good career and a good life, but when my mother asked me to come home and take over the business, I hadn't hesitated. The Merc, and Jewel Bay, are in my blood. Town surprised me in the ways it had changed—and the ways it hadn't—while I was gone. But the biggest surprise had been to find Adam Zimmerman living here, in my hometown, after a decade wandering the globe in search of outdoor adventure. Now he runs kids' programs and wilderness camps at the local athletic club.

Call it coincidence or fate. Divine intervention. I call reconnecting with him the best thing that ever happened to me. We'd gotten engaged last spring beneath an old tree in my family's orchard and were planning a Christmas Eve wedding.

We released each other from a long slow kiss. I ran a hand through my dark bob, then straightened my apron.

"I used to see Joe Crawford at the club," Adam said. "He's really aged."

"Funny how differently age affects people. Mom's sixty-five and she's like a kid compared to some people who aren't much older than she is." Though part of her sparkle came from her remarriage earlier this year, an event my siblings and I heartily approved of. "Nan's got to be seventy, but she's got plenty of energy. I always thought Joe was about the same age, but now he seems decades older."

"A touch of dementia? He was pretty mellow just now, but I'm sure it can be frustrating."

"More than a touch, I think. He was some kind of big-shot corporate finance guy. Summer people until he retired." They'd thrown themselves into volunteer work and community activities after moving here full-time, but from what I'd heard, he'd remained hard-driving. Or hard-ass, depending on your point of view.

By the time we got back outside, the Crawfords had moved up the street and Nan was chatting with Donna, owner of the liquor store. As usual, Donna was serving sparkling cider and mulled wine. Joe leaned over Nan's shoulder, and even from two doors away, I could see the twitch of exasperation on her face as she spoke to him. He turned, hands clasped behind his back, and grinned at passersby.

In front of the Merc, Tracy gave the tables one last loving touch, then headed in to mind the shop. I wriggled the produce cart outside. The season was winding down, but we still carried locally grown spinach, carrots, and squash, along with apples and plums. Braided garlic and clusters of dried morels hung from the canopy. I doubted we'd do much business today, not with the focus on food and friends. I adore summer in Jewel Bay—it's gloriously beautiful, and it's great to see town bustling—but I kinda don't mind when the craziness ends.

Lou Mary stood on the sidewalk, a faraway look on her face.

"Penny for your thoughts," I said.

"What? Oh. No. Not worth half that." She was a study in fall colors today, in an olive-green cashmere sweater and caramel pants, her coral nail polish the perfect complement to her reddish hair. Tortoiseshell readers hung around her neck on a gold chain. Though I'd worked with her for months now, much about her remained a mystery. Money, for example. She lived in the same pricey condo complex as the Crawfords. Her classic clothing looked expensive, stylish though clearly older. And yet, my mother had asked me to hire her because she needed a job. Whatever her secrets, Lou Mary could sell pasta to a hollow tree, and I'd learned a lot from her.

She handed me the clipboard holding the sign-up sheet for our category. Volunteers arrived with a motley mix of Crock-Pots, warming dishes, boxes, and coolers. My old school pal, Polly Easter Paulson, brought her chicken enchiladas, and her sister, Bunny Easter Burns, her tamale pie. You could always count on the Easter twins to be in sync, and to bring good food. Though I did think my enchiladas were better, thanks to the orange peel in the sauce. Heidi popped across the street to give us her eggplant Parmesan, in the ubiquitous red-and-white baking dish. Up and down the street, cooks delivered their entries to the appointed locations—appetizers, soups and stews, breads, pickles. Cakes, pies, and cookies. The very best of home cooking.

I dashed in to fetch my rigatoni and Nan's elk dish and nestled them into warming trays on the tables outside. Then the clock on the library tower struck noon. Lids were lifted, covers removed, and heavenly aromas filled the air—peppers and tomatoes, rich sauces, fragrant herbs. The sounds of conversation that had swarmed around us became the sounds of eating and appreciation. Volunteers helped Lou Mary and me fill plates.

"Ohmygosh," a woman from the bank said. "Those elk medallions are divine."

"If Nan ever says she's tired of bringing the same thing every year," Old Ned Redaway said, pointing his compostable fork at me, "you set her straight, Erin."

"Don't you worry," the bank woman interjected. "Nan likes taking home the prize too much."

We all laughed, but it was true. Nan Crawford wasn't the only one who turned what was meant to be a friendly cooking contest into a *Top Chef* rerun.

They drifted off and a round-headed, round-bellied man took their place. "You gonna take home the wooden spoon this year, Erin?" Gordon Springer asked. The pharmacist was an ardent supporter of anything involving food, which in a town that calls itself the food lovers' village meant plenty of opportunities to indulge.

"No, no. I'm just in it for the fun. Make sure your wife saves me one of her blondies."

"You bet," he said, taking his first bite of my rigatoni. "Mmm. Buffalo sausage?"

I nodded and he muttered an approving grunt, while two men in chef's whites surveyed the tables.

"I think I've seen this menu before," Ray Ramirez of the Bayside Grille said.

"Variety isn't a big spice among casserole cooks," I answered. "A taste of each? Except mine—I'm not entering the contest."

"Too bad," Tony Black said. He and his wife run the chalet-like Jewel Inn at the north end of the village. "Looks like it's Gordon's favorite."

"Gordon!" I play-swatted the pharmacist's hand as he helped himself to a second serving of rigatoni. "One per customer, or there won't be enough."

Tony and Ray were this year's judges. I give them much of the credit for Jewel Bay's culinary reputation, along with Wendy the baker and her husband, namesake of Chez Max, the French bistro. I like to think the Merc boosts the town's reputation, too, as do Kitchenalia and a handful of other establishments. A small town needs an identity and a draw, and we'd found ours.

From the looks the two men shared, I thought they'd found their winner. And I suspected it wasn't Nan and her elk medallions.

The chefs thanked us and moved on, Tony making a note on the back of an envelope.

"She can be a pain in the neck," the volunteer of the hour said in a low voice, and it took me a moment to realize she meant Nan. "But it's got to be incredibly difficult to see the man you married years ago turn into someone else. Joe is almost like a child at times."

"Excuse me, Erin," Lou Mary said. "I need a break."

Two spots of color bloomed high on her pale cheeks. I watched her step up the curb, her balance shaky. Her arthritic fingers clutched the doorframe as she paused, then stepped inside the Merc.

Was she ill? Had something she'd eaten disagreed with her? No one had complained about any of the dishes. I wasn't even sure Lou Mary had eaten anything—I hadn't. Once we start serving, the fun doesn't stop.

The thought of Lou Mary being seriously ill was too much to consider. We'd been going great guns all week and all morning. She'd be fine once she ate.

Another round of tasters converged on us and we served and chatted and served some more. I spotted the new sheriff's detective, Oliver Bello, better-dressed off duty than most men in town dressed for work. He'd moved here recently from Miami and the urban influence still clung to him. But he seemed to be enjoying himself.

There was nothing but a lonely mushroom left in Nan's casserole dish, so I took advantage of the lull to go inside for another pan of medallions.

As I'd predicted, the shop had made few sales and the Merc was empty except for Tracy and Lou Mary, sitting at the counter. A pile of used tissues sat in front of Lou Mary. Tracy shot me a worried look.

I put a hand on Lou Mary's back. "Is there anything we can do?"

She shook her head, the movement rattling the gold chain that held her glasses. "I'm sorry, Erin. After all these years, I shouldn't be such a mess. But seeing him today . . ."

Not understanding, I looked at Tracy, who mouthed a word to me. I frowned and she mouthed it again.

"Joe?" I said. "Why would . . . ohhh." How had I never put it together? When Lou Mary left me a note that a supplier had called or we were low on blackberry jam, she signed it with a bold *LM*, and the name on her paychecks was Lou Mary Vogel. But from the recesses of my brain, I pulled up her full name: Lou Mary Williams Crawford Vogel. As in Joe Crawford.

"And seeing what it's done to Nan," she was saying, "well, that could have been me. And I'm grateful and I'm ashamed and I'm worried."

"How long were you married?" I asked.

"Too long," she said, her tone hinting at the wisecracker I loved. "Joe was smart and hardworking and handsome as all get out. Tailor-made for the corporate world. He could see what everyone was doing and plan five steps ahead. And absolute hell to live with. We divorced ages ago, and I had twenty happy years with my David before he died."

David Vogel. I had never met him, but from Lou Mary's stories, it was clear they'd been a solid match.

"Sometimes it takes a second try to get it right," Tracy said, and she had reason to know.

"We vacationed in the area a few times, and I moved here after I was widowed. I never imagined they'd become my neighbors." Lou Mary added another tissue to the pile. "Still, it's hard to watch him deteriorate. Sometimes I think it's payback for what he put me through, but that's not a very charitable thought."

"But a perfectly understandable one." I straightened. "I'd better get back outside. Take as much time as you need. Head home, if you want."

I stepped around the counter into the kitchen—it was open to the shop floor so customers could watch while my mother rolled out her fresh pastas or Tracy made her chocolate truffles. The counters were covered with casseroles, many in the red-and-white dishes from Kitchenalia, and it took me a few tries to find another pan of elk medallions. The conversation with Lou Mary made me see Nan's obsession with the cooking contest in a new light. Kitchen therapy.

At the serving tables, I pulled the foil lid off Nan's dish and began cutting. The rich aroma of the thyme-studded sauce struck my nostrils, and as I served the next batch of guests, I tried to ignore the rumblings in my tummy.

Adam returned from his own volunteer duty, emptying trash cans. "Any chance you can break away for a bite?"

The Easter twins had just arrived to work the table for the final hour. "Erin, go," Bunny urged at the exact moment that Polly said, "Go, Erin." They made shooing motions with their hands.

And so we went, leaving them in charge. Mine isn't the only family of bossy women in town.

We were halfway up Front Street, halfway through slices of warm brioche spread with fresh butter from the creamery and raspberry jam that made the autumn day taste like summer, when I spotted Nan in the sculpture park next to the Playhouse. I followed her gaze to a tall bronze sculpture of a grizzly bear, ferocious even in still life. Joe darted out from behind the statue, raising his arms in a menacing imitation. I glanced at Nan, prepared to laugh with her at his antics. But as I watched, her expression turned from frustration to fear. A rock whizzed past her head and I glanced back at Joe, who had scooped up a handful of the egg-sized cobble surrounding the grizzly's giant feet. He threw another rock at Nan, who stood, frozen, then another. I screamed and dropped my bread, rushing to drag her behind a bronze mountain goat. It didn't give us full cover, but it helped, as Joe's rocks pelted the statue and bounced off with a metallic twang.

"Joe, stop," I heard Adam say. "Stop." I peered out. Adam had Joe's arms pinned behind his back, while Chef Ray held him from the front. Joe looked dazed, almost limp, next to the two younger, stronger men. Beside me, Nan whimpered.

I couldn't leave Nan to hunt for Detective Bello. I pulled the phone out of my apron pocket.

"No!" Nan cried. "Don't call the sheriff. He can't go to jail. Or the psych ward. He's not crazy. He's sick."

"He needs help, Nan. So do you."

"No," she repeated and unfolded herself from her protective crouch. "I'm his wife and I will take care of him. Joe, it's time to go home."

"If you leave now," I said, "you'll miss the announcement of the winners." Not that you need to be present to win, but it's more fun if you are. And from what I'd seen it seemed clear that Nan needed all the fun she could get.

"I didn't eat," Joe said, whining like a cranky toddler. "I want to eat!"

"I'll take him," Adam said. "We can snare a bite on our way."

"Better to take him straight home," Nan said. "I left a pan of elk medallions on the kitchen counter. It's a red-and-white dish, already baked. Just stick his plate in the microwave."

"Easy-peasy, as Erin would say," Adam replied, and I smiled despite the awful situation.

"Soon as he eats," Nan continued, "he'll fall asleep in his chair. Leave the TV on and come back downtown. He'll never know." She kissed Joe on the cheek, then turned to Ray. "Show time, Chef!"

"You sure about this?" I asked Adam in a low voice. "Want me to come?" Whatever fight had gotten into Joe seemed to have left him, but for how long?

"Nah. He can't be worse than some of the campers I've dealt with. Just bigger." He gave me that grin that made my toes warm. "You stay here. This is your deal." Adam enjoyed the village festivities, but just as much, he wanted me to enjoy them, and he knew events like this were good for both the town and the Merc.

"Okay. But don't hesitate to call for help if he gets out of hand, despite what Nan said."

I watched them leave, the tall, lanky, capable man my friends had dubbed Wilderness Guy and the white-haired man whose mind was deep in the grip of an unseen enemy. You make big decisions in life, like marriage, with big hope, committing to the unknowable future. But you never really believe the terrible things will happen to you, do you?

On the sidewalk lay my crumpled napkin and the bread I'd dropped. I knelt and scooped it up, not wanting someone to step in my mess.

"The Playhouse restrooms are open," Nan said, noticing my sticky palms. "Closer than the Merc."

"Perfect."

Fortunately, a woman on her way out held the door for me. I adore the Playhouse. The lobby had been remodeled since my days in the high school drama club, and the embossed ceiling tiles, mosaic-covered pillars, and painted benches give it a seriously whimsical mood. I washed the goo off my hands, then ducked into a stall. I learned long ago never to pass up the opportunity to pee in a clean, dry restroom.

"At some point, she's going to have to find a place that will take him," a woman said.

"Can you imagine?" another woman said. "She's got to think about herself. Her"—the sound of the water drowned out the rest of her words.

They had to be talking about Nan Crawford. I thought I'd heard the word "heart." Heartbreaking? My heart goes out to her? All that and more, no doubt.

The women were gone by the time I emerged and washed my hands a second time. Outside, on the sidewalk paved with bricks stamped with donors' names, I glanced around. Adam and Joe were long gone, down the street and across the bridge to the condo by the bay.

No sign of Nan. People were beginning to migrate toward the open area between Dragonfly Dry Goods and the Jewel Inn, the closest thing we have to a town square. Winners would be announced there.

I was suddenly ravenous. The closest tables were for appetizers. Pickings were slim, but I managed to score some yummy crab puffs and a hot artichoke dip on bruschetta that was light on the Parm and heavy on the mayo. Donna from the liquor store handed me a paper cup of mulled wine.

"Plenty more where that came from, darlin'," she said, her tone sympathetic. Word of Joe's tantrum had spread.

"Erin, I saved you some blondies," Margo Springer called from the cookie booth.

"Ohmygosh. They are soo good." She handed me a plastic bag and I slipped it into my apron pocket, then took the last lemon bar to eat now. "Perfect for later, after things quiet down."

She beamed. The staticky crackle of someone testing the sound system filled the air and we joined the crowd, eager to hear the results of both the scholarship drive and the cooking competition. My friend Kathy Jensen, chair of the event, climbed into the back of an old red farm truck, microphone in hand.

"Of all the festivals in Jewel Bay, Autumn Fest might be my favorite," she said. "This is the day when we come together as a community to celebrate the harvest and the great bounty of food, friendship, and generosity that has blessed our little town. Ticket sales and donations to our scholarship fund were more generous than ever, though we won't know the exact total until next week. Merchants, I need your ticket sales by Monday, please."

That reminded me that I hadn't yet turned in the proceeds from tickets we'd sold at the Merc. The envelope sat in the drawer of the antique brass cash register at our front counter.

Kathy went on to update us on previous years' scholarship winners and to recognize the major donors to the festival. Volunteers might power an event, but the expenses add up anyway.

"And now, the moment you've been waiting for. Chef Ray, Chef Tony." She handed off the microphone and Ray helped her down from the truck bed, then the two men hopped up.

"The envelope, please." Ray held out his hand. Tony pulled a long white envelope out of his hip pocket and brandished it before handing it over.

The crowd laughed. The chefs paid the requisite compliments to the organizers and volunteers and proclaimed that Jewel Bay truly was a food lover's village.

Then they started down the categories. The crab puffs won the appetizer award, with the second place spoon going to a puff pastry tart that sounded delish, and third to honey-mustard chicken bites that had been gone by the time I'd reached the table. They moved on to soups.

"Come on, come on," I heard a woman mutter. Nan, a few feet away.

The phone in my pocket buzzed and I pulled it out. Read Adam's text. *Courtyard. Need you NOW.*

I turned and ran.

When I say Jewel Bay is small, I mean it. I made the block and a half to the Merc in record time. I shoved open the front door and glanced around. Empty. Past the shop floor, past the kitchen, a hallway leads to our back door and the courtyard behind the shop. I rushed to the open door and stopped on the threshold. Over the sound of my thumping heart, I heard a siren in the distance. They'd have to come the long way, across the bridge and up Back Street, a.k.a. Back Alley, to avoid the crowd and the blocked-off streets.

Lou Mary lay on the cobblestones, Adam's fleece quarter-zip under her head. He knelt beside her while a few feet away, a highly disheveled Gordon Springer paced, speaking urgently into his phone.

I'd chalked her earlier pallor and imbalance up to the shock of seeing her former husband's condition. Had she been seriously ill and none of us had noticed?

"The EMTs are taking their time," Gordon barked into the phone. "Is there nothing else we can do before then?"

From the corner came the sound of someone choking back fear.

"Tracy!" I wrapped an arm around her shoulders. "What happened?"

"I don't know. They finished serving and everyone went to hear the winners announced. Lou Mary stayed behind. She wanted to fix a plate, but the dishes out front were nearly empty, so she helped herself from what was left in the kitchen."

Where we'd stashed the extra pans. The town cooks had been generous this year.

The siren was getting closer. Adam had two fingers on Lou Mary's neck. For the first time, I noticed the vomit covering the front of her sweater and caught a whiff of the sour smell.

"She came out here to eat." Tracy gestured to the courtyard, a sweet little refuge dotted with bistro tables and chairs. "Then, a few minutes later, I heard someone yelling to call 911. I ran out and found Adam kneeling beside her. Gordon came in while I was on the phone. He called an ER doc he knows. Erin, is she going to make it?"

That I couldn't answer.

"Stay here," I said, "in case they need anything." Tracy's lower lip trembled and I dashed back into the shop. Locked the front door and turned the sign to CLOSED. Cooks would come by to collect their dishes, and we'd need to tear down the tables out front, but all that could wait. I didn't want to have to think about the shop until I could think again.

In the kitchen, I grabbed several bottles of water. Casseroles, most in the familiar red-and-white dishes, littered the counters. Some were empty. One or two appeared undisturbed. Others, including my extra pan of rigatoni, had been opened and servings cut.

By the time I got back to the courtyard, the EMTs had arrived. Adam was leaning against the Merc's back wall next to Tracy. I handed them each a bottle of water. Adam took a long drink and pulled me close.

"Thank God you found her," I said. "What happened?"

"I don't know." His voice broke. "I just hope I found her in time." Adam had oodles of experience treating backcountry ailments and injuries, but this was a far cry from a bee sting or a sprained ankle.

Gordon sat at the nearest table, dwarfing the metal chair. I handed him a bottle and he took it gratefully. "The way the vomit smells—it could be poison."

"But from what? Everyone ate what she ate."

An EMT—his name escaped me—approached. "Her BP is stabilizing, and we got a line in. We're about ready for transport."

"That's good, right?" I asked.

"It's a good start," he replied. "Can you tell me about her medications, any health problems?"

Other than arthritis in her hands, I knew nothing about her medical history. I glanced at Gordon, who shook his head.

"I'll check her purse," Tracy said.

She was back in a flash with Lou Mary's mahogany leather bag. We found nothing medical inside except a tube of the balm she used for her hands. We sell it in the Merc, and she was its great advertisement.

"When the deputies arrive," the EMT said, "you'll want to give them her keys so they can search her home."

"The sheriff?" I asked. "You—you think there was a crime here?"

"Not for me to decide, but when something looks like it isn't natural causes . . ." He didn't finish the sentence. He didn't have to.

We watched as the EMTs loaded Lou Mary into the ambulance. At the last moment, I rushed to the gurney and grabbed her hand. "We love you, Lou Mary. Get better. You have to get better."

"Ell," she said, her voice barely a whisper. "Ell."

"Tell? Tell who?" She had no children, just a sister in another state. "Tell them what?"

Her forehead wrinkled in frustration. With her impaired speech or my impaired comprehension?

"The. Ell," she repeated, as an EMT prepared to close the door. I backed away, wondering what the ell she'd been trying to tell me.

I rejoined the others and turned to Adam.

"You get Joe settled?"

"Yeah. He didn't eat much—got kinda dizzy, said his stomach hurt. Started talking about hunting and his first wife. About the only coherent thing he said was that Nan kept Alka-Seltzer in the bathroom, but I couldn't find it. Tons of prescription bottles, but nothing for an upset stomach."

"That's strange. He said he was hungry, and Nan said the elk was his favorite dish. Ohhh, my gosh." I spun toward the alley but it was empty. The EMTs had left.

Lou Mary hadn't been saying "tell," or even "hell."

She'd been saying "elk."

"Call 911 again. Ask them to send EMTs to Joe and Nan's," I told Tracy. Then, to Gordon, "Detective Bello is roaming the village somewhere. Send him to the condo, STAT. Then find Nan Crawford."

They all nodded, wide-eyed.

"One more thing," I told Tracy. "Don't let anyone into the kitchen. Not even to collect a cooler or a dish. No one."

Our kitchen, I feared, had become a crime scene.

I grabbed Adam's hand and we sprinted down Back Street and across the bridge. When we got to the condos, he led the way to the Crawfords' place, a large end unit with a balcony and a killer view.

I wasn't at all sure that Joe had been asking Adam for Alka-Seltzer. I feared he'd been telling Adam that Nan had put something in the elk. She'd been too eager to get him home and fed. Had she poisoned the dish she'd left for him, knowing he'd scarf it down? But with what?

An image of Nan and that arm dripping with bracelets flashed into my mind. The easily-recognizable Tiffany silver links adorned with a simple heart. A Pandora bracelet dripping with beads and charms. And a medical alert bracelet. I could see it plain as day. A friend wore one for her bee allergy, another for diabetes.

And Nan's? I was betting on a heart condition. That's what Lou Mary had been referring to when she mentioned the toll Joe's decline had taken on Nan, and what the women in the restroom had been talking about. But I wouldn't know for sure until I saw those pill bottles.

For the second time this afternoon, I listened for the wail of an ambulance and urged it to hurry. I followed Adam inside.

"Joe?" he called. "It's Adam Zimmerman. Joe?"

We found Joe on the floor next to his recliner. I gagged at the smell.

Like Lou Mary, he'd vomited heavily, and when Adam checked his pulse, it was dangerously fast and irregular.

"Go watch for the EMTs," he told me. "Joe doesn't have time to lose."

My mission could wait. I ran down to the complex's main entrance and directed the ambulance to the Crawfords' condo. Then I slipped into the master bath. Covered my hand with the apron I was still wearing to sort through the bottles. Both Nan and Joe had a boatload of prescriptions, but one, for Nan, stood out. Three bottles, all empty.

In the living room, the EMTs continued to work on Joe. They were serious, intent, but I could tell they weren't holding out much hope. If—and it was a big if, but I'm not big on coincidence—Joe and Lou Mary had been poisoned by the same drug, had he gotten a bigger dose? Had the dementia weakened his system? Or was my beloved friend in as much trouble as her former husband?

They were strapping Joe onto the gurney when Detective Bello arrived. I couldn't hear his exchange with the crew chief, but the look on his face was grim. The EMTs wheeled Joe away, and moments later the siren began its cry. Bello finished stalking around the condo, then returned to the living room, where Adam and I huddled near the French doors overlooking the bay.

"Tell me all about it," he said. Adam went first, then Bello turned to me. "I presume you have a theory."

He may have been new in town, but my reputation had preceded me.

"Nan's specialty for the festival is a casserole. Elk medallions in cream sauce. She left a pan of them here for Joe, knowing he might want to come home before she was ready. She takes digoxin for a heart condition. There are three empty bottles in the master bath. I think she poisoned the dish, knowing Joe loved it. I don't know if she meant to kill him, or just make him sick enough that she could put him in a nursing home. Memory care. He's got dementia and it's pretty bad."

"So I hear," Bello replied, and I wondered if there was a history of trouble involving law enforcement.

"What I don't know," I said, grateful for Adam's arm around me, "is how Lou Mary was poisoned. Nan couldn't have known she'd eat the casserole. What if we'd served it as part of the festival? Half the town could have gotten sick. Unless something else happened to her. A reaction to a bad mushroom, maybe."

And I couldn't think of a reason Nan would go after Lou Mary. If Joe still paid her maintenance or alimony or whatever it's called, it couldn't have been much.

"We don't know what symptoms Lou Mary experienced before she collapsed," Adam said. "But at that point, her symptoms and Joe's were very similar."

"Even if someone had tampered with two dishes"—Bello was frowning—"how did one end up in the Merc?"

"What if," I said, remembering Lou Mary's comment that Joe could see five moves ahead of an adversary and beat them at their own game, "what if Joe poisoned a dish, intending for Nan to eat it later. Then she put it aside to take to the festival and poisoned another, for him? The dishes all looked alike." The bundle she'd been carrying, the extra dish that hadn't fit in the cooler.

I heard a muffled gasp behind me. Nan stood in the doorway, eyes wide, hands to her mouth. Gordon Springer stood behind her.

"Gordon," I said. "You're a pharmacist. Does what you saw in my courtyard look like digoxin toxicity?"

"Could be. But I'm pretty sure I've never filled a digoxin prescription for Nan."

I pictured the small orange bottles in the bathroom. The labels hadn't all been the same. Joe wasn't the only person in this marriage who could plan ahead.

"I don't know how she did it," I told the detective, "but I think you'll find that she filled her prescription at different pharmacies around the valley and built up a stash."

From the look on Nan Crawford's face, I thought we were going to have to call the EMTs yet again. But no vertigo or vomiting this time, no delirium or abdominal pain. It was the faint of the guilty. Gordon caught her before she hit the floor and Adam checked her pulse—strong and steady—while Bello called for backup. She was only out for a minute or two, and when she came around, she confessed, horrified to realize that the husband she had tried to poison had done the same to her. I was too horrified to ask any questions, leaving it all to Bello. There are times when the trained professionals really are the right people for the job.

Backup arrived, with a crime scene unit. Another was on its way to the

Merc. Deputies cuffed Nan and led her away. Bello took a call, motioning for us to wait before stepping into the kitchen, out of sight and earshot.

"Do you think she wanted him to die," I asked Adam and Gordon, "or just wanted out of the constant demands of caring for him? And what do you think Joe intended?"

But before they could answer, Bello returned, call finished.

"That was my deputy in the ER. Mrs. Vogel is doing well. They want to keep her overnight—"

"Can we see her?" I burst out.

"I imagine so. Unfortunately, Mr. Crawford died en route."

Murder or a mercy killing? I couldn't say, but the horror of it all hit me in the heart.

Any man's death diminishes me, I thought, recalling the poet's words, *because I am involved in mankind.*

That's what it meant to be part of a community. To feel the joy, and some days, the pain.

It was midweek before we reopened the Merc. The crime scene unit had finished their work in our kitchen and courtyard by Sunday, but I wasn't in the mood for selling soap and soup mix, for hawking honey and huckleberry jam. Lab tests confirmed that the mushrooms were innocent; digoxin was found in both the elk medallions Nan had left at home and an identical dish they'd brought to the Merc. I packed up my beautiful red-and-white pans and sent them to a friend. Adam and I were working on our wedding gift registry; we'd choose new bakeware, in another color.

Polly's enchiladas had won the casserole category. Margo Springer's Butter Rum Blondies took the cookie prize and she finally agreed to give me the recipe, in exchange for my rigatoni recipe and a pound of buffalo sausage. A pricey trade, but worth it.

Normally not much for letting other people help her, Lou Mary let Tracy, my mother, and me fuss as we got her settled back home. Turned out she was still the beneficiary of some of Joe's assets, and if Nan was convicted of murder, might well inherit a bundle.

"You could buy a new condo," I suggested. "One without a view of a murder scene."

"No," Lou Mary said. "This place is perfect. Plus, it's close to the Merc. I can walk to work."

"Oh, thank goodness," I said. "It wouldn't be the Merc without you."

"No," she agreed. "It wouldn't."

Later that week, I ran into Detective Bello at the liquor store.

"Well, if it isn't our friend the murder magnet," he said, gripping a bottle of gin.

"How can you joke about it?" I said. "Lou Mary could have died."

"She's too stubborn for that. Just like you."

"I prefer to think of myself as determined." Like generations of women before me, who helped build this town.

"That you are, Ms. Murphy," he said. "That you are. And it's our good luck."

The Christmas Stranger

*C*an you make copies yourself?"

I turned to see an elfin man, no taller than my five-five, dark-haired though he had to be well past seventy, his skin weathered from time spent in sunnier climes than northwest Montana.

"Oh, but you'd still have to wait in line to pay," he continued, eyebrows creasing in concern as he surveyed the crowded shipping depot.

It was eight days before Christmas and I was the last person in line. Six people ahead of me, each with at least one box to ship. Like me, half were multitasking, fiddling with their phones while they waited.

"Busiest day of the year," I heard a clerk say, "and the computers are cranky. Everything's taking twice as long."

At my feet were three large plastic tubs filled with packages headed all across the country. Not my personal holiday shopping, you understand, but locally made jam, pasta sauces, and soap, all ordered from the Merc, the business I run in my family's hundred-year-old grocery in the heart of the village of Jewel Bay. Not to mention bags of Cowboy Roast, our custom-blended coffee, and boxes of truffles.

So. Many. Truffles.

"I'll show you," I said. It was the last day we'd promised delivery in time for Christmas, though I suspected I'd be standing here tomorrow and the day after that. "It's easy. You can sneak ahead to pay—no one will mind."

I slipped my phone in my bag and led him to one of the three giant machines that stood against the wall. In the modern world, copy machines seem like techno-tyrannosaurs, gulping up your documents at the touch of a button and doing mysterious things before spitting them out again. On this particular model, you never knew which mouth or other body part the copies would emerge from. I didn't blame the man for being daunted.

"Two copies," he said, handing me his original and standing well back, clearly expecting me to make the copies. No biggie.

"Do you want me to unstaple them, or can I fold over the top page to copy the second?"

"What? Oh, no. Whatever's easier. I hate technology." He lowered his voice on that last comment, as if he didn't dare utter such a dangerous opinion in public.

"Line it up like this," I said, "then push Copy and the quantity, and hit Start."

"Two," he repeated, and I lowered the lid and pushed the buttons. We waited while pulleys pulled and lights lit up, while the copier drew paper through its cavernous bowels, then went silent. I lifted the lid and positioned the second page.

"Seems like it's taking over our lives," he continued, still on the techno rant, but as rants go, it was mild. Almost sweet.

"It does," I said. "I run the Merc, the local foods market next to Red's Bar, and I'll admit, between the sales and inventory system, social media, and our own online sales platform, sometimes I feel like all I do is wrangle wayward computers."

The machine swallowed, chewed, and belched, and I slid the copies out of the belly of the beast. Gave them a quick glance to make sure they'd come out okay. A college transcript. Curious. At thirty-three, I hadn't needed my college transcript in eons. Why did a man his age need copies? I lifted the lid and reached for the original, actually a well-worn copy, the paper thick and slippery, the ink faded.

Probably an engineering major, I thought, laughing to myself. If the transcripts were his. I'd never seen him before and hadn't looked closely enough to read the name on the records.

"Hey, Murph, you get a new job?"

The ribbing came from an old high school classmate who'd just walked in. I grew up in Jewel Bay, though I left after high school and only moved back a year and a half ago. I waved, then smiled at my mystery man.

"Murph?" he asked. "Are you the Murphy girl?"

"One of them," I replied. "Along with my sister and a couple of cousins. I'm Erin." I resumed my place in the line, which hadn't moved, and he followed me.

"Tom Murphy's girl," he said, persisting, and I nodded. "Tom was a good man. Such a shame, what happened to him."

I bit my lower lip. My father was killed in a hit-and-run my senior year of high school, the case unsolved until I finally put all the pieces together last winter, nearly fifteen years to the day after the accident. The man responsible was now in prison. He wasn't a bad man, and I knew he'd punished himself plenty. Though the delay had caused my family deep pain, justice had been served.

But I would never stop missing my father, especially this time of year.

I pulled out my phone. The details of running a business can be a useful distraction.

"A good man," the mystery man repeated, with a touch of sadness. How did he know my father? He wasn't local, I was sure. Between growing up here, running a shop, and getting dragged into every event from judging high school drama team meets to organizing holiday decorating in the village, I had at least a passing acquaintance with nearly everyone in town.

"How much will it be?" he said, bringing my attention back to the copies. He glanced at the line and the busy clerks.

"Forty cents. But I've got a copy card, so it will only cost me twenty cents. Merry Christmas."

He tilted his head, not understanding.

"My business keeps a prepaid account," I explained. "We pop in, make copies, and leave without having to wait to pay or get a receipt. Plus, we get a price break. I'll pay for your copies so you can take off. Merry Christmas."

I could almost see the gears turning in the man's brain as he grasped my meaning.

"Thank you," he finally said. "Thank you. Merry Christmas."

He left, the bell on the door ringing behind him. The woman in front of me smiled and I smiled back. Christmas is like that, in the village.

I thumbed my phone, glad to see an email update on a shipment of compostable bags for the pasta my mother makes. They'd been delayed by a snowstorm in the Midwest, but would be delivered this afternoon.

The door opened, a blast of cold air hitting my backside, and the little man stood next to me. "How much did you say that cost?"

"Forty cents," I said, not bothering to explain the prepaid account this time.

He stuck his hand in the pocket of his baggy corduroys and pulled out a book of stamps. "Let me give you a Christmas stamp."

"Okay, sure," I said as he tried to tear one out of the book. The first stamp ripped and he tried another, the stiff peel-off paper resisting his efforts. He shoved his hand back in his pocket and brought out a small leather card case. Drew out a stamp and handed it to me with a grin. "Merry Christmas."

Then he was gone, before I could thank him or wish him a happy holiday. I tucked the stamp, a portrait of the Madonna and child, in my wallet and dropped it back in my bag. My classmate, who got his mail in a box here, paused on his way out and we chatted about the holidays and how great it was to see the town buzzing and our plans for watching this weekend's parade. Then it was my turn. The computers had picked up speed, thank goodness, and I finished my transaction, stacked my empty tubs, and headed back to the Merc.

Sure enough, another day, another pile of packages. I lugged the last tub up from the basement—not the best spot for a pack-and-ship station, but the building had passed the century mark a while back and options were limited. I set my load by the back door, grabbed my bag and keys, and popped up front to tell Tracy, the Merc's assistant manager, and Lou Mary, saleswoman extraordinaire, that I was leaving. Tracy was busy helping a woman choose truffles for her office Christmas party.

"Oh, would you drop off my Christmas cards?" Lou Mary asked. "I'm short one stamp. Let me get some change—"

"No worries. I've got a Christmas stamp right here." I found it in my wallet and held it out. "Although when did you last see a stamp you actually had to lick?"

"What? Let me see that," Lou Mary said, lifting the readers she wore on a beaded chain into place. Today's chain was made of bumpy red-orange beads that looked like coral, almost the same shade as her hair. Even with the glasses, she had to squint and hold the stamp up to the light. "Where did you get this?"

I told her the story.

"Humph," Lou Mary said. "Let me do some research." What she knew about stamps or how, I had no idea, but I knew better than to question her.

The shipping depot was quieter today, and I didn't have to wait long. As I piled my packages on the counter, I told the clerk about the mystery man baffled by the copy machine. "But then, I completely forgot to pay you. So charge me for four copies."

"No way," she said. "Merry Christmas!"

"No, really, he was willing to pay. He just didn't want to break into the line, and I didn't think he should wait, so let me—"

"No," she repeated. "I love this story so much. I'm not letting you pay."

"Thanks. Any chance you know who he is?"

She shook her head. "It was so hectic, I barely noticed anything. I did see you making copies, but I didn't give it another thought. Figures the computers would choose yesterday to act up."

We finished with the packages, then I bought Lou Mary's single stamp and mailed her cards. I made one more attempt to pay for the man's copies, which was soundly refused, and I left, the joy of the season on my face. After a couple of other errands, I drove back to the village, a.k.a. downtown. A parking problem is a good sign during the busy season, so I didn't mind that the only spot was a good hike from our back door.

There are few more beautiful sights than retail shops filled with customers. I hung up my coat and stashed my bag, then grabbed an apron and got to work.

A regular bought gift packs of jam for each of her visiting children and grandchildren, and added a jar of huckleberry, the crème de la crème of jams, for herself. "I fill my own Christmas stocking," she said, wagging her eyebrows. "That way, I know I'll get what I want."

Then I helped a college student choose handmade soaps and lotions for his mother and sisters. Next came a couple picking up Christmas gift baskets they'd ordered, filled with a variety of our treats, and a woman who bought wine, pasta, and sauces for an easy Christmas Eve dinner.

The front door closed, the place momentarily quiet. I poured myself a cup of Cowboy Roast, the rich aroma almost enough to perk me up without a sip. I perched on a stool at the stainless steel counter that divides the shop floor from our commercial kitchen. My mother found the red-topped chrome stools years ago in Pondera, pronounced Pahn-duh-RAY, the nearest big town, all of thirty thousand, thirty miles away. They'd come from a long-closed soda fountain, and customers adore them. Unlike the wide plank floors, tin ceilings, and milk glass pendant lights, the kitchen and counter weren't original to the building, which my great-grandfather built in 1910 when he opened the town's first grocery, but they fit in perfectly. The Merc was my happy place, my home away from home, and when I came back from Seattle, after a ten-year stint as a grocery buyer for SavClub, the international warehouse chain, I knew right away that this was where I was meant to be. I'd reconnected with Adam Zimmerman, who'd crushed on me in college, though I'm embarrassed to admit I barely remembered him, and life here in Jewel Bay was just about all a girl could ask for. This girl, anyway.

"I made a call," Lou Mary said as she plopped onto the next stool. "An expert in Pondera will see you this afternoon. You and the stamp."

"What?" Her swift action took me by surprise. "In case you've forgotten, it's a week before Christmas. I'm not going anywhere until the new year."

"No," she said. "You need to do this now. I called your mother. She's on her way in to spell you."

I should have been irritated. After all, I do run the place, though my mother owns it. And this was our busy time, second to the ninety days of summer when we live and breathe for tourists. But I'd learned to trust Lou Mary's instincts.

"Can't we text him a picture? Or email it if he's old school?"

"He is seriously old school," she replied. "Not to mention old. He needs to see it himself, with his own eyes and a magnifying glass."

I heard the back door open and shut, followed by footsteps. A moment later, my mother walked in. Everyone calls Francesca Conti Murphy Schmidt "Fresca." I've been training to call her that myself, instead of Mom, when we're in the shop.

Worry creased her normally smooth brow and darkened her normally bright brown eyes. She has great genes and I pray every night that I've inherited a fraction of them.

"Did you hear what happened to Lynette Barnes?" she said, skipping hello and the usual hugs and kisses.

"Lynette the cleaning woman? No. What happened?" I asked.

"You know she rents that little house by the entrance to the Nature Trail, with the hideously steep driveway?" The Nature Trail, a.k.a. the River Road, runs past the village high above the Jewel River, and it's popular in all seasons.

"She goes to work at some ungodly hour," my mother continued. "Five o'clock in the morning, cleaning the bank before they open. Her car hit a patch of ice and missed the turn at exactly the wrong spot. It's a miracle she wasn't killed. A dog walker found her."

"Ohmygod. Will she be okay?"

"Broken wrist, broken ribs, cuts and bruises, a touch of hypothermia. Who knows when she'll be able to work again."

Demanding, physical work. I doubted she'd been able to tuck away much savings. Sounded like she'd been lucky, though. Her car could easily have tumbled all the way down to the icy water, where it could have been hours, even days, before she was spotted.

An accident like that could happen to anybody. I rubbed the three lucky stars tattooed inside my wrist.

"I ought to go see her," my mother continued, but Lou Mary gave an almost imperceptible shake of the head. My mother always listens to Lou Mary.

I didn't want to go to the hospital. I didn't want to go see this stamp dealer. I had plenty to do right here at the Merc, selling pickles and popcorn and pork chops from pigs who'd been raised not five miles from our front door. But it was the season for the unexpected.

"Give me that stamp," I told Lou Mary, then looked at my mother. "I'll swing by the hospital to see Lynette."

After promising to be extra careful on the roads, especially driving home in the dark, I headed out.

I drove through downtown Pondera and up the hill toward the independent living community where the aptly named Mr. Silver had moved after retiring and closing his coin and stamp shop. The tangle of winding streets and new-to-me buildings was confusing, but I finally found the address Lou Mary had given me.

The lobby was tastefully decorated with garland and red and gold accents, a well-dressed noble fir next to the reception desk. I signed the registry and told the woman on duty that I was meeting Sam Silver.

"He's waiting for you in the library," she said and pointed the way.

A pair of French doors stood open, each festooned with a holiday wreath. Two tall arched windows, a grandfather clock between them, let in the soft gray light of mid-December. Bookcases lined the other walls, the rows of colorful spines neatly organized and dusted. At one of the classic library tables sat an elderly man who rose when I walked in.

"Miss Murphy," he said, extending a hand. The word for Sam Silver was "rotund." He wasn't much taller than I, his dark suit pants belted around his very full waist, his white shirtsleeves rolled halfway up his forearms, his hand fleshy but his grip firm. "Come in, come in."

"Thank you for seeing me." At his gesture, I slid into a chair and he resumed his seat.

"Any friend of Mrs. Vogel is a friend of mine."

I never think of Lou Mary as "Mrs. Vogel." I hadn't known her late husband, but knew she missed him deeply.

"And besides," he added, clear blue eyes shining, "I hear you have a mystery to solve."

I fished a small box meant to hold a trio of truffles out of my bag. Lou Mary had refused to let me slip the stamp back into my wallet, instead lining the box with a bed of tissue and nestling the stamp inside. I slid it across the table.

The old man adjusted his glasses, cleared his throat, and lifted the lid. "Oh, my. Yes. Quite right, quite right." Using a pair of metal tongs, he raised the stamp to the light. Brought it toward him for a closer look, then turned his wrist to inspect the back.

Then he laid the stamp on a piece of thick white paper and slipped a magnifying device onto his head. Lowered the lenses into place and focused on the front of the stamp for several long moments. Raised the lenses and without a word, pulled a fat paperback out of the stack of books at his elbow. He found the page he was looking for and ran a finger down a long column. Muttered something I couldn't hear. Removed the headset and sat back, arms folded across his belly. For the first time since he'd lifted the lid of the truffle box, he looked directly at me.

If I'd thought his eyes were shining before, now they positively glowed.

"Young lady, you have quite a treasure."

I waited, the only sounds in the room the ticking of the clock and the pounding of my heart.

"I believe," Mr. Silver said solemnly, "that you have been given a 1917 three-center. Stamps had cost two cents, but late that year, rates were increased temporarily to help fund the war effort. A special Christmas stamp was issued, in a limited edition, as a morale booster. I've seen three, none in nearly mint condition, like yours. Stamps are meant to be used, after all, not saved. I want to call a friend to be sure, a reputable dealer and a member of the American Philatelic Society, who pays close attention to current prices. But I suspect that a knowledgeable collector would pay you upwards of seventeen hundred dollars."

He was pulling my leg. He had to be.

"You're a skeptic." He dropped his arms and reached for a handheld magnifier. Held it so I could look through the thick, warbly glass. "See the perforations? Perfectly crisp. The gum is undisturbed." He used the tongs to show me the back, then returned the stamp to the blotter. "No cancellation marks, no wrinkles from moisture. This stamp has not only never been used, it's been well-preserved. Light can damage the colors on stamps this old, and it is slightly faded, enough to tell us that it's an original. Though while it's worth some money, it's not valuable enough to tempt a forger."

My head was spinning. I had to find the man who gave me the stamp. He couldn't have known its value—he'd given a perfect stranger a seemingly ordinary object in fact worth a small fortune in exchange for almost nothing. Forty cents' worth of copies. Twenty cents to me, with my prepaid discount.

"Mrs. Vogel told you how I got this stamp, didn't she?" I asked, and he nodded. I described the man who'd given it to me. "Do you recognize him at all?"

"I'm sorry, my dear. I have no idea who your benefactor might have been."

Why hadn't I paid more attention? Because it had been a brief interaction, and I'd been preoccupied with the holiday rush. There had been nothing truly memorable about the man or the moment. But I had to find him. Because I didn't just have a Christmas stamp.

I had a Christmas problem.

"It was the strangest thing," Lynette said. She was a small woman, made smaller by the white sheets, the white bandages covering her arms and one side of her head, and the tubes and monitors. The room had that mix of hospital odors—antiseptic tinged with the smell of the uneaten food on the lunch tray that hadn't been cleared yet and the scent of chrysanthemums in a get-well bouquet. "I felt like there was a hand protecting me, keeping me from going over the cliff. Don't tell the doctors. They'll think I'm crazy."

"I've heard similar stories," the woman in the bedside chair said. I wasn't surprised to see the Reverend Anne Christopherson here, despite the shocking fact that my sister's childhood friend had become a Methodist minister. She's a full-figured woman who favors loose, flowing tunics, but today, she wore a dark gray ministerial shirt and clerical collar. I supposed the collar helped open doors in places like this, saving her from constantly explaining her presence. "It's quite common, actually."

Though Anne's tone was calm and matter-of-fact, her words gave me the chills. Had my dad felt an unseen hand, an unseen force, when the speeding car sideswiped him on that icy night so long ago? The sheriff had always said it was a miracle that his car hadn't plunged over the side of the bridge into the bay. I found myself torn between gratitude that he'd been spared that fate and fury that he'd been killed anyway. Why hadn't the hand protected him?

"I've been in touch with the volunteers guild," Anne was saying. "You'll have plenty of help when you get home. The bank president told me they'll keep paying you, even though you won't be able to work for a while, and I'm sure your other clients will do the same."

"The Merchants' Association can probably chip in," I said.

Anne raised a finger and gave me a look. "I have another project for you and the association. We'll talk outside."

What did she have in mind? The merchants get hit up for every fund-raiser imaginable, especially this time of year. But if the season was a good one, as it looked to be, they'd be in the giving spirit.

"If it weren't for that dog walker," Lynette said, "I could have laid there for hours."

"Who was he?" I asked.

"I have no idea," she replied. "I've never seen him before."

"Rings no bells for me, either," Anne said. She lives in a tiny cottage near the church, not far from the trailhead. "That's about the time I start my morning prayers. Unusual to see anyone out walking a dog that early, especially when it's so cold and dark. Truly a miracle."

Lynette's eyelids were drooping and she was sinking lower into the pillows, so we said our goodbyes. As we wound through the hospital's corridors to the front door, Muzaked Christmas carols following us, I told Anne about the mysterious man in the copy shop. I did not mention the stamp or my visit to Mr. Silver.

But she didn't know the stranger.

"I wish I'd paid more attention, but I was too busy," I said. Too busy waiting in a slow-moving line, updating our Instagram feed from my phone, replying to texts and emails that had meant more to me than the stranger had, once his copies were made.

"What matters," Anne counseled, "is that you had an opportunity to do a kindness for a stranger, and you did it."

I wasn't convinced. My kindness had been dwarfed by his generosity. Besides, he'd known my father, and I hadn't even asked how, or asked his name.

"Now, here's what I need you to do," she said. "You know about the refugee family the church is sponsoring."

"Sure." Everyone in town knew the Syrian couple with the two darling little girls. He'd been hired as a school janitor and she worked in the school cafeteria.

"They came here with nothing. We helped them with jobs, housing, furniture. They work hard. They're good members of the community. But their travel loan, for the airfare to get to the U.S., is due in January, and they don't have the money." She raised a hand. "I know, everyone thinks the clergy can make a call and get a donation, but it isn't always that easy."

"How much do you need?"

"Seventeen hundred," she said. And a shiver as cold and swift as the Jewel River shot through me.

∞

Back in Jewel Bay, I stopped at the grocery store on the highway. When it opened forty years ago, it all but closed the doors of Murphy's Mercantile. The same thing happened to the hardware store, and over time, downtown businesses found the highway offered room for expansion and customer convenience, a.k.a. parking. The village nearly emptied out, but gradually developed a new identity. Restaurants, galleries, a children's clothing and toy shop, a bookshop, antique store, and liquor store all thrived in the tiny triangle bordered by the Nature Trail, the river, and the bay.

It took my family years to find a business model that worked, but now, the Merc was thriving again. I aimed to take us from a boutique offering specialty items to a place where people shopped for everyday food and drink, but despite our mission, town would always need a full-service grocery.

On my way out, bags in both hands, I heard the telltale chime of the Christmas bell. In Jewel Bay, holiday bell ringers raise money for community projects, like Christmas decorations and the annual parade honoring the new high school graduates. I fished in my pocket for spare change.

"Hey, Polly. Merry Christmas!" I plunked my coins in the kettle, then leaned in to air-kiss my old friend's cheek.

"Merry Christmas, Erin! Isn't this just the best time of year?"

Polly Paulson was one half of the Easter twins, and like her sister, Bunny, had never felt the need to leave Jewel Bay. Both are perpetual volunteers, as quick to get involved as they were to prank a new teacher in our school days.

"Pol," I said, as an idea took shape in my brain, "I won't bother you with the details, but something odd happened that makes me wonder. You've been ringing bells for years, right?"

"Oh, for ages. Starting in high school. Bunny and I shared a shift, ringing as a duet." She stomped her feet, in black boots trimmed with faux fur, to keep warm.

"You hear stories sometimes about an anonymous person dropping a gold coin in the kettle. Anything like that ever happen here?"

"Gosh, no, not that I've ever heard. Why?"

"It's nothing. Hey, if I don't see you before the big day, have a great holiday."

"Ho, ho, ho," she called, then greeted another customer making a deposit.

Sounded like my surprise stamp had been a one-off gesture, not the sign of a serial philanthropist. Which made it harder to find the man and return his too-generous gift.

This late, I had no trouble finding a parking spot behind the shop. Inside, I helped Tracy and Lou Mary tidy up and readied the till for the next day. Sales had been good, and that brightened my holiday spirit. I turned off the lights and we headed out, Lou Mary through the front door to walk to her condo across the one-lane bridge, Tracy and I out the back.

"Hey, Erin!" Kim Caldwell, my BFF since the sixth grade, called as she crossed the alley, hand in hand with my big brother, Nick, aiming for Red's Bar. "Grab a beer with us."

"Great," I answered, and glanced at Tracy, who shook her head and said she'd see me tomorrow.

Nick held the back gate, then the three of us hustled through Red's beer garden into the warmth of the bar. I love sitting outside with a burger and a brew when the weather permits, but right now, it definitely did not permit.

Kim is a sheriff's detective, and even when she isn't in uniform, people often stop her with a question or a complaint. She'd taken a break for a few months earlier in the year and joked that one reason she came back to the job was that no one could remember she'd left. Nick and I had already ordered for the three of us and nabbed our favorite high-top table when she joined us.

"Questions about the accident," she said as she slid onto her stool and picked up her beer. "I was first on the scene, because I live so close. I even beat the ambulance."

"I stopped to see Lynette when I was in Pondera today," I said. "She's pretty banged up, but it's obvious what happened, isn't it?"

"We still need to do a full investigation," Kim replied. "Any time anyone's injured or there's serious property damage. There's all kinds of statistical information to report, including that she had no insurance—"

"You don't ticket someone for that, do you?" Nick asked. "Under the circumstances."

"Sheriff's policy is no ticket if the driver is alone and injured, but he does make them get insurance and prove they've kept it for a year. We also give the road department the info, so they can decide whether to make any changes, like put up a guardrail." She took a long sip of her Moose Drool. "Mmm. This hits the spot."

"So who was this dog walker who found her and called for help?" I asked. "Did you see him, or get his name?"

"No. No idea. He was gone before I got there. I'd like to know—he's a witness, and I hate leaving a blank on my report."

Could it have been the little man I'd met at the shipping depot? He'd seemed spry enough.

Now I was the one talking crazy.

Nick and Kim decided to order burgers, maybe shoot some pool, but I wanted to go home and put my feet up. Retail is hard work.

First, though, I took a quick detour. I drove up Hill Street toward the trailhead. Stopped the car and grabbed the flashlight from my console. Finding the spot where Lynette had skidded across the road and hit the embankment was easy. The tire tracks were plainly visible, but there were too many scuffed footprints to make out any individual prints. No doubt they belonged to Kim, the EMTs, and all the walkers who'd passed this way since morning. But what I did not see was a single set of footprints coming from the direction of the houses, a set of paw prints beside them.

That didn't mean anything, did it?

The next day was as busy as the last two and I barely left the shop. Fortunately, that gave me plenty of chances to ask about the mysterious man. No one knew him. In summer, that wouldn't have surprised me—our population quadruples in July and August. But midwinter? Town hadn't grown that much, had it?

I am a creature of good habits and most mornings, I stop at Le Panier, the French bakery next to the Merc, for a latte and croissant. But a high school friend was in town visiting her parents, and we'd agreed to meet for breakfast Thursday at the Jewel Inn. Just down the hill from the scene of Lynette's accident, the chalet-like building anchors the north end of the village. When I was a kid, the racks mounted on the walls creeped me out— how could I possibly eat my huckleberry pancakes with a moose, an elk, and a Rocky Mountain goat all staring at me? Now I find the taxidermy part of the charm. Nothing says Christmas spirit quite like a stuffed bobcat wearing a Santa hat.

"You girls splitting those huckleberry pancakes again, or you gonna live dangerously?" Tina, our waitress, asked as she set two cups of coffee on our table, unrequested but most welcome.

My friend stared, disbelieving, but I laughed. Like most good waitresses,

Tina has a fabulous memory. Order something twice and the next time, she'll ask if you'd like your usual. I could not have remembered what I'd ordered here last week, let alone what my friend and I ordered last year, if my life depended on it, but to Tina, that was all in a day's work.

"As long as you still vouch for them," I said.

"You know it, darlin'," she replied and marched off to the kitchen, leaving us to the serious business of catching up.

More than an hour later, she topped off our coffee for the umpteenth time. "Get you anything else, girls?"

"Thanks. Just the check," my friend said.

"Don't you dare. It's my turn," I told her, then raised my gaze to the waitress. "Tina, memory test."

"Ooh. My favorite kind." She cocked a hip flirtatiously and ran a hand through her short, curly hair.

"There's an older man in town, short—about my height, slender. I'm guessing seventy-two, but it's hard to tell. Dark hair. He might have a dog. He might be an early riser, and he might collect stamps."

I could almost see her flipping the pages of her memory.

"When the economy hit the last big downturn," she said, "my husband lost his job. People weren't eating out as much, and I wasn't making nearly enough to tide us over. Then my son broke his leg wrestling, and that about wrecked us."

She caught her lower lip between her teeth and exhaled heavily. "A man came in for breakfast—two eggs over easy, whole wheat toast, no butter, and a glass of grapefruit juice. Ate up, left cash on the table, and walked out the side door without a word. It might have been him. From your description, it mighta been him."

The back of my neck began to tingle. "How much, Tina?"

"That man—" Her voice broke and she choked back a tear. "That man left me a one-thousand-dollar tip on a ten-dollar ticket. Soon as I found that wad of cash, I went running after him, but he was gone. I told the owner. I insisted we had to find him, I couldn't keep the money, I just couldn't. She told me to calm down, be grateful, and put the money to good use. And I did."

That had all happened before I moved back. If my mother had heard the story, she'd never mentioned it.

"Then my husband found a better job, and my son made the honor roll—when he couldn't play sports, he actually studied—and I started believing in people again." Tina gestured toward the big bank of windows overlooking the corner of Front and Hill. "I've got the best view in town and there isn't anything wrong with my eyes. But I have never seen him again. Not back then, and not since."

"You're sure about that?"

"Honey, I am never in doubt." She let out a cackle. "Occasionally mistaken—don't you tell my husband I said that—but never in doubt."

I'd chided myself for not having paid better attention. But if I didn't know the man, if the Reverend Anne couldn't identify him, and his description rang no bells for Polly Paulson, Detective Kim Caldwell, the clerk at the shipping depot, or my mother, and even sharp-eyed Tina hadn't spotted him . . .

Talk about a mystery.

The closer it gets to Christmas, the more people spend and the less time they take to do it. It was true in the giant SavClub warehouse and it was true in village retail. In fact, it might be the one thing the members of the Merchants' Association agreed on. And it was certainly true this year, thank goodness. My first few months running the Merc were shaky, especially when my mother had trouble remembering she'd hired me to run the place so she didn't have to. But my first full year as manager was coming to a close, and we were going to finish with a flourish.

I thanked Tracy and Lou Mary for their hard work and locked the doors behind them. I had a few details to wrap up, making sure the day's receipts matched what our system said we'd sold, and getting the shop ready for Sunday. Only a half day, but guaranteed to be crazy busy.

The phone in my apron pocket rang. I didn't recognize the number.

"Miss Murphy, Sam Silver calling. About that stamp."

"Mr. Silver. How nice to hear from you. I hope you're well." I perched on one of the red-topped stools.

"And I hope you're sitting down, young lady."

I assured him I was.

"I talked to a dealer in Denver. He's my nephew, but that aside, he's the sharpest young man I know in the business. Young." He laughed. "Fifty is young to me these days. Two years ago, he got fifteen hundred dollars for a stamp like that, in not as good a condition, and he's quite certain he could get a little more for yours."

"You're joking."

"Young lady, I never joke about philately."

Phil-what? Oh, stamp collecting.

"Did your nephew tell you where he got it?" Maybe we had a chance of finding my mystery man. Anne had given me the perfect opportunity to put the money to good use, to excellent use, but I still felt the urge to find him. To correct the mistake, and raise the funds for the refugees another way.

"A most unusual occurrence," Sam Silver said. The stamp that crossed his nephew's desk had not been dropped in a Christmas kettle or left as a tip, and it hadn't been given to a stranger in exchange for forty cents' worth of photocopies. No, it had been tucked inside a card handed to a woman on a Denver bus by a nondescript older man, short, slender, with surprisingly dark hair for his age. A woman who had left her abusive husband on Christmas Eve and was on her way to a shelter with her two young children. She'd been sure the gift was a mistake and the nephew had searched high and low, using all his contacts in the business to trace the stamp's prior owner, with no luck. So, finally, he'd sold it to a collector and gave the woman the full proceeds, refusing to take a commission. He himself, Mr. Silver told me, had not been aware of the discovery at the time; he'd been in the hospital with pneumonia and his sister, the stamp dealer's mother, had feared the story would distress him and set back his recovery. "Stuff and nonsense," he said. "Stamps don't distress me. Stories don't distress me. What distresses me is men who beat their wives and terrify their children. That there are hardworking people with too little and lazy bums with too much."

What could I say to that? I thanked him for his kindness, promised to be in touch, and stepped out the front door. Gazed up and down the street. The shoppers and shopkeepers had gone home, leaving behind windows filled with magical scenes. A light snow had begun to fall, and in the glow cast by the bulbs woven into the garland that hung from every roof and eave, the flakes sparkled.

I'd lived in Jewel Bay more than half my life, leaving for college, then worked in Seattle, a city I loved. But if I'd ever had any doubt that coming home had been the right choice, that doubt was gone. Adam and I were in agreement: Jewel Bay was where we belonged, and where we meant to stay.

A gust of wind blew a blast of wet snow in my face, and I dashed back inside.

After Mr. Silver's news, there was no way I had the presence of mind to reconcile our accounts tonight. But a nervous energy coursed through me, so I got the coffee maker ready for the morning. Checked our bestsellers to make sure we were fully stocked and cleaned the bathroom. Walked every corner of the old pile of bricks, debating, deciding. But I knew what I had to do.

I realized I had always known.

Adam had offered to drop me off this morning, knowing my reluctance to take a parking space better left for a shopper, but I'd chosen to drive in case I needed to run an errand that required wheels. I'd tucked my car at Riverbend Park, well away from the shopping district, on the other side of the old one-lane bridge. I wrapped a muffler around my neck and zipped up my parka. Pulled a knitted cap over my ears, looped my leather bag over my shoulder, and locked the door behind me. The closer I got to the bridge and the river, the heavier the snowfall, and I shoved my gloved hands deep in my coat pockets, head down to keep the cold, wet flakes out of my eyes. The wind had whipped the snow up onto the bridge, making the narrow walkway along one side impassible, so I stepped onto the bridge deck.

As if out of nowhere, a hand clapped against my chest and pushed me backward. I staggered, my feet slipping on the ice beneath the snow, arms flailing as I tried to catch my balance. My hip hit the high guardrail at the end of the bridge and I grabbed the rail. The deck boards rattled. A horn blared in my ear and a delivery truck zipped past me, into the village.

I blinked, the truck's headlights still flashing in my brain. Instinctively, my gloved fingers reached for my lucky stars. A few feet away stood the man I'd been looking for all week.

"You," I said, stupidly. "You saved me."

He said nothing.

"I've been searching for you, asking about you. No one knows who you are."

In the glow of the Christmas lights strung high on the steel trusses, I saw him grin.

"You saved Lynette from going over the side of the road." If he did have a dog, it was nowhere in sight. "And a few years ago, you gave Tina the waitress a huge tip that helped her keep her family afloat and gave her back her hope. Now you gave me that stamp, just when a deserving family needs exactly what it's worth."

He waved an ungloved hand in front of his face, whether to wave away my comments or chase the snow from his vision, I couldn't say.

"And you knew my father," I said. "Who are you?"

"Sadly, my dear, I can't save everyone."

The deck boards rattled again and an unfamiliar pickup came across the bridge. But I was safely out of the way this time, and so was my rescuer. The truck passed and I turned to speak to the man, to ask his name, to ask him to let me take him to meet my mother, to ask how he knew that stamp was worth exactly what the refugee family owed and why, oh why, had he chosen to give it to me.

But the stranger was gone. In his place was nothing. Not even a footprint.

I closed my eyes. Pulled off my hat and tipped my head back, letting the snowflakes fall from the sky and kiss my face.

A Death in Yelapa

The waves broke over the bow of the water taxi and the cold salt spray misted my face. I smiled up at my husband. The sea breeze whipped his dark curls, his sunglasses reflecting the diamond glint of a January day off the western coast of Mexico.

My husband. Adam and I had been married all of twenty-three days, but our Christmas Eve wedding on a dude ranch in Jewel Bay, Montana, might as well have happened on another planet.

"Bahia de Banderas is the seventh largest bay in the world," said the blond man seated in front of me, his voice rising above the roar of the outboard motor. "The name means the Bay of Flags."

His wife, her highlighted hair tied back with a black chiffon ribbon, turned her gaze in the other direction.

"Erin, look." Adam pointed at a school of fish leaping through the water, not thirty feet off starboard.

"Dolphins?" I asked.

"Dorado," he said. Adam had spent a few months in Mexico after college, hiking and kayaking. He'd planned our slightly belated honeymoon himself, telling me to make sure my passport was current and that I had a good bathing suit. Then, three days ago, he'd said we'd be vacationing in our own private casita on the most unspoiled beach in western Mexico.

Is there any wonder I'm head over heels for the man?

"Mahi-mahi. Dolphinfish." The blond man rested his arm on the back of his wife's seat and spoke over his shoulder. "Not to be confused with Flipper." He cackled.

"Oh, shut up, Max," his wife said. "No one wants to hear your stupid jokes." In profile, I could see her prominent cheekbones and strong jaw, makeup so expertly done you almost couldn't tell it was makeup. Full lips in a trendy red-orange, though I suspected the pout came naturally. Chic tortoiseshell sunglasses. I was sure I'd seen her browsing in an art gallery off the Malecón, when we were in Puerto Vallarta.

The two women sitting next to us raised their eyebrows, and one winked.

Max faced forward with another chuckle, and Adam and I exchanged a quick smile before turning our attention back to the jumping fish.

Twenty minutes and a hundred fish later, we landed in Yelapa. My mouth fell open, literally, at the sight of the picture-perfect village wrapped around the calm, blue inlet. A row of three-story haciendas, each a different color, faced the water. Some were private homes, others small hotels. Then came the charming casitas with their deep porches and a cluster of open-air bars and restaurants. Bright umbrellas dotted the beach.

Adam and I grabbed our backpacks and scrambled onto the pier, new since his last visit. Max stood in the boat, surveying the surroundings, while his wife tried to disembark. Her white skirt was too narrow for her to get both feet on the pier easily and she stumbled, hands flailing as she shrieked, one cork-soled sandal flying.

Adam caught her. I rescued the errant sandal.

"Thank you, thank you," Max said. He stepped onto the pier, hand out. "We're Max and Parisa Porter, from Calgary."

"Oh, for Pete's sake, Max," she said. "You were willing to let me fall in the water. They don't care who you are."

"Teresa? Nice to meet you. I'm Erin Murphy, and this is my husband, Adam Zimmerman. From northwest Montana."

"PUH-reesa," she said. "Like Paris with an *a* on the end."

"You been here before?" Max had the manner I associated with a college football player-turned-stockbroker, but not the size—halfway between my five-five and Adam's six-one, neither fat nor slender, he had thick lips and parted his hair in the middle.

"I have, she hasn't," Adam said. "It's our honeymoon."

"I knew it," Max said. "Didn't I tell you, sweetheart? On the boat. They gawk at each other like newlyweds."

We said a quick goodbye, though not before agreeing to meet them some evening for a margarita. "Or that *raicilla*," Max said. "Bootleg booze. Puts hair on your chest and ideas in your head. You know—*loco*." He pointed a finger at his ear and twirled it.

A few minutes later on the beach, I paused to kick off my flip-flops, eager to feel the golden sand between my pale, northern toes. On the pier, Parisa stood beside a huge pile of luggage, arms folded, while Max waved his hands at the boatman.

"Negotiating for delivery?" I speculated. "To one of the big houses?"

"This ain't the Grand Hyatt," Adam replied and gestured to a turquoise casita with a palm-thatched roof.

The perfect honeymoon hotel.

"Well, if it isn't our American newlyweds," Max Porter called when he spotted us the next afternoon from the beachfront *palapa*. The palm-thatch canopy covered a few white plastic tables surrounded by white plastic chairs. "Looks like you've been out making waves. Not what we did on our honeymoon, eh, Parisa?"

What was your first clue? I wanted to ask. The bathing suits? The snorkels, the paddleboards?

A dark-haired young woman delivered a basket of chips, a bowl of salsa, and two frosty margaritas. Max beckoned. "Join us for a drink."

Chips and salsa and a cold Pacifico or two had been our plan but not with the Porters.

"Uh, thanks," Adam said, then turned to me. "I could do with a quick shower. What about you?"

Saved. "Good idea. Maybe if you two are here later—"

"Ohmygod, this is awful!" Parisa Porter flung her tortilla chip onto the table, bits of salsa splattering across the white plastic. "They can't even wash dishes right. It tastes like soap." She shoved her chair back—not easy to do in the sand—and flounced off, also not easy to do in the sand, especially in platform sandals.

Max's jaw tightened and his nostrils flared, then the jolly look returned. "My wife knows what she likes. We'll catch up with you two lovebirds later. When you're not out adventuring." He cackled and followed her.

Adam picked up the chair Parisa had knocked over, and by unspoken agreement, we sat, trying not to laugh.

I dipped a chip in the salsa and took a tentative nibble. "Oh, it's fine. It's got cilantro in it, that's all."

Adam cocked his head.

"About fifteen percent of the population thinks cilantro tastes like soap. Maybe less down here." We gave the waitress our order, and she picked up the Porters' untouched drinks. "I read about it recently. It has to do with your ability to detect certain bitter compounds. So some people taste soap while the rest of us—"

"Get to eat all the chips and salsa," Adam said, sporting the crooked grin I love. The waitress set a tin bucket of beer on the table and popped two caps. Adam raised his bottle toward me and we clinked.

"I'll drink to that."

∞

On our third morning in Yelapa, our luck ran out. We'd taken a guided sunrise kayak trip and were now relaxing under the *palapa*, sipping fresh juice and waiting for our *huevos rancheros*.

"Look who the tide washed in," Max said. He sat, not waiting for an invitation. I glanced in the direction he'd come from and spotted Parisa. She'd given up on her shoes, the sandals dangling from her well-manicured fingertips as she slipped on the loose sand.

Adam popped up. "Max, Parisa, hello. Join us?" He pulled out the fourth chair and Parisa sank into it gratefully. At least, I thought she looked grateful, the way her shoulders dropped and she heaved out a ragged breath. I couldn't tell for sure—she kept her sunglasses on, despite the shade.

Our plates came. I didn't hear Max's order—I was too busy salivating over the glorious fried eggs dressed with *pico de gallo* and perfectly placed on a crisp tortilla, a sliced avocado and a spoonful of refried beans and rice on the side.

But I did hear Parisa ask for a Bloody Mary, and I didn't blame her.

"Fascinating place, you know," Max said, and started in on the history of the indigenous people—he called them the Yelapanese, though whether that was a real word or one he'd made up, I had no idea. We heard about First Contact, supposedly with a military man who was a cousin to Cortez, the early missionaries, and the treaties with the King of Spain. Since we were eating, we were a captive audience, and the history was interesting, if too detailed.

"Whatever their intentions, those old Spaniards recognized paradise when they found it," Max continued. "The Mexican dry forest—monsoons half the year, tolerable in winter and spring."

Parisa sipped while he recited average temperatures for late January—sixty-two point one degrees for the low and eighty-three point eight for the high.

"For you, that is," he said with another cackle. "Much cooler for us. Sixteen point seven and twenty-eight point eight."

The old Fahrenheit-Celsius bait and switch.

"You must sleep with the guidebook under your pillow," I said, and a smile flitted across Parisa's face. "I love how it's all so local. No chain restaurants or hotels. The people who live here run the businesses. Everything we're eating is grown or caught right here."

"Except the beer," Adam said.

"What do you two do back home?" Max asked.

"I run a local foods market," I said.

"She's the heart and soul of the place," my beloved added. "And the brains. I run a wilderness camp for kids. What about you?"

"Financial planner," Max said, confirming my guess. When I glanced at Parisa, he answered for her. "My wife's job is to make me look good."

Turned out the Porters had signed up for the same afternoon tour as we had, along with the two women we'd seen on the boat and a handful of other tourists. At the edge of town, away from the bay, we boarded a small bus painted in vivid shades of green. To blend in, I supposed, as if any wild bird or animal would be fooled.

The Porters sat across the aisle from us. To my surprise, Max did not continue his recite-the-guidebook routine as we wound through the forested hills, deferring to the actual guide who sat behind the driver on a tall stool and told us all about the region's flora and fauna.

The bus stopped for lunch in a hillside village. Somehow, we managed to get separated from the Porters and sat with the two women, Jackie and Jill, who turned out to be mystery-writing buddies from Washington State.

"We flew into Puerto Vallarta from L.A. with them," Jackie said. "I don't know who's worse, him or her."

"Oh, him, for sure," I said. "Though maybe only because she doesn't talk as much. Are you scouting for victims for your next book? And how do you write together?"

Over chips, salsa, and cold beer, the two women chatted about their books and writing process. Turned out one lived in Seattle, the other in Spokane, but distance didn't slow them down, thanks to email.

"It's good that we live three hundred miles apart," Jill said. "Keeps us from killing each other."

After chips came gazpacho, the thick tomato-cucumber soup garnished with fresh cilantro. I could hear Parisa's exclamation of disgust from twenty feet away, and revised my opinion on which Porter the mystery writers should dispatch.

Back on the bus, our guide announced a side trip upriver to the *Cocodrilo* Sanctuary.

"Crocodiles," Max said loudly, in case anyone couldn't figure it out themselves.

I had honestly never considered the breeding habits of crocodiles before, nor even seen one live, but they were fascinating. As long as they stayed inside their fenced, jungle-like swamps. The guide explained how this facility helped preserve the biodiversity of the species through a selective breeding program.

"Crocodile Nazis," I heard Max say. "Good place to get your crocodile boots."

"In our next book," Jackie joked in a low voice.

Another function, the guide said as he cradled a baby croc in his arms, was education. Did we know how powerful a *cocodrilo*'s jaws were? "Thirty-seven hundred pounds per square inch. Greater than any other living animal." He let that sink in, then lunged forward, holding out the baby, who snapped its jaws and we all screamed. "But, they prefer chicken."

On the boat ride back down the cool green river, I sat next to Parisa, the two of us between Jackie and Jill.

"You like all this outdoor stuff?" Parisa asked, and I nodded. She shuddered. "Don't go out on your own. It isn't safe. Don't you live near grizzly bears?"

"Yes, and I do hike on my own, even though my mother and sister tell me not to." Somehow, that led to me pulling out my phone and pulling up wedding pictures.

"You and your sister could be twins," Jill said.

"I have a cousin who looks so much like me," Parisa said, "that people are always confusing us, even though Calgary is a big city and we don't spend much time together. I hate it."

I thought it quite wonderful to look so much like one of the people I loved most, but I kept my mouth shut.

Back in Yelapa, we all collapsed into beach chairs. The beach sellers must have been waiting, because the moment we were settled with drinks and snacks, they swarmed us. The colorful pottery was stunning, and I bought a set of serving bowls, though carrying them home would be tricky. The silver jewelry didn't tempt me. But the pie. Oh, the famous Yelapa pie. I chose coconut cream, Adam banana cream, and we traded bites.

I was about to wave "no" to the little man carrying a bundle of sundresses when a fringed knee-length number in shades of blue caught my eye. Alas, it caught Parisa's, too, and before I knew it, Max had paid the man full price for it and two more, not even pretending to bargain.

"There's another one in the same fabric," Adam pointed out, but it didn't have the fringe so I shook my head. The man picked up his load, considerably lighter now, and trundled down the beach.

A moment later, Max stood. "Gotta stretch after all that sitting," he said, and wandered off.

We swam, napped, and devoured fish tacos. When the sun finally set, the tourists cheered, and the locals laughed and shook their heads as if we were crazy. *Loco.*

The next morning, Adam and I got up early and headed inland to a village where he'd lived briefly. The road was winding and narrow, like the mountain roads back home. I loved every bumpy minute, peering into the jungle for the birds we'd seen yesterday, grabbing Adam's hand when a tree-climbing snake stared back at me.

We strolled the cobbled streets Adam remembered fondly and found the house he'd shared with three other crazy *Americanos*. We toured the church with its shrine to a saint I'd never heard of. On the main street, in search of lunch, we spotted a sidewalk café next to a hole-in-the-wall clothing shop.

"Grab a table," I said. "I'll just be a minute."

I ducked inside and let my eyes adjust after the bright sunlight. A rack of sundresses stood in the middle of the room. I was reaching for an orange-and-yellow print when the hanger moved and I spotted a woman on the other side of the rack, flipping through the dresses.

"Hey," I said, but she turned away. Her hair was held with a silver clip today, not the usual ribbon. She'd already bought three dresses on the beach—why did she need more? But then, a woman like Parisa always wanted more dresses, didn't she?

I felt hot and wiggly, embarrassed. Like I should have known she wouldn't want to talk to me when she had the choice. I didn't want a dress anymore. I just wanted to leave.

"I'm sure it was her," I told Adam five minutes later, after a long draw on my beer. We were sitting in the ubiquitous white plastic chairs at one of the ubiquitous white plastic tables, dipping the freshly fried chips into salsa redolent with peppers and herbs. Tinny music from an old boom box filled the air. "Why would she ignore me like that?"

"Strange. I thought they were going fishing. Granted, shopping does seem more her style."

"Yeah, but after what she said about going out alone? And she would never take that bus if she didn't have to."

"No other way to get up here," Adam said. "Unless she hopped a cargo truck."

Which is how we got home, after we downed too many tacos, walked too far up a dry riverbed, got lost, and missed the bus. We didn't see Parisa or Max, or anyone we knew, and that was just fine.

"Did you hear?" Jill said. She was standing on the front porch of the lemon-yellow casita next to ours. I'd taken a quick shower after our delightful misadventure, and kinda wished I hadn't been so hasty in the clothing shop—a cool cotton coverup would be perfect right now.

"They found a woman's body near the river mouth," she continued. "She was partially eaten by a *cocodrilo*. Her body is so badly damaged they can't identify her."

My stomach felt like a *cocodrilo* had bitten it. According to Jill, who spoke fluent Spanish and heard the story from the girl at the beachfront café who'd been interviewed by the *policía estatal*, no one remotely matching the victim's description had been reported missing.

We didn't see Max or Parisa that evening. The mood among the tourists was subdued and I imagined that the Porters, like many others, had stayed in for the night. After dinner, we returned to our front porch, and the sun set with only a handful of solemn witnesses.

We didn't see them the next day, either. In truth, we didn't see much of anyone except each other. When we left the casita, it was to grab a quick bite, then hike up the stone trails carved into the hillside to the swimming hole, where we swam and splashed in the waterfall. Though the death of the unidentified woman highlighted the dangers of foreign travel, there was nothing we could do and no point letting it interfere with our plans.

Early one morning, we went fishing with a local crew, returning to shore just as other vacationers were ordering their *jugo de naranja* and *huevos rancheros*. That night, we ate dorado we'd caught ourselves, and pronounced it the most delicious dinner ever. We went kayaking again, and Adam talked me into parasailing. We visited with the mystery writers and other tourists, lounged in the sun, and enjoyed not-so-restful siestas in our casita.

One afternoon, Adam decided to actually nap during siesta time, but I was feeling restless. Instead of staying on the beach, I took the trail behind the haciendas up the hillside and over, down toward the river. The trail was well-used and I wasn't worried, even though I had it to myself. Jungle flowers dotted the dense greenery with color. I heard birds I couldn't see, and my skin drank in the cool, damp air.

I strolled along the river, eyes and ears alert for snakes and *cocodrilos*. The river began to widen and I saw an opening in the thick growth where it met the ocean.

This must be where it happened. Where the unknown woman died. I shivered. There was no crime scene tape, no *cocodrilo* bones, no signs of death or mayhem. The sense of gloom was all in my head.

I turned to leave and slipped on a pocket of mud. I reached out to catch myself on the nearest tree and as my hand hit a branch, my fingers snared something else.

A black chiffon ribbon.

∞

Calling the police in a foreign country isn't as easy as you might think if you've never done it before. Adam's leftover Spanish wasn't up to the job, and when we told the waitress what we wanted and why, she grabbed her throat and her eyes rolled back in her head. While Adam tended to her—you don't run a wilderness camp without some serious medical training—I scanned the beach for other help.

Jackie and Jill were sitting under an umbrella with books in hand. Jill made the call with ease, while Jackie went in search of the young waitress's mother.

The *policía* arrived by boat and interviewed me at a table under the *palapa*. We spoke in English, thank goodness, since my Spanish hadn't progressed much beyond *cerveza* and dorado. And you don't usually need to talk about beer and dolphinfish when you're being interviewed by the police.

"*Gracias, señora,*" the uniformed detective said and rose, signaling the end of our conversation. I noticed how easily he managed the plastic chairs in the sand. "We'll notify the embassy, and if we need more *información*, we'll—what's your phrase? Be in touch."

"What's going on?" Max's voice interrupted. "You two lovebirds get caught doing something you shouldn't have?"

The detective faced him. "Your name, *señor?*"

"Max Porter. My wife and I are visiting from Calgary. That's in Canada. What's this about?"

A flicker of recognition that needed no translation crossed the detective's face. "We are just asking questions, *señor*, about the body found by the river. No need to be alarmed." He gestured toward us. "We missed this observant American couple when we did our initial interviews. We missed you and *Señora* Porter as well, did we not?"

He drew out the first syllable of "Porter," gesturing with one hand in a manner so cordial that he might have owned the place. For all I knew, he did.

"We don't know anything worth saying," Max replied. The day was hot and a thin bead of sweat formed behind his ear.

"Nonetheless, I should like to speak with you."

"Ah, sweetheart, here you are," Max said. "These men would like to chat about the poor woman found in the jaws of the crocodile. Such a tragedy."

Parisa crossed the sandy beach easily, wearing a pair of black leather flip-flops instead of her usual cork-soled platform sandals. As she tilted her head to listen to her husband, I noticed that her hair was held back in a silver clip. I'd seen one like it somewhere. Maybe in one of the beach sellers' trays.

We ordered beer and snacks and sat under an umbrella out of earshot as the officers spoke with the Porters. What Parisa might have known about the *cocodrilo*'s victim, I had no idea. But I knew she'd been in the jungle near the river. I only hoped she'd seen something that would help the police solve the mystery.

The Porters didn't come down to the beach that evening. We saw them the next morning when we came in from snorkeling, sitting at their usual table talking intently. To my surprise, they didn't call out to us. We waved but didn't stop. It was our last full day in Yelapa, and we wanted to catch another glimpse of the reedy-voiced Mexican parrotlet and take another swim beneath the waterfall.

The late afternoon sun had turned the inlet into a sea of diamonds when we joined the mystery writers for margaritas before dinner. They were bubbly and full of chitchat, and I knew I would enjoy reading their books when we got home.

Max and Parisa joined the crowd on the beach in time for dinner. She was wearing the blue dress I had wanted. I had to admit, it looked great on her. Everything did.

"It would have looked even better on you," Adam whispered into my ear. How did he always know what to say?

For our last night, the tables were covered with bright cloths, a candle and a jar of hibiscus flowers in the center. I tucked a red blossom into my dark hair. A creaky sound system cranked out a motley mix of Mexican songs, reggae tunes, and classic rock.

The Porters were seated a few tables away. I kept sneaking glances at them. Something puzzled me, but I couldn't say what.

No chips and salsa tonight. We started with *ceviche*, the snapper so fresh it was practically still swimming, seasoned with lime and chiles, garnished with cilantro leaves. After that, we had our choice of *cochinita pibil*, the classic slow-roasted pork shoulder with onions pickled in citrus juices, or cilantro salmon with a tomato-*habañero* salsa. We chose one of each to share.

"The only problem with vacation is that it ends," Adam said. "Look. Even Parisa's enjoying herself."

I laughed. That's what was different. She was actually talking to Max, her features lively, instead of studying her nails or staring off into space. A bottle of tequila sat on their table, and Max was clearly indulging.

Our dinner came and we dove in, savoring every fresh, spicy bite. I glanced at the Porters. Max had a hand on Parisa's leg where her dress had ridden up and I knew what had confused me earlier.

No fringe.

And Parisa was eating.

She was eating cilantro.

I pushed back my chair and found Jill. Bless the woman, she asked no questions but made the call, translating my words for the police dispatcher. The American witness had new information that could identify the victim in the Yelapa death, she said, information that would also prove it had been a crime and identify the killer. They should come immediately.

They did, in two marked boats that drove right up on the shore. Half a dozen officers jumped out, armed, uniformed, and stony-faced. The detective we'd met earlier took Adam and me aside and quizzed me. Then he fired instructions at his men. Two officers spoke to the waitress, who pointed and gestured, giving directions, and the men marched down the beach to where the locals' tiny houses clung to the hillside. Several barefoot children—where had they come from?—ran ahead, laughing and shouting.

It seemed the officers were well-known and not unwelcome—friends and relatives.

Around us, the other visitors ate and drank, though I could feel curious glances sweep over us. No one left. Something about armed officers standing on the perimeter of a space tends to keep people put.

A few minutes later, the two officers returned with the little man who sold dresses to tourists.

"*Si, Señor* Detective." He confirmed that Max had followed him off the beach and bought the second blue dress, the one without the fringe. No, he hadn't asked why. Why would he?

Why indeed?

Señor Detective gestured and his men took Max by the arms. "I am arresting you, *Señor* Porter from Calgary, for the murder of your wife."

"What? What are you talking about? This is my wife." Max tried to wave a hand toward the woman in the blue dress without fringe, the woman in flat sandals with a clip in her hair instead of a ribbon. The woman who could eat cilantro without making a face. The woman I'd seen browsing in an art gallery in Puerto Vallarta the day before Max and Parisa arrived on the same flight as Jackie and Jill. The woman who hadn't recognized me in the village shop because she had never seen me before.

"She's your wife's cousin," I said. "The one who looks so much like her that even your friends back home can't tell them apart. The one your wife can't—or couldn't—stand."

Max, the man who knew the guidebook backward and forward, had picked this village because it was remote enough that he could take Parisa out into the jungle and be assured of finding harm for her to fall into, yet easy enough for her cousin to reach on her own and take her place.

The detective sent for the bus driver, who confirmed that he'd brought an extra passenger back to Yelapa earlier in the week. We hadn't seen her on the return trip because we'd gone exploring, missed the bus, and hitchhiked back in the bed of a rusty pickup driven by a man we didn't know, but who surely lived nearby and would vouch for our story.

"She's *loco*," Max said. "She's been drinking that *raicilla*. She's seeing things."

But I had never been more sober, or more sure.

We had time for breakfast the next morning before the water taxi came. Jackie and Jill sat with us—they were leaving, too—and the waitress brought our usual orders.

The eggs were fried to perfection, the corn tortillas bursting with flavor, the tomatoes and avocados the fruit of the gods. Fingers pinched together, I plucked off the cilantro leaves and set them aside.

Vacation may be good for the soul, but it can be murder on the appetite.

Put on a Dying Face

"Remember Cats on Broadway, in Missoula?" Adam asked as we settled into our seats in the Playhouse. Good seats, thanks to the generous donation the Merc had made to this year's summer theater program.

"The vet clinic?" I said. "The sign always cracked me up."

"I actually saw this show on Broadway," he said.

"The real Broadway? The one in New York?" My sweetheart never ceases to amaze me. We'd been married not quite six months, though we first met at the University of Montana when he crushed on me and I was too oblivious, or self-absorbed, to notice. We met again fifteen years later when I returned to Jewel Bay to take over the Merc, my family's hundred-year-old grocery in the heart of the village. Thanks to my mother's vision and my long hours, it's now a thriving market focused on local foods. Adam had been lured to the tiny lakeside community to run kids' programs at the athletic club, including the wilderness camp that would take him into the woods for most of the summer. This was our last Friday Date Night before his departure. He's an utterly amazing guy and I count myself utterly lucky that he gave me a second chance.

But—musical theater? In New York?

"She musta been pretty cute," I said. When you reconnect with a guy at thirty-two, you know you missed a lot of history. And you don't ask too many questions. But honestly, I couldn't imagine Adam Zimmerman, who loves music and movies but hates crowds and collars, going to a big-city theater for any reason other than a very attractive woman.

His jawline flushed. *Bingo!*

The lights dimmed. I smiled and squeezed his hand. In moments, we were enthralled as the stage of our small theater in northwest Montana became the back alleys of London, overtaken by magical creatures with impish black noses, wickedly long whiskers, and tails that had lives of their own.

The costumes were incredible. Especially considering that, according to the village rumor mill, the costume manager had quit less than a week before opening night. My sister and other local designers had pitched in to help fit the rented costumes for *Cats* and adapt costumes from the company's storehouse for the other productions.

A slinky, minky feline sidled onto the stage. I almost didn't recognize Emily Davies, the actor beneath the makeup and fur. Summer stock is a big draw for our little town, but it doesn't pay much. Like a lot of "theater kids," Emily needed a part-time job that could be squeezed in between rehearsals and performances. I'd hired her at the Merc to pack and ship online orders, sending Montana-made jam, jerky, and truffles to lucky folks across the continent. At busy times, she helps out on the sales floor. She often sings as she works, and when customers catch a line from *Oklahoma!* or *Singing in the Rain*, a few join in. I like to joke that at the Merc, earworms are free.

On stage, cats snarled, clawed, and scratched as they pranced and prowled, singing all the while. After a particularly fractious exchange and another refrain, Emily snapped her tail at the offending cat and flounced off into the wings. As the action continued, the auto-replay function in my brain was still singing about Jellicle Cats.

And all that might explain why I recognized Emily's voice when I heard the scream.

Chad Stevenson did not look good. When Emily screamed, the actors on stage paused briefly, then carried on in loyal theater tradition. But I'd elbowed Adam and we'd edged our way down the row to the aisle. Over the years, I've spent a lot of time in the theater. I was on stage rehearsing for the senior play the February night when my father was killed.

So despite the dark, I had no trouble finding the stairs, hidden by a half wall, that led to the L-shaped junction between stage and green room. Where Stevenson should have been on duty, script and pocket flashlight in hand, one eye on the action and an ear on any waiting actors. As stage manager, it was his job to cue them, make sure the necessary props were at hand, and generally keep things rolling.

I glanced at the stage, where the show went on, and slipped into the green room, Adam behind me.

Emily stood against the nearest wall, one black-gloved hand covering her mouth. The room looked as it always did. A high-top table near the door was jammed with pop cans and water bottles. More bottles and scripts littered a large table on the far side of the room, and a gigantic whiteboard covered with the production and rehearsal schedules filled one wall.

In the middle, in a clearing where actors often paced, muttering their lines, lay Stevenson. His eyes were open but blank. What I could see of his skin—forehead and cheeks—appeared dark, almost purple, though in life he'd been a fair-skinned white man. Some sort of scarf or muffler, made from that fuzzy yarn that looks like it's shedding even when it isn't, was wrapped tightly around his mouth and nose.

Adam crossed the room and dropped to one knee. He laid two fingers along the man's neck, checking for a pulse, while I slipped an arm around Emily, her small body quaking, the gray and black faux fur of her wig quivering.

"Is he—?" She couldn't finish the question.

Not for the first time, I gave silent thanks for Adam's wilderness medical training, though I had no doubt that Chad Stevenson was past saving.

Adam's expression confirmed my fear.

"He's gone," he said, almost in a whisper.

Ohmygod.

I turned to Emily. "How long until intermission?"

She glanced at the wall clock. "Three minutes?"

Adam gave my arm a gentle squeeze, then strode out.

I pictured him standing in the shadows, waiting for the curtain to fall. Redirecting the actors to keep them from barging in on a crime scene. Because Chad Stevenson's death was clearly no accident.

I slipped away from Emily, fumbling in my bag for my phone. Stevenson lay on his back, legs outstretched. I snapped a few pictures, wondering how the killer had managed to wrap the scarf, or whatever it was, around his head tightly enough to kill him without signs of a struggle. Anyone who's ever seen a late-night horror movie—and who hasn't, on a sleepless night—knows that if someone wraps something around your face or neck, you grab it. You pull, you jerk, you fight.

But Stevenson's arms lay by his sides, fingers closed. Not in fists, but loosely, as if wrapped around something.

I leaned in, not daring to touch him. One hand held a lime-green object, the other a few inches of hot pink yarn. I caught a whiff of jasmine perfume. His? Odd for a man.

Had he fought with someone, grabbed bits of a costume? Emily's was dark and sparkly, but I thought I'd seen spots of color on other cats.

I took a few more shots, close up.

Stevenson wore black, the better to stand unseen at the edge of the stage. An average-sized man; not big, not small. It couldn't have been easy for one person to move him, dead or alive. And he couldn't have been dead long. We were still in the first act.

Then I heard Adam, calling from the edge of the stage, "Is there a doctor in the house?" I tucked my phone in my bag and stood near the door, next to Emily. Wide-eyed and trembling, she shed no tears. A surprise, frankly, as I'd found her to be sweet and sensitive in the few weeks she'd worked for me. Artistic control, or a fear of ruining all that makeup?

Moments later, footsteps approached.

Adam entered, followed by a fiftyish woman in black linen crops and a white lace-trimmed tunic.

Her attention went straight to the body. "Strangled?"

"Suffocated, I think. Smothered. Red spots in his eyes." Adam gestured to his own black-coffee eyes, pinched with worry. "And I don't see any neck injuries."

Her blond bob swayed slightly as she did what Adam had done, surveying the area around the body, then crouching to check for a pulse. She slipped her fingers underneath the scarf and lifted it up, giving the mouth and nose a closer look.

"Who's in charge?" she said, standing. "And what is this man's name?"

A dark-haired man I'd known most of my life emerged from the shadowed hallway. "I am. I'm Kip Taylor. Christopher Taylor. My family and I run the summer productions. He"—Kip gestured, his hand shaking—"is Chad Stevenson. He's our stage manager."

"Carolyn Cook," the woman said as she straightened. "M.D. Visiting from Tucson for a few days. My condolences."

"What—?" Kip asked. His gaze skittered from Dr. Cook to the body on the floor and back. "He's dead? Heart attack? Isn't he too young for that?"

"I'm afraid not," Dr. Cook replied, not sounding frightened at all. "I'm not a medical examiner, but I'd say this death looks suspicious."

A collective gasp came from the actors gathered in the dark hallway.

Emily gasped, too, and I pulled her close. With that single word—*suspicious*—Dr. Cook had put her finger on exactly what had been bothering me.

Though I didn't know what was wrapped around his face or what had been tucked into his hands, and hadn't the foggiest idea why he lay on his back in the middle of the green room floor, it was crystal clear that Chad Stevenson's body had been deliberately arranged.

Staged.

I've always cherished the patterns of the day that give it rhyme and reason. And the ritual cup of morning coffee with Adam—in good weather, on the stone terrace outside our newly remodeled home, overlooking the orchard my great-grandparents planted—is sweetness itself.

But that cup of coffee, delicious as it had been, had worn off by the time I got to work Saturday morning. Happily, right next to the Merc is a touch of Provence, a French bakery called Le Panier. I drove down Back Alley and parked behind the Merc, then headed over for a Saturday morning special: a double latte and a *pain au chocolat.*

Okay, that's my Monday through Friday special, too, but let's not quibble.

And I admit, I was particularly curious this morning to hear what the townspeople and visitors were saying about Chad Stevenson's murder.

The Playhouse is a major part of life in Jewel Bay. The elder Taylors founded it more than fifty years ago, and while community and student productions fill the house in the off-season, it truly shines in summer. Aspiring actors from around the country audition, hoping to gain experience and credits. It's repertory theater, rotating four plays and musicals a season. That's brilliant, if you ask me. Theater lovers in Montana and beyond make the trek their seasonal ritual. And tourists visiting Jewel Bay or passing through on their way to Glacier National Park delight in discovering an unexpected gem.

The money they spend in our hotels and inns, our restaurants and grocery stores and gas stations, keeps this town afloat. Not to mention what they spend in shops like mine.

While Kip Taylor, the middle child, had taken over the summer theater from his parents, his younger sister, Wendy Taylor LaFontaine, had found her calling in flour and yeast. She runs the bakery, while her French husband runs the adjacent bistro. If the Merc, founded in 1910, is the heart of Jewel Bay, Le Panier is its stomach.

The outdoor tables were already half full. Inside, I was greeted by whiffs of caffeine and sugar and the whistle of the espresso machine. Heavenly. A woman examined the pastry case. Behind the counter, a barista attempted the intricate ballet of lattes and cappuccinos, this milk or that, extra foam, and shots of flavor.

"Was that skinny mocha double or single?" she asked.

"Double. The capp's a single," Wendy answered. Wearing a summer-weight white chef's tunic and black cotton pants festooned with red chili peppers, she juggled giving instructions, taking orders, and plating croissants.

"Hey, Wendy," I called. "How goes the grind?"

Bad puns are half the fun of working in food and retail.

She tossed me a half smile, her eyes dark and intense. She's two years older than I, the same age as my sister. Since I came back to Jewel Bay two years ago and took over the Merc, we've become good friends.

The woman in front of me added a lemon tart to her coffee order, then turned to her husband. "So, what should we do tonight? Since the show is canceled. At least we've seen *Oklahoma!* before."

The cancellation wasn't a surprise. Though it seemed likely that Stevenson was killed where he was found, the sheriff would view the entire theater as a crime scene. I imagined the Sunday matinee a no-go, but hoped his team finished scouring the building in time for next week's shows.

"Linger over dinner, I guess," the man replied as he pulled out his wallet. "What else is there to do?"

"There's a folk duo playing in the park tonight," I said. "Other side of the one-lane bridge. The galleries and shops are open late and several bars and restaurants have live music."

"Anywhere to dance?" the woman asked.

"The Jewel Inn. The chalet-like building at the north end of town."

"Oh, we saw it. It's darling," she said. "Such a terrible business, murder in the theater. When we heard the scream last night, we thought it was part of the show."

How could you? I thought, but bit my tongue. Literally—a salty pang shot through my mouth.

"Honestly," she continued, "we had no idea anything was going on. And the town looks so safe."

"Sheriff Hoover is top-notch. I'm sure he'll wrap this up quickly." I rubbed the three lucky stars tattooed inside my left wrist.

"I hope so." She took the wide white coffee cup her husband handed her. "Thanks for the suggestions."

"The usual?" Wendy asked me and I nodded. Behind her, in the bakery in back, I saw a young man shovel loaves into the brick oven while a woman slipped in and out of view, bearing large metal trays of something delicious.

"You shorthanded this morning?" I asked as Wendy slid my croissant into a white takeout bag.

"I'm down two theater kids," she said, holding up two fingers. "At least Bianca texted me that she was too upset to come in. Braden didn't bother. I had to move a baker up front to pull shots. I don't know when we'll get the dishes washed."

I'd barely known Stevenson—we'd met at the annual welcome party the Merchants' Association throws for the cast and crew, and I often saw him strolling down the sidewalk in the afternoon on his way to work, sipping from a can of flavored Pellegrino. But even I found his death deeply distressing. I could imagine how hard this was on the kids who worked with him. Sheriff Hoover, who had been the deputy in charge of investigating my father's death all those years ago, had once told me that if violent or untimely death didn't bother you, you were a poor excuse for a human being.

"How's Kip taking it?" I asked.

"He ordered a triple shot," she said. "Not sure if he was that upset, or just isn't used to getting up in the morning."

Too funny. And while I'd never heard the sheriff say you should wonder about your humanity if you didn't occasionally laugh in the middle of tragedy, I was certain he'd agree.

∞

Outside, I stopped and raised the cup to my lips. The substitute barista didn't quite have the knack; the foam was too thick to let the good stuff through. I pried the lid off and was about to take a sip when a young couple approached, hand in hand, eyes only for each other. He leaned down, she lifted her face, and they kissed, still walking.

"Hey!" I stepped back, but not fast enough to avoid getting bumped. My coffee sloshed over my hand.

"Oh my gosh. I'm so sorry," the young woman said. "Are you okay?"

I set the dripping cup on the stone wall separating the bakery's patio from the sidewalk and shook my hand. Milky coffee had splattered my short denim skirt and was now dribbling down my leg. In half a second, it would pool into my sandal. The woman who'd ordered the lemon tart was sitting at the closest table, and I gratefully accepted the napkins she offered.

"I'm so sorry," my accidental assailant repeated. "I guess we weren't watching where we were going."

Too focused on each other.

"Here, Erin. I got napkins," the young man said as he emerged from the bakery, the screen door banging shut behind him. He was one of the athletic club's year-round employees and a camp counselor. The swimming and boating instructor, if I remembered right, though I could not pull his name out of my rattled memory. She was a summer hire.

"And I ordered you a new coffee," he added. "Sorry about all that."

"Thanks. It's okay." Did Adam know they were together? We weren't so old and married that we didn't understand all-consuming new love—I pegged this couple at around twenty-five—but I knew Adam worried about staff relationships. Hormones sometimes meant staffers weren't always the best role models for the kids. Plus, if a fling went wrong, there he'd be in the wilderness with three dozen teens and tweens and two employees spitting at each other. I waved off their concern. "Don't worry about it. It's only coffee."

They apologized again, then wandered off, glued at the hip, but not at the lip. Wendy brought me a fresh latte, and gratefully, carefully, I headed the other direction.

The Merc is the oldest building in the village, what we call downtown.

It's a pile of century-old bricks that regularly gives me headaches and sends me scrambling to replace broken windows, repair soffits, and tinker with the locks. It's cramped and drafty. You wouldn't want to play marbles on the sloping plank floors. And the only space for storage and shipping is down a steep, narrow flight of stairs.

But it's my happy place.

I am particularly happy when it's busy. As it was this Saturday, starting the moment Tracy, my assistant manager and creative director, unlocked the door at ten sharp. She and Lou Mary, sales clerk extraordinaire, work full-time, and my mother helps out now and then. We focus on Montana-made food and drink, along with locally made pottery, soap, and other goodies. A pair of gardeners grow veggies for us, and I hauled the sidewalk produce cart outside.

Then I sent Emily a quick text to make sure she was okay, since she wasn't scheduled to work today.

I managed to clean myself up reasonably well. Faked a pleasant smile when a customer said that a place as old and venerable as the Merc must practically run itself.

A handful of folks mentioned the tragedy and tonight's cancellation, and I admit, I did worry. If the shutdown went on, the lost ticket sales would be a serious drain on the theater's finances. If it led to canceled travel plans—by those who, like the couple in the bakery this morning, didn't know what else to do in Jewel Bay—the merchants would suffer. We've got the ninety days of summer to make a year's worth of income, and if something interferes—rain, wildfire, murder—we're in big trouble.

By noon, we'd run out of both huckleberry and cherry jam and I dashed to the basement to restock.

On the big worktable lay a copy of the script for *Brigadoon*, which wasn't scheduled to open for another week. Emily must have left it here Friday afternoon when she finished her shift. Tucked inside the front cover was this year's cast and crew list and their roles.

Bianca Calderon, Wendy's part-time barista, was listed as Fiona, the Scottish girl who charms the lost American hunter. I remembered her as a dark-haired dynamo who, like Emily, enjoyed surprising customers by singing to them. I couldn't picture Braden, the other part-timer Wendy had mentioned, even though I'm in Le Panier far too often.

Emily had said no other actors were coming on before intermission, and no one had been in the green room when she left the stage. In the dark, in a hurry, she hadn't noticed that Stevenson wasn't at his post.

So who, or what, had lured him away? Cast or crew? Male or female? An incident or an intruder? I couldn't even guess, not without knowing more about the cause of death.

I tucked the list in my apron pocket and picked up two cases of jam. Upstairs, Tracy was talking truffles with an older couple—her huckleberry chocolates are to die for—and Lou Mary had stepped out for lunch. The front door opened and a woman entered. I set my boxes on the counter.

"Dr. Cook," I said, recognizing the vacationing doctor in an instant. "We met last night in the theater. Sort of. My husband is the medic who summoned you. I was comforting the young woman who found the body—she works here part-time. I'm Erin Murphy. Welcome to the Merc." I held out my hand.

"Carolyn Cook." Her handshake was quick and firm. "Such a sad business. Did you know the man?"

"A little. I hope he didn't suffer." I was fishing.

"Most likely not," she said, avoiding both bait and hook. "Those picnics to go, in your window. Are they available here?"

"You bet." I ran down the options—cheeses, crackers, wild game salami, pasta salads. And of course, wine and truffles. "Refill the basket as often as you like." One of my innovations, and quite popular, especially for evenings when outdoor concerts were scheduled.

She filled a basket, then chose a few soaps shaped like pine trees and bears as gifts for friends back home. But she said nothing more about Chad Stevenson or the cause of death, despite my subtle probing.

I plucked a wedge of cheese and a green salad from the cooler and climbed up the half flight of stairs to my tiny office under the eaves. As I ate, I glanced over the cast and crew list a second time. Fingers crossed that no one quit because of the murder. Every year or two, a cast or crew member got sick or injured, left because of a family emergency, or flaked out. Most were young, college students or new graduates. The Playhouse was a training ground for crew members as well as actors—set designers, sound engineers, musicians. Stevenson was a veteran, traveling from company to company. I'm well aware, as the wife of a onetime ski bum, that the itinerant life appeals to some people, but Stevenson had to have been at least thirty-five, an age when most people choose to settle down. Loved his work, apparently.

Emily's cast and crew sheet listed the costume manager, the one who'd quit without warning, as Amanda Swallow. If she'd been at the welcome party, I'd missed the chance to meet her.

I texted Chiara. *Why did Amanda leave the theater company?*

No idea. Surprised everybody—to come back after all these years then wig out.

Any theories? Where did she go?

Don't know. Gotta run—baby's awake—see you tomorrow.

Sunday. The weekly gathering was a family tradition that stayed with the house when my mother remarried last year and sold the place to Adam and me. Depending on the season and our schedules, it could be brunch, lunch, or dinner. This Sunday, we were eating early so the family could wish Adam good luck before he left. Whether he needed more luck with the kids or the wilderness was a toss-up. And now, he had a potential staff issue.

I finished my lunch, drained my water bottle, and got back to business. It takes a lot of work to make a place run itself.

"Not that I'm surprised," Adam said that evening when I told him about my literal run-in with his staffers. "But I am disappointed. She's new, but he saw what happened last year when the cook wouldn't leave one of the counselors alone. It was flat-out harassment. I had to let him go midsummer, but happily, the counselor stayed and didn't sue. We didn't get a new cook for a week. Everybody had to pitch in."

I remembered. He'd come home a champion pancake flipper.

"And we're leaving tomorrow at noon," he continued. "I can't afford to lose anyone."

With my small staff, I hadn't had to deal with serious personnel issues, but in my days in Seattle as a grocery buyer for SavClub, the international warehouse chain, I'd witnessed both innocent coworker romance and supervisors who'd abused their power. We talked about his options as we sat outside with a glass of wine, watching the evening sun turn the tips of the waves on the lake to diamonds. We kept talking over dinner—my mother's fresh pasta with basil pesto, and a salad Adam put together from the Merc's produce cart.

In the end, he decided the simple approach was best. Talk to the couple, separately and together, and make sure the relationship was what it seemed. Remind them it couldn't interfere with their responsibilities to the kids, and warn them against tent-hopping. Kids would see and parents would hear. Adam would keep a close eye and reassess after the first session.

The cats had come in with us after dinner, and now full-figured Pumpkin lay on the living room rug, a late patch of sun warming her soft orange belly. From the couch, I watched sleek Mr. Sandburg, half her age and size, swat a fuzzy cat toy shaped like a piece of sushi, right down to the white stripes on the faux salmon, occasionally sending it her way. Whether he was teasing her or enticing her to play, I couldn't tell. Human or feline, romantic or otherwise, the male-female relationship is often hard to decipher.

But then, something struck me.

I reached for my phone and scrolled through my crime scene pictures. My finger was poised to send a pair of close-ups—one showing a clump of lime-green felt held loosely in Stevenson's hand, the other a strand of pink yarn—to Chiara and ask if she recognized them from any particular costume, when I thought better of it. She wouldn't want me to get involved—she never did. Plus, she was busy with a new baby and a seven-year-old. Better to show her the pictures tomorrow, when she couldn't ignore me.

But no luck. Sunday morning, my six-month-old niece woke up feeling punk and Chiara kept her home. My brother-in-law and nephew traipsed from their place to ours through the woods, and I scooped up Landon, savoring that little-boy smell. My mother arrived with my stepfather, whom I adored and who, more importantly, adored her. My brother Nick came with his fiancée, my BFF Kim Caldwell, coincidentally a sheriff's detective.

"Not my case, Erin," she said, her first words after a quick hug.

That, I knew. It had been her counterpart, Detective Oliver Bello, late of Miami, Florida, and now practically a native after a year in Montana, who'd questioned Adam and me at the theater Friday night. I swear, I never go looking for trouble—it seems to know where I live and work without being told. And Kim had reluctantly come to admit that I have a talent for asking the right questions and seeing things the pros sometimes missed. But now that she was about to join the family, I thought it more critical than ever not to trade on the friendship that stretched back to sixth grade. If she volunteered info about the investigation, fine, but I wasn't going to ask.

"This season seems cursed," my mother said. "First the costume manager quits, and now this."

"Don't you need more than two bad things to call it a curse?" Adam asked. "You know, bad things come in threes and all that."

"Hush your mouth," I said. "You know how much can go wrong in the theater." Like the near-disasters the night we'd caught my father's killer in the alley outside the building. But I wasn't going to think about that right now. "Mom, did you know the woman who left?"

"Mandy? I met her briefly in Dragonfly before the season started," my mother continued. "She was picking up a torn costume Kathy had repaired. One of those skimpy skirts from *Oklahoma!* Turns out she was an actress here ten years ago, the last time they did *Oklahoma!* But then she just up and quit. No one seems to know why."

Mandy. Amanda.

The plot thickened. In my imagination, anyway. As if I didn't have enough to do without chasing after killer cats and missing costume designers.

The buses were already waiting when I pulled into the athletic club parking lot at eleven o'clock.

"I miss you already." From the passenger seat, Adam took my hand. "But I'll be back in two weeks." Trading the first group of kids for the next, with two luxurious nights at home in between.

"Twelve days," I said. There would be no cell service once they left base camp, though I knew he carried a GPS device and a radio for emergencies.

"It's summer in retail. You'll be too busy to miss me."

I gave him a kiss I hoped proved otherwise.

A few moments later, we spotted the staffers who'd spilled my coffee the day before. He'd spoken with them last night, but wanted another word, in person, before they all left civilization.

"I'll wait," I said. I jerked a thumb toward my old friend Bunny Burns, née Bunny Easter, dropping off her oldest for her first summer at camp. "Bunny will be a blubbering mess. She'll want to talk."

I watched Bunny going over the camp checklist with her daughter, who looked exactly like Bunny and her twin sister, Polly, had looked at twelve. How was it that my friends had kids going off to camp and I was still hoping for that first twinge that told me our first baby might be on the way? Because they'd gotten started early and I was getting started late.

And because Bunny was always early for everything. Parents and kids were starting to arrive, and her daughter turned her attention to her friends, as young and adorable and nervous as she was.

As predicted, Bunny was both chatty and choked up. "I figured as long as I was here I'd take in a yoga class," she said, gesturing to her knee-length black exercise pants and pink T-shirt. "That's the only way to get me out of my jammies before noon on Sunday. And there's the new teacher arriving. She may not improve our down dogs, but she'll up our fashion game, for sure. You should start coming to class again."

I followed her gaze to a slim, dark-haired woman in black leggings with mesh panels up the sides and a red-and-black bra top, a canvas duffle emblazoned "Jewel Bay Summer Theater" over her shoulder. Was that the missing Bianca, a silk scarf tied flapper-style around her temples and flowing down her back? No. This woman was a good ten years older. Close to my age. A bit taller, maybe five-six or seven, but like Bianca and Emily, she had a dancer's grace that no amount of yoga would ever give me. Or Bunny.

Then Bunny and I exchanged air-kisses and she bounced over to give her offspring one last teary farewell. Adam joined me after his talk with the counselors.

"They promised to behave," he said. "Fingers crossed."

I gave my tall, dark, and handsome guy another kiss, then drove into the village. Turned off Front Street and parked on Back. Inside the Merc's rear courtyard, I stopped.

Emily sat at one of the bistro tables we'd added last summer. She wasn't scheduled to work today.

I had a bad feeling, even before I saw her swollen eyes and heard her shaky voice.

"I—I'm sorry, Erin. I hate to quit, but I have to. I need to get my things. And my final paycheck?"

Whatever I'd expected, it hadn't been this. I firmly believe that it's a lot easier to get someone to talk when they have a hot drink in their hands. Plus, I needed a dose of caffeine, toot sweet, and we didn't have time to go next door for the fancy stuff. The girl was skittish as a new colt, and as likely to bolt.

Inside, I flipped a switch and the old milk glass pendant lights began to glow. Behind me, Emily's clogs echoed on the plank floor. Oh, the stories this old Merc could tell.

In the commercial kitchen in the back of the shop, I started a big pot of Cowboy Roast, the custom-blend coffee we serve as samples and sell by the pound.

While it brewed, I gestured to the chrome stools lined up along the stainless steel counter that divides shop from kitchen. My mother rescued them years ago when an old soda fountain closed in another small Montana town and recovered them in red vinyl. They always make customers smile. Me, too.

We sat, and I reached for Emily's hand, half expecting her to pull away. Instead, she gripped it like a lifeline.

"How well did you know Chad?" I asked. "And have you told Kip you're leaving?"

She shook her head, blond ponytail wagging, though whether in answer to my first question or my second, I couldn't tell. The coffee was ready. I filled two cups and slid the sugar dispenser toward her.

"Are you getting any sleep?"

Her eyes flashed, then almost as quickly, her face closed down.

Emily's talent and passion for the theater shone brightly, but she was young. And I knew from our conversations that while her family was supportive, they weren't flush. How would she get back home, thousands of miles away?

"Are you sure you want to leave?" I continued. "It's awful, I know, but there's no reason to think anyone else involved with the theater is in danger." I hoped not, anyway.

"Oh, Erin. I never meant—we thought . . ." She covered her mouth with her hands, her eyes cast down, seeing—what?

The back door opened and Tracy called out a greeting. She and Lou Mary alternate Sundays.

I leaned forward, not quite touching Emily's knee. "You've had a huge shock. But you don't have to decide what to do right now. I know you need the money, so stay here today and help out, and we'll talk again. Just put on a happy face."

Her spine straightened and the clouds disappeared. "From *Bye Bye Birdie*. I love that song," she said. "I played Rosie in my high school production."

"Atta girl."

"Umm, Erin? I need a new water bottle—they took everything we'd left in the green room. Can I use my employee discount to buy one of yours? They're super cute."

"Take one," I said. "On the house. My sister designed the logo."

As we got the shop ready to open, my brain replayed Emily's words. What had she never meant? What had they thought? Who was the "we"? Not that Chad Stevenson's death wasn't tragic enough, but was something else troubling her, too?

Was my mother right, and a third tragedy was waiting in the wings?

With Emily there to help Tracy, I slipped out a few minutes after we opened and walked up the street to Dragonfly Dry Goods, a totally yummy quilt and yarn shop. I have no arts and crafts skills—my sister got that gene—but I do love drinking in the colors and petting the soft wool. Kathy Jensen, the owner, came here eons ago as a costume assistant, then returned after she left theater work. Jewel Bay is the kind of town people like to come back to. Her shop is a major draw all year long, but especially in tourist season.

After a few shopkeeper pleasantries, I got to the point. "I hear you've been helping out at the theater this summer, with fittings and repairs."

"Costumes get ripped. It's inevitable, with all that dancing and running and the quick wardrobe changes. Fixing a torn skirt is easy, but thank goodness they don't do *Cats* very often. I still can't figure out how that girl ripped her costume the way she did." She gestured to the wall of yarn. "The tail was completely gone. I couldn't match it. I had to make a new one, then add a new sleeve and insert a piece on the leg so it didn't look like I'd stuck the hind end of a zebra on a giraffe. We won't be sending that one back to the rental company."

I scrolled through my phone and found the photo. Cropped it so she didn't have to see everything I'd seen, just the fabric wrapped around Chad Stevenson's mouth and nose. "Did the original tail look anything like this?"

Even without the full photo, she knew what she was seeing. "Ohmygod. Where did it come from? Who?"

"I was hoping you could tell me. Do you recognize these bits and pieces? Does anyone in *Cats* have a costume with these colors?" I showed her the pictures of Stevenson's hands, clutching the shocking pink and lime scraps. As if he'd grabbed at something. Or someone.

"No. Those costumes are pretty fanciful—feathers, fur, eyelash yarn. Not like any cats I've ever known, which I guess is the point. But no, nothing like that."

Strange, indeed.

Though tourist season wasn't in full swing yet, the Merc was hopping all afternoon and I didn't have much chance to mull over Kathy's comments about the costumes. When we'd locked the door behind the last customer, I spoke to Emily.

"Promise me you'll take a few days to think things over. Leaving the company is a big decision. Besides, look at all the orders that came in over the weekend." I showed her the stack I'd printed out. "I really need your help. You can work as many hours as you want."

She caught her lower lip between her teeth. I rubbed my lucky stars, and finally, she agreed.

"Thanks, Erin," she said, and picked up her new water bottle. "For believing in me."

And as she headed for the back door, I heard her singing softly. "*Gray skies are gonna clear up. Put on a happy face.*"

You'd think Monday mornings in a tourist town would be quiet. You'd be wrong. Lots of folks stretch the weekend an extra day or two. And it didn't help that I'd overslept, forgetting Adam wasn't there to wake me, or that I'd tripped while sidestepping the cats' faux fur sushi roll and banged up my knee, requiring ice, Band-Aids, and a wardrobe change of my own. I skipped the morning stop at the bakery and got straight to work.

And breathed a sigh of relief when Emily showed up, right on time.

It wasn't until midmorning that I had a chance to take a break in my tiny office, icing my battered knee. The cast list I'd found in Emily's script lay on my desk. Emily had mentioned some of her cast mates, and I'd met a few. I ran a finger down the names.

If I remembered right, that costume Kathy had virtually remade belonged to the cat played by Bianca Calderon. She also had a role in *Oklahoma!*, a show involving a host of twirling skirts. And she was the girl who worked for Wendy in the coffee shop but begged off Saturday morning.

I limped down the stairs and out the front door, wondering who to quiz first—the brother or the sister?

The decision was made for me when Kip Taylor emerged from the theater and crossed the street to the bakery.

"We could reopen tomorrow," Kip said a few minutes later, "if we ran the show without the green room. Which they won't let us have back until they finish some forensic doo-dah. Toxicology, I think the detective said. He's thinking Wednesday, maybe Thursday. Gonna be hard to find a replacement stage manager, especially mid-season. I can fill in for now, but not forever."

We were huddled at a mosaic-topped table inside, in the corner. The air was thick with the mingled scents of sugar, bread, and caffeine. Wendy set a triple shot in front of her brother but stayed on her feet, ready to get back to work the moment a customer entered. I'd declined her offer of espresso. My brain was buzzing without any extra help.

"You still shorthanded?" I asked, and she rolled her eyes. *Yes.* I laid my purloined copy of the cast and crew list on the table and turned to Kip. "Which means you're missing actors. These two." I pointed. "And a third is ready to quit."

Give him credit for looking stricken. If I was right, he'd be looking far worse pretty soon, and I wouldn't feel one ounce of guilt.

"Stevenson's been badgering those girls, hasn't he?" I continued. "And not just the twenty-year-olds. That's why Amanda Swallow left, isn't it, because Chad Stevenson was pestering her."

"No! She never—she didn't—" It takes a cool cucumber to run a theater company year in, year out, with all the moving parts, all the things that can go wrong. But Kip was flustered now, and his reaction confirmed that

Stevenson had been more than a hard-nosed coworker. His sister picked up on it, too.

"Kip," Wendy snapped. "You knew that man was harassing the women who work for you and you didn't do anything about it? You have a responsibility to protect them."

"Look. It happens, right? It's wrong, and we do everything we can to stop it, to prevent it. But I can't solve a problem if they don't tell me about it. No one ever said a thing. I just thought we had a couple of actors who couldn't get things right. That happens, too."

He was insistent, and I didn't want to doubt him. But it's all too easy to close an eye to things you don't want to see. You have to be willing, as Adam had been, to look beyond the surface. But with replacements so hard to find, Kip wouldn't be the first employer to convince himself he didn't have a problem.

No wonder Stevenson liked the work. It gave him ready access to ambitious young women who put up with unwanted attention because the season was short. Girls, some of them, afraid to make waves and risk capsizing their plans. One whiff of trouble and it would be their fledgling careers in ruins, not his.

A shortage of qualified competition meant theater owners looked the other way. And the traveling life made it all easy-peasy. Odds were he'd left a trail of trouble behind him.

I stood. "Drink up. You're taking me to the wardrobe room."

Inside the theater, I followed Kip through the semi-darkness to the basement.

"I'm not sure I should let you in," he said, "though the sheriff didn't tell me not to."

"They've already searched down here, right?" But did they know what to look for, a bunch of men, mostly, pawing through full skirts and feather-flocked leotards and cowboy getups.

"They searched the room. I don't know how closely they looked at the costumes. I wasn't here."

Dressing areas were separated by gender. In each, makeup stations lined one wall. Huge metal rolling racks held the costumes for this season's shows, the racks for each show clustered together. The fanciful *Cats* wardrobe was easy to spot.

I flipped through the rack, searching for Bianca's costume. I ran my fingers over the soft faux fur, the spiky nylon feathers, the smooth Spandex. Kathy's work was impeccable. You'd never know the costume hadn't been designed this way from the start. You'd never know there'd been another tail, and that it had been wrapped around a man's face.

No sign of any new rips or tears. I had half hoped—okay, I had fervently wished—to show that he had attacked Bianca again. That she'd taken revenge, improbable as it might seem, in response to yet another attack.

But this costume didn't prove it.

"Kathy worked a miracle," Kip said as I returned the costume to the rack. "I can't remember when we've had an actor who was so hard on costumes."

"Show me. What did she wear in the other productions?"

"Costumes are organized by actor, hung in the order they'll be worn, for quick changes." He pointed to the rack marked *Oklahoma!* "She was one of the dancers. We try not to feature the same actors in every show."

Bianca had worn two outfits, a gingham homesteader's dress and showgirl's cancan skirt and bodice. The "skimpy skirt" Kathy had mentioned to my mother. I could see where the nylon underskirt beneath the black netting had been torn loose at the waist and ripped all the way to the hem, then neatly repaired.

"What else? She's in *Brigadoon*, right?"

"It opens next week. We've only done a couple of rehearsals in costume. This is hers." He pulled out a dress with a full skirt that fell to mid-calf, a tartan scarf draped over one shoulder.

I lifted the skirt, scanning inside for signs of repair. Sure enough. A ripped seam had been repaired with safety pins. A new tear, or had she been afraid to report yet another torn costume?

"Were Bianca and Emily close?"

"Roommates, I think."

Criminy. I had to call Detective Bello. After I talked with Emily. Assuming she hadn't gone missing, too.

I stood outside the Merc, in front of one of the twin display windows, catching my breath. My banged-up knee had not liked me rushing up the theater's long staircase, across the lobby, and down the street, but it was worth the pain to see Emily at the front counter, ringing up a sale. Smiling brightly, no longer the sad-eyed waif of yesterday. Either she was a good actor, putting on the happy face, or retail is balm for the soul and the happy face was genuine.

Or had she been acting when she told me she needed to leave, that the murder was too upsetting? Had I misread her? Did the girl who literally sang and whistled while she worked know more than she was telling me? Could she be a killer?

The customer picked up her bag and headed for the door. I watched as Emily's shoulders deflated, as the smile drooped, as the sadness returned to her eyes. I held the door for the departing customer and walked in.

"Erin," Emily said, making a visible effort to square her shoulders and put on the pleasant retail expression that I always tell my staff is the first rule of business. The gray skies didn't suddenly clear, and I couldn't brush away all the clouds. There was still a killer in town.

But at least I was reasonably sure the killer wasn't working in my shop.

"Take a break with me," I said, pointing out back. "I have news."

Her chin quivered. On her way past the kitchen, she snared her new water bottle from behind the counter.

We use the courtyard for special events, like bridal showers or charity fundraisers. Sometimes, we open the gate in the wooden fence separating our place from Red's Bar, for larger shindigs. Right now, lunchtime chatter and wisps of '80s rock drifted over the fence. A delivery truck rumbled down the alley, followed by an acrid belch of diesel.

"I know what happened," I said. "Though I don't think you meant it to turn out the way it did."

Emily's cheeks flushed and her fingers went to her throat, then clutched the neckline of her embroidered peasant blouse. She wasn't acting now.

"Cast members leave their water bottles on the high-top table inside the green room. When you come off stage, you can grab yours, catch your breath, wet your whistle. Stevenson didn't use a water bottle. He drank flavored Pellegrino." I pictured the cans on the table. "I used to see him walk by the shop on his way to the theater, and he always had one in hand. Never a Coke or a Mountain Dew. He was a creature of habit." Some habits good, some very bad.

"I don't know what you put in the can," I continued, "but I do know that the state crime lab will figure it out. And the sooner you tell the truth, the better."

"It wasn't—I didn't—"

"A man is dead." I knew I sounded harsh, but I was losing patience. "I know he was a creep. I know he was bothering Bianca, and maybe you, too. I suspect he hounded Amanda Swallow right out of a job. But murder—"

"He wasn't supposed to be dead," she blurted, eyes filling and features twisting. "He was only supposed to fall asleep on the job and get in trouble. We knew Kip wouldn't fire him. Even if Chad suspected he'd been drugged, he couldn't have said anything without admitting that he'd been—well, you know. But we wanted him to know what we'd done and leave us alone. That's why we left the mice."

"The mice?"

"They were part of a running joke. Early on in rehearsals, Braden, one of the other actors, brought in a toy mouse, the kind cats play with."

The kind my cats played with.

"But more realistic," she continued. "Gray and rubbery. He used it to scare Bianca, because he liked her."

Ah, kids.

"And then—" Her voice broke and I waited while she took a long drink. "It grew from there. We all started bringing in toy mice. Some were bright-colored, some had bells, some feathers. We'd leave them for each other in funny places, like in a tap shoe or the pocket of a costume. Stevenson tried to get in on it, but it was just between the actors. He kinda took the fun out of it, you know?" She glanced at me nervously, needing me to understand. "But when he woke up, he would know we'd done this to him. And he'd stop harassing us."

That explained the bright objects clutched in his hands.

"What did you give him?"

"Chloral hydrate. It's an old remedy for sleep and anxiety. My mother takes it and I brought a bottle with me. She's got a prescription—I don't. But I only gave him a couple of doses. Two or three teaspoons, max."

As she talked, I Googled the stuff on my phone. "Enough to knock him out and make him feel sick afterward."

She nodded. She looked miserable.

"Who else knew what you were going to do? Your roommate, Bianca?"

"He was awful to her. Me, he teased. Touched my back and made comments about my breasts—they do stand out in some of those costumes. But he attacked her. More than once. How far he went, I'm not sure, but she was determined to get him back. It—it was her idea."

"And you think she took it a step further. Took the old tail from her costume and wrapped it around his nose and throat, suffocating him while he slept."

"She couldn't have. She was on stage. I didn't even know she'd kept the tail." She shuddered. "Weird souvenir."

I tried to picture the Act I choreography but I didn't know *Cats* well enough. I'd never been in it, and too much had happened since Friday night. Didn't matter; I believed her.

From the bakery next door came the yeasty scent of bread fresh from the oven. That reminded me that Wendy was missing two employees.

"Did Stevenson bother boys, too? Ohh. You said Braden liked Bianca. Are they dating?" They'd worked side by side in the theater and at Le Panier. Dating among the cast might present a few problems, but it didn't create the same risks as dating among camp counselors, and a rule against it would have been nearly impossible to enforce. "But wouldn't he have been on stage, too?"

"He was a chorus cat," Emily said. "He could have disappeared for a minute or two, easy."

An actor on stage left could have slipped behind the curtain and snuck into the green room. Found Stevenson passed out, done the deed, and slipped back into position, barely missing a beat. These kids were triple threats—actors, singers, and dancers. Fancy footwork was their hallmark.

"Did Detective Bello ask if you'd seen anyone leave the stage?" Shortly before her own exit.

"Yes. And I didn't lie. I didn't see him go. But—" She broke off, wagging her hands in dread. "I was center stage, singing. Braden could have set off fireworks in the back row and I wouldn't have had a clue."

I sent Emily inside to grab my bag and tell Tracy we were leaving. I pulled my phone from my apron pocket.

"Ms. Murphy," Detective Bello said after I identified myself and told him I had information. "Imagine my surprise."

Did I mention that Bello and I got off on the wrong foot when he first came to Jewel Bay? I've tried to put that behind me. He hasn't bothered.

"Detective, we don't have time to play cat and mouse." Poor choice of words, I know, but I swear, they just popped out. "And I don't have time to give you all the details. I know you're waiting on forensics before you release the green room and give the theater the okay to reopen. Tell the crime scene people and the ME to look for chloral hydrate." Assuming it was detectable in chemical analysis or on autopsy. I didn't know and I didn't have time to ask Google. "Forget the water bottles. You're after the flavored Pellegrino cans from the table inside the door. That was Stevenson's drink, and that's where the drug was."

"I'm listening."

"Send someone to the theater to secure the wardrobe room. You're going to want to take a close look at several of the costumes, but we don't have time to get specific right now. Then meet me at the theater dorm. The actors you're looking for are Bianca Calderon and Braden something."

"This better not be some wild-goose chase, Ms. Murphy."

"I promise you, Detective. We've got very human prey."

With Emily in the passenger seat, I zipped up Back to Front, then zigged and zagged out of the village. Wound my way past the small, older homes clustered at the top of the hill and through a newer residential district to the dorm where the theater's summer hires bunk.

Emily's hands trembled as she unlocked the dormitory's front door. The smell of microwave popcorn hit my nose. A bass rhythm thumped in the distance.

"Upstairs," she said. "Second floor, second room on the right."

The room with the open door. Where one bed had been stripped, half the drawers emptied, and one side of the small closet cleaned out, except for one last cardboard box.

"Did she sleep here last night?" I asked.

"No. I thought she was with Braden. Guys are on the third floor. We're not supposed to, but . . ." Emily made a "what can you do?" gesture. "She must have packed up this morning, when she knew I'd be at work."

So Bianca didn't want Emily to know she was leaving. Why?

We reached the same conclusion at the same time. I opened the medicine cabinet above the sink. Also half empty. No prescription bottles.

Emily was rummaging through a zippered canvas duffle. "It's gone," she said. "The chloral hydrate."

I sat on the edge of the bed and gestured for her to join me. "Tell me exactly what you did Friday. How you got the drug into Chad's drink."

"That was easy. I'm the last person on from stage left, from the green room, so I poured a little into his can, then slipped it back in my bag. We're not supposed to bring anything but scripts and water bottles into the green room, so I opened the outside door and left my bag behind one of the shrubs in the alley. No one knew."

"Except Bianca and Braden." Everybody knew the actors often propped open the door, to let their friends from town sneak in for a show, or to pop in and out without making any noise.

She pressed her lips together and nodded.

I frowned. "So after the deputies let you change back into street clothes, you ducked down the alley and grabbed your bag."

"And I never checked. But the bottle's gone."

Which meant the other two had feared getting caught more than Emily did. Even though it was her mother's name on the prescription and the bottle had been in her bag.

Footsteps pounded down the hallway. I had expected Bello and his deputies to be quieter.

But it wasn't them. It was Bianca. She grabbed the doorframe and skidded to a stop when she saw us.

"Aren't you—weren't you supposed to be at work?"

Emily roared back, like the cat she'd played on stage, "You were just going to leave? Go back to Indiana without saying a word?"

"I—we didn't know what to do." More footsteps. A male voice called out, "Bianca, hurry up. Grab the box so we can leave."

Then Braden came up behind Bianca. He might have been a chorus cat, but with his boyish features and curly dark hair, I'd have bet a bundle he played Curly in *Oklahoma!* and took a star turn in *Brigadoon.*

"How could you?" Emily said. "Both of you. We only meant to send him a message. To make him stop. Not . . ."

Not kill him.

"We didn't mean to hurt him," Bianca said, half sobbing. "We—we thought you were being too cautious with the stuff, so Braden snuck back in and dumped an extra dose in his can. You said it wouldn't hurt him, not seriously."

"Wait," I said. Adam had thought that the man had been suffocated, not strangled. Dr. Cook had appeared to agree. The soft fabric wrapped around Stevenson's face would have been enough, if he was already out of commission. "That was the old tail from your costume wrapped around his face, wasn't it? If you didn't smother him with it, who did?"

"It wasn't us," Braden said.

Bianca's olive skin paled. "The tail came off when—when he attacked me. I didn't know what to do. Amanda had told me, after he ripped my showgirl costume, not to let it happen again. Like it was my fault. But then she quit. Kip said if we had problems with costumes to take them to Kathy at the Dragonfly."

"Did you tell her what happened?" I couldn't imagine the straight-talking artist, quilter, and retail mainstay keeping quiet about a stage manager harassing an actor.

Bianca shook her head. "No. No. I didn't want to cause any trouble. I knew . . ."

"You knew he would have denied it," I said, "and made things worse."

"Not just worse. Impossible," Emily interjected. "He's supposed to cue us on, make sure all the props are in place and everything goes smoothly. That everybody knows about last-minute changes in the rehearsal schedule, or the blocking on stage. There are a million ways he could have sabotaged us. He *did* sabotage us. To keep us in line."

The real reason Kip Taylor thought he had a couple of actors who couldn't get things right. Chalk that up to Stevenson. "How did the killer get the tail? I've talked to Kathy. She had to make a whole new one."

"I don't know," Bianca said. Her eyes were wet. "We're not allowed to take the costumes home, so I left it in the wardrobe room. When I came back the next day to get it and take it to Kathy's shop, the tail was gone."

"Bianca," Braden said. "My car's outside. We have to go."

"Hold on, cowboy. You're not going anywhere."

Heaven help me, I was actually glad to see Detective Oliver Bello. A deputy stood behind him. No doubt another had an eye on Braden's car.

"Are we under arrest? Are you charging us? We didn't kill him." The three young actors didn't wait for any cues or prompts, talking over each other.

"I know that," Bello said. "I've talked to the ME and the chief toxicologist. The chloral hydrate didn't kill Stevenson. But drugging him is a form of assault. You need to tell me everything." He glanced around the half-empty dorm room, not exactly a comfortable place for an interview. But then, I've been in the sheriff's interview room. It's not a space meant to make you feel comfortable. "At the station, please. Deputy Oakland will show you the way."

Emily turned to me. "I'm going to be late for work. Should I call my dad?"

"Don't worry about work. And calling your dad's not a bad idea."

The actors left with the deputy. No surprise that Bello stayed behind, or that he trained his very serious peepers on me.

I summarized what the girls had said about Stephenson and the plan to send him a message. "Bianca said the tail disappeared before she could take the costume to be repaired, and I can't see either Emily or Braden taking it. It doesn't fit with the rest of the plan. He passed out, then he was suffocated with the tail, right?"

Bello grunted and glowered. "Why didn't they report the perv?"

"Detective," I said. "Oliver. You know why. Young women these days know what Stevenson did was wrong. But even the bravest and boldest isn't going to speak up if she doesn't think it will do any good. Not that I condone drugging a man, but they did try to solve the problem themselves. Rather creatively, in my opinion. Since you asked."

As he obviously wished he hadn't.

"Come in and give a formal statement." He checked his watch. "Say, two o'clock? We should be finished with our young thespians by then. I've got a couple of other witnesses coming in, but those interviews should be quick."

I agreed and walked out with him. The car needed gas, so I drove out to the highway to fill the tank. Realized I was famished and needed to fill my own tank, too, so after gassing up, I pulled into a slot outside Perk Up, the breakfast-lunch-coffee joint next to the gas station.

"Hey, Cyndi," I called to the woman behind the counter. "How about one of your fancy grilled cheeses?"

"Onions and tomato? Stay or go?"

"Yes, and go, I guess." I searched in my bag for my phone—might as well check my email and our social media while I waited. The program from the other night was stuffed in the bottom of my bag. I smoothed it flat and paged through. The cast lists I'd seen, but not the bios. Bianca wasn't from Indiana, as Emily had said, but Illinois. Close enough. Braden McNally hailed from Southern California. Would the trouble over Stevenson bring the curtain down on their summer romance before the season ended? Kip couldn't keep them in the company if they were charged with criminal assault, could he?

I flipped through more pages, then stopped. Flipped back. The souvenir program, the one I'd paid two bucks for, compared to the free playbill for that night's show, included bios for the full cast and crew. It had been printed before the last-minute changes, and it included a woman with shoulder-length dark hair and a serious expression.

Amanda Swallow's hair had been cut collar-length when I saw her Sunday at the athletic club, going in to teach a yoga class. Not uncommon for dancers to study yoga, and once she left the theater, she'd needed a job. Why had she stuck around? Because as I'd said of Kathy and myself, Jewel Bay is that kind of town. And she knew Stevenson would be leaving in September.

I wasn't a regular, didn't know the schedule, but took a guess that class ran at the same time every day. I stuffed my phone and the program into my bag and grabbed my keys. No sign of Cyndi.

If my hunch was right, I didn't have time to wait.

I was halfway to the car when Cyndi came running out, a go-box in hand. I thanked her and did my best to heed her caution to drive carefully as I wound my way above the lakeshore, past the golf course, to the athletic club.

Why had Amanda done it? I had little doubt that she'd snuck in the side door—she'd have known the actors often left it propped open. She'd found Stevenson passed out and seen an opportunity she couldn't pass up. The tail was an even bigger message than the toy mice Emily had tucked in the stage manager's hands, but one he'd never see. A message he would never get, because Amanda Swallow had taken their prank a step too far.

I'd been irked with the former costume manager's admonishment to Bianca after the assault that tore her skirt to not let it happen again. Like it was the girl's fault, I'd thought. But no. It was not that, and more than that, at the same time. Amanda had been an actor once, and she knew. No one would listen. No one would stop guys like that. You had to look out for yourself.

She couldn't have known about the chloral hydrate, just as the three young actors had not known about her. She had taken matters into her own hands—strong hands, used to sewing and to supporting yoga poses. She had taken revenge for what Stevenson had done to her, and taken action to keep him from attacking yet another young woman who feared the consequences of speaking up even more than she feared him.

I parked outside the club. No sign of her. I had no idea what she drove. Was I too late?

"Erin!" Bunny was coming toward me, in her yoga clothes. "If you're here for yoga with Amanda, it's canceled today. Besides, you're late. And you're not dressed."

"Bunny. The new teacher, with the dark hair and the trendy clothes. Is that Amanda?"

"She's terrific. I guess she's sick today, one of those summer colds. I ought to swing by and check on her, but I think I'll head home instead."

"You know where she lives?"

"Sure. She rents from Polly, the apartment over the garage. I keep telling you, come to class. You'll love her."

"Thanks. It's so hard to make time in the summer." We air-kissed and I followed her car back to the highway. She turned south, toward home. I went north, to her sister's house.

I was not one bit surprised to reach the place and find a car parked outside the garage, the rear hatch open, boxes and suitcases inside. It was apparently the day for theater people to load 'em up and move 'em out. I blocked the car with mine, careful of Polly's roses. Her husband had built the apartment for his parents, but they'd bought a condo instead, and Polly used it as a retreat and gathering place. I'd been here once for a Pampered Chef party.

The people door at the bottom of the stairs stood open. I ignored the twinge in my knee and started up. A few steps later, Amanda emerged from the apartment, dressed in leggings and a tank, a cardboard box in her arms.

"Who are you? What are you doing here?"

I held out both hands in the universal signal that I came in peace. "Erin Murphy. I run the Merc, in the village. One of the theater kids, Emily Davies, works for me."

A look of fear mingled with defensiveness crossed her face.

"I know how these guys work," I continued. "Stevenson and his ilk. He pestered Emily, but it was her roommate, Bianca Calderon, who was his real target. After you left, that is." Apparently he had a thing for slender brunettes.

"I don't know what you're talking about." She came down a couple of steps, obviously hoping I'd back up. Or back down, literally and figuratively. As she got closer, my nose picked up the scent of jasmine.

"I think you do. He went after you and you pushed back. He got more insistent—I won't pretend to know what he did, but it must have been pretty awful for you to leave a job you loved. After all, you came back to Jewel Bay intending to stay, didn't you? You couldn't let a creep like that ruin things."

She took another step, and so did I. Neither of us could see where we were going, she because of the box, me because my eyes were fixed on her.

"You did your best to protect Bianca," I continued, "but when you left, he focused all his attention on her."

Another step. "I told her not to let it keep happening. To find a way to stop him."

"But you didn't mean for her to kill him. You wanted to do that yourself."

"What do you want me to say? That I killed him, but I'm sorry? Because I'm not." She took another step. Were we close to the bottom yet?

"How did you get the tail? And what did you plan to do when you snuck in during the first act? You couldn't have known about the chloral hydrate." Her face said I was right, that she'd had no idea. "Sleeping pills. Liquid, actually. They spiked his pop can so he'd pass out and get in trouble."

"Orange Pellegrino. He's addicted to the stuff."

I used to love it, too. No more.

"They tucked little fuzzy mice in his hands, as their calling card," I said. "So he'd get the message."

"I wondered what those were."

"You wrapped the tail around his face and smothered him. You're wearing the same perfume now that you wore that night—it must have rubbed off from your hands onto the tail fabric. But where did you get the tail?"

"After I quit, I came back to get my things and I spotted it on the floor beneath the costume rack. I recognized it right away as part of Bianca's costume. When I saw how badly he'd damaged it, I knew I had to do something."

"So you came back . . ."

"My hatred was keeping me from enjoying something I loved. I thought if I came back and walked around during a production, I'd fall for the place all over again and forget about revenge. But when I saw him lying there, sleeping on the job, it was like a sign. That the time had come. That he'd never stop unless I stopped him."

Criminy. She'd admitted it. "Come with me. Tell Detective Bello what happened. All of it, including what Stevenson did to you. They'll understand."

I didn't know if they would or not. If the law would consider his harassment, his assault, a mitigating circumstance. If her actions were legally defensible. I couldn't defend them, but I understood them.

Amanda pushed the box at me, shoving me against the wall. She started to scoot by and I stuck out a foot, hoping to trip her. No luck. She was a former dancer, after all, leaping easily down the last few steps and dashing out. I staggered to my feet, pain shooting through my knee. From outside, I heard a car engine start. I stumbled to the door and out into the bright sunlight.

Amanda put her car in reverse, cranked the wheels, then pulled forward and backed up again at an angle. If she kept it up, she might be able to squeeze around my car, but only if she took out Polly's rose bed. Polly would never forgive me, and neither would Bunny.

And I'd never forgive myself if I let a killer get away. Even if her victim had been despicable. He deserved to be punished, to be reminded every day of the terrible things he'd done, robbing young women of their dreams, their confidence, their futures. But to suffer, he had to live.

I didn't have time to rub my lucky stars. And with my knee throbbing, I couldn't run after her.

The contents of the box lay scattered at my feet. The miscellaneous box, the last things you pack. I picked them up, one by one, and began pelting Amanda's car. The alarm clock bounced off the windshield with a metallic clang. A coffee cup decorated with comedy and tragedy masks, the symbols of drama, smacked the side-view mirror and shattered when it hit the ground. As Amanda wiggled the car back and forth, I stooped, grabbed, and threw.

"What is this racket?" Polly's cry pierced the air. "Erin Murphy, what are you doing? Don't you stomp on my roses."

"Call 911," I shouted. "A killer's trying to get away."

Bless her, for once, Polly Easter Paulson did as she was told. Detective Bello pulled up just as I was hurling the last item within reach at Amanda Swallow's car. I missed the car, and if he'd ducked when I yelled, it would have missed him, too.

Oh, well. Getting smacked with a pastel rainbow Beanie Baby unicorn is hardly the worst indignity a cop has to endure.

Turned out I was right. Amanda had been in the company for two seasons a decade ago, singing and dancing her way through *Oklahoma!*, *Footloose*, and even *Bye Bye Birdie*. She'd have kept on singing and dancing if an injury hadn't stopped her. She pivoted to costume design, jumping at the chance to come back to Jewel Bay. She'd truly loved the Playhouse and the Taylors, and had hoped to make a full-time career with them. That was part of the reason she'd kept her mouth shut when Stevenson began harassing her.

You can't solve a problem you don't know about, Kip Taylor had said. But I wasn't going to let him off the hook. To his credit, he completely agreed that he'd failed in his responsibility to keep the young women in his employ safe, and promised to do everything he could to make the theater a safe workplace. I had a hunch his sister had played a role in his sudden understanding.

Amanda had been driven to murder as much by protectiveness as by personal revenge. Would that help her in the legal system? I hoped so. My knee recovered and the theater reopened. Emily, Bianca, and Braden all agreed to stay for the rest of the season. Misdemeanor assault charges were filed, with a promise that they'd be dropped if the actors completed the season without any further trouble and cooperated with the authorities. Emily continued working at the Merc, and before long, we were all singing with her, as the wind came sweeping down the plain and swept the gray skies away.

You didn't think I'd get all the way to the end of the story without saying it, did you?

The show must go on.

An Unholy Death

"*G*entlemen. We'll have no such rough language in Murphy's Mercantile," Kate Murphy told the two loggers as she plucked their change from the drawer of the brass cash register and slid the coins across the glass-topped counter. "About the sheriff or anyone else. Besides, it's too pretty a day for talk about thieving."

Both men cackled, their bushy beards in need of a good trim, then dropped the coins into the pockets of their wool pants and gathered up their supplies.

"Thank you, Mrs.," the older one said. "We'll be well fed for another week in the woods. Maybe next time we come into town, we'll visit the barber." He gave her a broad, blue-eyed wink, as if he'd heard her thoughts about his beard.

"Off with you now," she said with a wave of her hand.

The men laughed. "She's a feisty one," the younger man told his companion, a beefy hand reaching for the brass thumb latch on the front door. "Paddy's got his hands full with her."

At that, Kate's embarrassment turned to anger. *Don't let it show,* she warned herself. *You know what they say about the Irish.* In less than two years, Murphy's Mercantile had gone from a supply tent to a whitewashed shack to this grand building made of locally fired clay bricks, with plank floors and wide display windows and milk glass lights hanging from the tin ceiling. Paddy had sunk everything he had into the business and she dare not do or say a thing that might jeopardize its future. *Their* future.

She'd been Paddy Murphy's wife for thirty-one days now, the last twenty-two here in Jewel Bay, Montana. The town wasn't anything like what she'd expected, nothing like their hometown in Wisconsin. Paddy had been honest in his letters over the six months before their marriage. The older cousin of a schoolmate, he'd come from Ireland at twelve and worked hard to get a start in the new country. A boy she'd known but never given any serious thought, until he'd come back to Wisconsin for a visit last winter. They'd locked eyes in an understanding, though she'd just turned twenty-one, and when he left to return to Montana, they entrusted their courtship to the postal service and planned a late August wedding. Then what was already being called the Great Fire of 1910 swept through the region, endangering millions of acres and thousands of people. Thankfully it had spared this valley. After their wedding and two nights in a grand hotel in St. Paul and the long railroad trip west, here she was.

No, Jewel Bay was nothing like she'd expected. Both more, and less, and every day full of surprises.

"Don't you mind them," said a woman in a yellow dress, lace and a green ribbon trimming the stand-up collar. She wore no hat, the dark hair fashionably coiled on top of her head accentuating her height, and her warm smile eased Kate's tensions. Or maybe it was the hint of lavender that surrounded her. "The valley's full of men like that. More comfortable with squirrels and silence than a pretty young woman. I'm Laura Peterman. I think you've met my husband, James, at the bank."

Kate felt herself blushing again. Was that going to be the way of things, at least until she'd met all the customers and figured out where all the canned goods were shelved and who paid cash and who had credit? Surely the Petermans had credit. Paddy had shown her the books, but he'd gone out to make deliveries, leaving her here alone for the first time.

And she wasn't pretty, not by a long shot. Short and slight, with fair skin and hazel eyes, brown hair and a pointy chin. A heart-shaped face, if you wanted to put it kindly. She didn't look Irish at all. Paddy said maybe not, but she wore her heart on her sleeve as well as her face, and that made her the sweetest lass to him.

"Kate Flan—" she began, then corrected herself. "Kate Murphy. I'm not quite used to it yet."

Laura Peterman's lips curved, but there was less warmth in her expression this time. Had Kate offended her? She couldn't imagine how.

"We're so pleased with all that you and Paddy have planned for the Mercantile," Mrs. Peterman said. "Now that residents will be able to get everything they need right here on Front Street, more families will put down roots. Town will prosper."

"That's all Paddy," Kate replied. "I only take credit for marrying him. Shall we see if we can fill that order?" She gestured to the list in the woman's gloved hands.

When Paddy applied for a loan to build the Mercantile, in the heart of town, not everyone at Jewel Bay State Bank had been sure of him. The West, with its logging and mining camps that sprung up almost overnight and closed down almost as quickly, was full of get-rich-quick schemers. But James Peterman had grasped that Paddy was not just another itinerant Irishman out to make a fast buck. He had plans, for himself and for Jewel Bay. Peterman had been impressed by Paddy's sketches of the storefront and the columns of figures showing what he expected to sell in each of the first five years. When the loan came through, Paddy had written to her that he felt as tall and broad as the Douglas fir and Engelmann spruce that studded the nearby slopes, their future secure.

Now, the two women reviewed the list. Kate stacked cans of tomatoes and corn and peaches next to bags of flour and sugar on the long counter. Then she pointed to the list, in Laura Peterman's graceful cursive. "Those we'll have to order from Pondera," she said, the name of the bigger town thirty miles away still unfamiliar to her mouth. *Pahn-duh-RAY.*

"James is eager to teach me to drive his new Packard," Laura said, "but I'm content with driving the horse and buggy into town. I'm grateful to Miss Lang at the school for suggesting you take over my daughter's piano lessons. Elizabeth is improving already. You should come to the house and play for us sometime soon."

"I'd be delighted." Kate had seen the Petermans' large white house, as fine as any back in Baraboo, on the north shore of the lake. Elizabeth had talked about their grand piano.

"It's settled then," the other woman said, and laid a hand on her list. "I trust these other things can be delivered?"

"Yes, certainly." The man Paddy had hired to make deliveries had taken his last wages and left town, and they hadn't found a replacement yet. Paddy was doing his best, loading up the wagon and driving the mule himself, but the extra work was taking a toll.

"Very good. Put all that on our account, please, but I'll pay you now for some licorice for the children." Laura Peterman drew out a small coin purse.

"That is exquisite," Kate said. She'd always been drawn to shiny things.

The monogram on the silver clasp read *LLC*, the initials of the first and maiden names smaller than the *L* in the middle. Monograms were a rite of passage for a newly married woman; she'd been stitching her own on linen towels in the evenings. "My older sister has one much like it, a gift from her mother-in-law when she married. How many children do you have?"

"Three." The other woman laid a coin on the counter and quickly thrust the coin purse into her kid leather purse. Kate lifted the lid of a large glass jar and pulled out three sticky black sticks.

"Do be careful on your way home," she said as she handed over the bag of licorice. "If there is a band of thieves, as those loggers said . . ."

"Hard to imagine in broad daylight, isn't it?" Laura Peterman said. "But yes, a woman must beware of danger, and keep herself safe."

May the Good Lord keep us all safe, Kate whispered as the front door closed.

∞

"It's worrisome, Paddy, it is," Kate Murphy told her husband later after filling him in on the talk about the thieves. "And it wasn't just those two loggers, trying to rattle me. All afternoon, everyone who came in asked what I'd heard, whether they'd struck again, what Sheriff Gibson is doing to track them down. People are frightened."

"Daniel Gibson isn't the sheriff. He's a deputy, though an able man," Paddy Murphy replied. "I'm sorry you had to hear harsh talk on your first day tending our wee shop on your own."

It was not just "a wee shop." Kate was astonished that he had built this fine general store, as fine as any she had seen. Astonished that they owned it, determined to make it prosper.

"But you're not worried? We do keep some cash here, and heaven knows where you go making your deliveries."

"No, lass." He took her in his arms, there behind the counter, and she glanced around. They were alone. And they were married. After a long, sweet kiss, he released her, the look on his face echoing the joy in her heart.

She was married.

"Jewel Bay's a gem," Paddy said, "but there's grousers here just like back home. Men who'll grouse when it rains and complain when it stops. They're not wrong about the sheriff, but Daniel Gibson will find those lowlifes and give them what-for. Now, me, I've got to find a delivery man. I can't be headin' out all hours of the day with bags of nails and flour and whatnot."

"There must be someone. A man who can drive the motor car as well as the wagon." The Model T couldn't go everywhere; the roads were too rough, too rutted and steep. A man might own a horseless carriage, but if he owned a business, he still needed a horse. Or a mule.

"Aye, but who, lass? When you talk to the Good Lord, ask Him to give you a name."

"Think of your hand as a mama bird, your fingertips the beak dropping food into her chicks' open mouths," Kate told her pupil, making her own hand a bird pecking the air. "A firm but gentle touch."

Grace Haugen was a serious child of eleven, her blond hair caught above her ears by a pair of barrettes. She barely smiled as she bent her head over the keys. But she could play, even if she was more determined to do things right than to make a joyful noise.

The Flannery sisters had all taken piano lessons and learned to draw and paint, and after she'd finished school, Kate had given lessons in the parlor of the family home. So when Anne Lang, one of the Jewel Bay elementary school teachers, had asked her to take on a few pupils after school, she'd readily agreed. She and Paddy had no piano, not yet, though she hoped they would in a few years when they built a real house, maybe with an orchard and a view of the lake. But the battered oak upright in the smaller of the school's two makeshift classrooms was sturdy enough to withstand the pounding the children gave it, and it held a tune decently.

"LAH-dah-dah-da," she sang, leading the girl through the melody of the Bach bourrée. "Very good. That's very good. Now, let's add the bass line."

On they went, a phrase at a time.

"Good heavens," Kate said, glancing at the clock. "We've gone far too long. It will be getting dark. I'll walk with you and apologize to your father for keeping you."

They bundled into their coats—the October days were clear and sunny, but temperatures dropped with the setting sun. Grace retrieved her school bag and Kate followed her outside. The makeshift school in the church hall was cramped, but students and teachers were managing while plans were made for a new, dedicated school. No high school, though a handful of local students boarded in Pondera during the week to attend classes.

"Will your father let you practice on the church piano?" Kate asked.

"Sometimes," Grace said. "Though I think hearing me makes him sad. The first time he saw my mother, she was playing the piano in church. He always says that's what convinced him to serve God."

The girl's tone was serious, not quite grasping her father's joke. Kate had only met the Reverend Arval Haugen a time or two, but he struck her as kindly and gentle, if perhaps more attentive to his books and his flock than to his daughter. He might not notice that she was late, a thought that made Kate frown.

"His work makes him happy, Mrs. Murphy," the girl said.

"Of course it does," Kate said quickly, chiding herself for not keeping her feelings hidden. It was a fault, one her mother had cautioned her against many times.

"My mother played beautifully, almost as well as you, and she taught me as much as she could before she died. I wish . . ."

The words went unspoken, but Kate let her thoughts fill them in. *I wish she were here.*

They reached the minister's small frame house. It was dark, the chimney quiet. The gate in the white picket fence squeaked as Grace pushed it open, and Kate followed her into the yard.

"Where's Buster?" Grace asked.

The dog, Kate assumed. The reverend must be resting. She watched the windows, expecting a light to come on and the reverend to open the door and welcome them. Would he have supper ready for his daughter, or was cooking part of her chores? The parsonage had no garden that she could see, just a pair of young apple trees. Surely the churchwomen kept an eye on the absentminded widower and his daughter, dropping off spare eggs, beans, and potatoes.

But the house remained dark. Kate knocked and called out. Turned the handle and stepped inside, calling again. The house was neat and tidy and empty.

What should she do?

No point borrowing trouble. Most likely, he'd gone to visit a church member and lost track of time, as she and Grace had, though they'd been caught up in eighth notes, not tea and sympathy.

"Grace, does your father keep a horse and buggy?"

"He borrows one from Mr. Peterman or the sexton if he needs to go somewhere too far to walk or ride his bicycle."

It was a common sight, the man in black, a hat jammed on his head, riding a bicycle along Jewel Bay's dirt roads and up its hills, a speckled brown dog trotting beside him.

"Does he often go visiting this time of day?" *And leave you to fend for yourself.*

Grace nodded. "But he's always home in time for supper. Or nearly always."

Not the encouraging words Kate hoped for. "Well, shall we start supper?"

Inside, Kate turned on the lights. Thanks to Jewel Bay Power and Light and its capable manager, Ivan Gregory, most homes and businesses were electrified. Most had running water, too, though only a few had telephones, a service the power company had begun earlier in the year. After several tries, she got a flame going in the cookstove's firebox and put on a pot of water for the potatoes and carrots the girl was peeling. Though it was Wednesday, there was a good chunk of Sunday's roast in the icebox. She tucked the meat into a small roasting pan and added hot water. Before she left, she'd slip it in the warming oven.

Within minutes, the potatoes were boiling and the table was set for two. The kitchen was almost cozy.

"Well, then." Kate brushed one hand against the other. "Your father will come home to a nice hot supper. You can start your schoolwork while you're waiting." She hated to leave the girl alone, but it wouldn't be long, and she wasn't a small child. Grace would be fine.

"Thank you, Mrs. Murphy."

"Remember." Kate pinched her fingers together as she had during their lesson. "Like a bird," and the girl smiled.

Outside, dusk had deepened and it would be full dark by the time Kate got home.

But something tugged at her. She pulled her coat tight and retraced her steps to the church, a simple frame building so different from the brick-and-stone St. Joseph's in Baraboo with its spire and bell tower, the church where she had been baptized and married. As she approached, a dog came running toward her and stopped at her feet. His paws were muddy, and he smelled like pine pitch.

"You must be Buster. Where have you been?"

In the shrubbery beside the main doors, a bicycle leaned against the white clapboards. Just as she'd thought. Clearly, Grace had not noticed it. Kate herself had only seen it out of the corner of her eye, the sight not entirely registering.

She opened one heavy door. The air was still, though it bore a hint of the wax used to polish the pews and altar table. Not a large space, no bigger than the Mercantile. And empty.

To the left of the raised altar were two closed doors. One, she suspected, led outside, the other to the reverend's study. She'd give him a piece of her mind. What was he thinking, sitting here with his books and prayers while his daughter sat home alone, pretending not to worry?

She started across the nave, her hand already raised to knock. Glanced to her right, for no reason that she could explain then or afterwards.

Behind the altar table, on the raised wooden platform, lay a man in black. Crumpled—knees bent, one arm outstretched, hand open. His eyes were open, too. They'd once been blue, she could see, but the color had begun to leave them, as it did in the first few hours after death.

That, and the bloody gash on his forehead, a good three or four inches long, told Kate Murphy beyond any doubt that the Reverend Arval Haugen was, in fact, dead.

Ivan Gregory motioned Kate back, but she followed him anyway. She'd already seen the body; seeing it again was not going to make her nightmares worse.

The power company manager crouched and placed two fingers on the side of the reverend's neck. He was one of those men who, like Paddy, seemed to know exactly what to do in a difficult situation, and as soon as he answered her knock on his door, listened to her story, and stepped into action, her worry had eased. Not that everything would be all right; it would not. A man was dead, and a motherless girl now fatherless, too.

Gregory raised his eyes to hers, his expression confirming what she already knew.

"Would you offer a prayer, Mrs. Murphy, while we wait for Deputy Gibson?"

After finding Reverend Haugen, she'd gone outside, not wanting to check for a telephone in his office, and had seen the light on up the road in Gregory's two-story yellow house. She'd stood inside the front door while he telephoned the deputy. When Kate fretted about leaving Grace home alone, he'd instructed his nephew, a slender boy of about twelve, to fetch Miss Lang, the teacher, and escort her to the parsonage to sit with Grace. The boy asked if he should come to the church afterwards, a mix of horror and excitement in his eyes, but the uncle had said no, he should stay with the women, and it was clear from the way the boy straightened his shoulders and nodded solemnly that he took his duty seriously.

What sort of prayer could an Irish Catholic and a Scot, as Gregory's name suggested he was, say together over the body of a dead Norwegian? No matter. They were all Americans. Montanans. God's children.

She cleared her throat and Gregory bowed his head, hands clasped in front of his chest. "Father in Heaven, we ask you to receive the spirit of Arval Haugen into your hands. To forgive his sins and accept him into the company of the angels." She paused briefly, wondering if Mr. Gregory or Reverend Haugen believed in angels. "You who listen to the cries of the injured and bereaved, who cares for the orphans . . ." Her words faltered, as she thought of Grace.

The church door opened. A tall man in a brown wool suit removed his hat and entered.

"Ma'am," Daniel Gibson said, a hint of the South in his voice. Her mouth opened and closed without a word. Then he acknowledged the power company manager with a quick nod. "Ivan."

She had met Daniel Gibson once, when he'd come into the Mercantile to see Paddy. With the county seat so far away, the residents of Jewel Bay were fortunate, and grateful, to have a resident deputy. Who the two men were who came in behind Deputy Gibson, she couldn't say. Locals he'd rounded up to assist if needed? She had no idea what might be needed. One man stepped into the small office and a moment later, the electric sconces mounted on the walls began to glow.

Oh, how she wished Paddy were here. He'd be locking up the Mercantile and heading home, expecting to find her working in the kitchen. He'd worry at her absence, with the band of thieves on the loose. But he knew she was giving lessons; if it got too late, he'd come to the school to fetch her. Dismay over worrying her husband vied with her concern for Grace, and she shuddered.

"Good of you to come so quickly," Ivan Gregory said, and Kate was struck by the stiff formality of his tone. What could be the reason? Surely she was imagining things, in the terrible moment.

"Doc is on his way," the deputy replied.

Gregory gestured to the body. Gibson stepped onto the altar and crouched to check for a pulse, then leaned closer to inspect the wound on the dead man's forehead. Raised the man's outstretched hand, turned the wrist gently, then laid it down again. Stood and let his gaze move slowly around the room. It stopped at the altar table, continued its circuit, and returned to the table.

"Where are the candlesticks?"

They all looked around, as though the missing objects were simply waiting to be noticed.

"Tall. Silver. Matching pair." Gibson held one hand about ten inches above the other. "A gift from a parishioner. Most valuable thing in the place, I suspect."

"The thieves?" Kate asked, surprised to hear her voice shake. "Could—could they have done this?"

"You never know what a greedy man will do, Mrs. Murphy, I'm sorry to say," though Gibson didn't sound sorry. "You shouldn't be here. One of my men will take you home. We'll get a search party going."

"I'll wait for the doctor," Ivan Gregory said, as much to her as to Daniel Gibson, who did not reply, already discussing plans with his men.

Kate found herself reluctant to leave. She hadn't known Arval Haugen well—she didn't know anyone in town well aside from Paddy. But she'd liked him and was genuinely fond of his daughter. This wasn't her church—there was no Catholic church in Jewel Bay—but their God was her God, and as

Deputy Gibson's man took her elbow and led her out, she sent a quick prayer upward, asking God to send His comfort and strength to all those in need.

And His mercy, and justice.

∞

"I can't take her home with me," Anne Lang whispered as the two women huddled in the kitchen of the parsonage, the cookstove radiating a warmth Kate's every bone craved. "Not with Frank . . ."

The teacher's younger brother, who lived with her. There was something wrong with him. Kate didn't know what.

The deputy's man had wanted to take Kate straight home, but she'd insisted on coming here. The wagon had barely stopped when the dog bounded past and threw one paw against the front door. Grace had opened it, seen him, and raised her face to Kate. "Where's Papa? What's happened?"

Now Kate glanced at the teacher in her navy skirt and white blouse, blond hair braided on top of her head, her back stiff and her eyes wary. It was Kate who'd found the man, and she who had to break the news.

"Let's sit," Kate said, gesturing to the kitchen table and taking the seat across from the girl. "I'm so sorry, Grace. We don't know exactly what happened. He–he may have tried to stop some thieves and been attacked. He's–"

"He's dead, isn't he?"

Kate nodded, not trusting her voice. It had never failed her the way it had twice in half an hour. But then, she had never before found a man dead or had to tell his daughter.

Grace's eyes filled, but she didn't cry.

"Mr. Gregory is with him," Kate continued. "In the church. Deputy Gibson is starting a search party. You'll come home with me for the night. There's a man waiting outside with a wagon."

Anne Lang touched the girl's shoulder. "Go pack your nightgown and clothes for tomorrow."

Wordlessly, the girl rose and left the room. Anne sank into the empty chair. "How could such a terrible thing happen? Such a good man, and that poor child."

"I lost track of time on our lesson—she's making such progress. The school was dark when we left. So was the church."

"I walked right by it, but I didn't notice a thing."

"Did you see the reverend's bicycle?" Kate asked. "Against the wall by the front door." Of no interest to the thieves.

"No. Best to keep her home tomorrow. Give her a day to let the news sink in."

What was she going to do with a grieving eleven-year-old? "Has she no family in the area?"

"No." Anne got to her feet. "I'll be off now. My brother will be wanting supper, if he's home, though I can't stomach the idea. Let me know if she needs anything. I'll talk with the other teachers and students tomorrow."

The two women stood, silent. Kate grasped Anne's hands and they locked eyes. Not quite friends, but not quite strangers, drawn together by tragedy. And by the needs of a young girl.

Anne left and Kate made her way to the girl's bedroom. From the doorway, she watched Grace tuck a small pile of clothing into her carryall. Then she took a framed photograph from the top of the oak dresser and slipped it into her bag.

Her mother? A family portrait?

"Ready, then?" Kate asked gently, only to see a tear sliding down Grace's cheek.

And she folded the sobbing girl into her arms.

Kate's spirits lifted at the sight of lights in the window of their little log house, a beacon in the gloom. The wagon slowed, the front door opened, and Paddy emerged, summoned by the sounds of wheels and hooves. He was in his shirtsleeves, his suspenders dark against the white shirt, his sandy hair catching the light behind him. Kate didn't wait to be helped but grabbed her skirt and jumped.

"Paddy, oh Paddy!" she cried as she ran to him.

"Slow down, lass. What's a matter with yeh?" He caught her by the arms and she searched his face. He didn't know. He looked past her to the man and child in the wagon. "And who's this?"

"Oh, Paddy," she said again, then explained about finding Reverend Haugen dead in his church. Paddy listened, his fair skin paling beneath the freckles, concern in his wide blue eyes. By the time Kate finished her story, their escort had helped Grace down and brought her to them, the child clutching her small bag, the dog beside her. Kate lifted a hand to touch her shoulder, then pulled it back.

"It's gotta be them thieves," the man said. "Daniel Gibson's getting up a search party."

"I'll get my coat and my rifle," Paddy said. "If you'll wait on me a minute or two. Obliged to you for bringing my wife home. And the girl."

Kate led Grace inside, Paddy following.

"Paddy, no," Kate said. "You're not going with them."

"I am, lass. They'll need all the men they can get. The Model T would be faster, but I can't be sure of the roads where we'll be going." He tugged on his coat, then spoke in a low tone. "I'm taking the rifle, but you've got the shotgun. And the dog."

She'd almost forgotten about the dog.

"Yeh'll be all right, you and the girl," he said.

Would she? Would they? They had no telephone at home. The closest neighbor was well out of shouting distance. If the thieves were bold enough to strike in town, in daylight, would they target the Murphys, assuming a shopkeeper with a fine new brick building was prosperous, never mind that it was built on borrowed money? Never mind that their cash was locked in the Mercantile's safe, and that they owned little else of value?

She almost laughed. Any thief with his wits about him would see this place, barely more than a cabin, and ride on by.

Daylight, she thought, her mind spinning backwards. Would thieves strike in daylight, so close to the school and homes where they might be seen?

"We'll be back before yeh know it," Paddy said. Then he kissed her on the cheek, picked up his rifle, and was gone.

Kate stared at the door. Reached out and locked it.

"Well, then." She blew out a big breath. The girl hadn't eaten; she'd been waiting for her father. Kate hadn't eaten in hours. Wasn't sure she could keep anything down. Not after seeing the reverend's vacant eyes, the bloody gash. "You'll have to sleep on the sofa. It's a bit scratchy, but we'll find you a spare quilt. And light the fire, if we need to."

"Please, Mrs. Murphy," Grace said. "May I have a bowl to give Buster some water?"

"Oh, good heavens. Yes." Kate led the way to the kitchen, where she filled a good-sized enamelware bowl—small as the place was, at least Paddy had been able to bring running water inside, though he'd never gotten around to bringing the outhouse in. She set the bowl on the floor, and the sound of the dog's tongue lapping up the water seemed to fill the room.

A few minutes later, after she'd shown the girl where to put her things and the privy out back, they dished up the supper they'd brought with them, not wanting it to go to waste. Grace cleaned her plate. Kate set hers on the floor for Buster, then put the kettle on. Cut two slices of apple cake.

What next? School work? Impossible. What else might a child do after school and chores and supper? When Kate had been Grace's age, she and her sisters had read, quietly or out loud. They'd sketched or sewn. Played the piano and sang. Here, most evenings, she and Paddy talked. He'd tell her about the customers. Who was setting up a homestead or building a barn. Who came in hoping to sell extra produce or wool, or hoping he'd take a lamb in trade. The sewing machine he'd ordered for the doctor's wife, and where on earth would he find a new delivery man. Her husband could talk the ears off a hollow tree, but she loved every minute, every tidbit, as he told her about Jewel Bay and the logging camps and the steamships that plied Eagle Lake, the farmers nearby, the Indians who crossed the valley.

But Paddy wasn't here. She had to figure this one out on her own.

She poured boiling water into the porcelain teapot and set a glass of milk on the table for Grace. They sat, with their cake.

"I haven't gotten used to the quiet yet," Kate said. "Back home, in Baraboo, I lived with my parents and the sister just above me. My younger sister is attending art school in Chicago, if you can believe that. She's only eighteen, but so talented."

Grace lifted her fork to her mouth, her gaze fixed on Kate. Her eyes were sad, but not afraid, and clearly interested, so Kate went on.

"My oldest sister, Alice, is married and lives a few blocks from our parents. Her husband is on the railroad, as our father was before he retired. She's got two little ones and they drop by almost every day. So there is always something going on."

"Where's Baraboo?"

"In Wisconsin. Not far from Madison, the capital."

"My grandmother lives in Chicago."

"Oh." The tea had steeped by now so Kate poured herself a cup, steam from the dark liquid carrying the rich, floral aroma of the Darjeeling her mother had sent with her. Paddy sold a rough, inexpensive brew. He wasn't convinced yet that more subtle varieties would sell, but she was sure that as the town grew and more ladies settled in the area, they would need to stock a few finer things. "Your father's mother or your mother's? We must write and let her know what's happened. Or telephone her in the morning, from the Mercantile."

"My mother's mother," Grace said softly. "But she won't care."

Kate was taken aback. Her maternal grandmother, small and Irish and always in black after being widowed at thirty-seven, had lived with them as long as Kate could remember, until her death a few years ago. Her father's parents had farmed outside of town and she had seen them every Sunday of her life until they too had died, months apart.

"Do you have other relatives? In Montana, by chance?" Though Anne Lang had thought not.

"Not that I know of."

"We'll write your grandmother tomorrow," Kate said. "I'm sure she'll be deeply saddened."

Grace's jaw tightened and she lowered her eyes. "No. She won't. She warned my mother against marrying my father. She said he was a dreamer and an idealist who could never support a wife and children. My mother died when I was eight, and my grandmother told my father it was his fault, that he had no one but himself to blame and we were not welcome in her home again. That's when he decided to move west, and the bishop sent us here."

Kate was shocked. How could the woman speak so cruelly? Out of grief and anger, yes, but even so . . . Perhaps she'd softened. But Kate could not say that. She could not raise false hope.

She leaned forward, a hand on the table. "You are very young to be alone in the world. I believe Deputy Gibson and his men will find your father's killers and bring them to justice, but that will take time. Meanwhile, you'll be safe and cared for."

Was that enough? It was all she could say, all she could promise, right now.

Grace set her hands in her lap and lowered her chin. It quivered, and she caught her lower lip with her teeth. Buster leaned against her leg, and she rubbed his boxy head and scratched behind one floppy brown ear.

Then the dog laid down, the girl picked up her fork and took a bite, and Kate let out her breath.

She had more questions, but they could wait. She'd as much as promised to keep the girl for now. What Paddy would think, she could scarcely imagine.

After they'd finished their cake, Kate washed up the dishes. "What did you and your father do in the evenings?"

"He read, or worked on his sermons. Sometimes I read to him."

"Oh, what an excellent idea. Would you like to read to me, while I work on my sewing?"

Grace's eyes brightened. "Miss Lang lent me a book of poems. I could read from that."

Kate switched on the electric lamp in the front room—she couldn't pretend the cramped, low-ceilinged room with its log walls was grand enough to call a parlor—and Grace rummaged in her bag for the book. Kate picked up her sewing basket and sat on the sofa beside the girl. Drew out the troublesome tea towel, an elaborate M traced lightly on the creamy white fabric. So graceful, so perfect before she pierced it with her needle. Needlework had never been her talent. Her sister Alice could make the needle sing, but in Kate's hands—well, it was as if the fabric turned grubby and the stitches crooked almost before they were done.

"My mother could sew anything. She made all my clothes as well as her own. Papa likes to say—" Grace interrupted herself, swallowed hard, then spoke again. "Papa liked to say there wasn't anything she couldn't make, or make prettier with a bit of lace."

Kate returned the towel to the basket. "Tell me about her."

And Grace talked. She talked about her mother's soft gentle hands and the tenement in Chicago where they lived while her father served the poor. About her father's determination to make a home for the two of them, serving God and the people of Montana. She talked about school and books she'd read and how hard the piano was and how much she loved it. She talked about the dog. She talked until she fell asleep. Kate slipped off the girl's shoes and slid her legs onto the sofa, turned out the light, and sat in the kitchen with another cup of tea and the dog and the eddy of her own thoughts swirling like the rushing waters of the Baraboo River until Paddy came home.

∞

The dog lay at Paddy's stocking feet. Paddy had kept watch when he let the dog out to do his business, making sure he didn't try to find his way down the hill to the parsonage. But the dog seemed to know this was where he needed to stay, close to Grace.

"Hide nor hair," Paddy repeated, cake finished, a fresh cup of tea in front of him. They were going to need a third kitchen chair. Maybe they could bring one from the parsonage. Although it belonged to the church, not to Reverend Haugen. Did the chairs belong to the church, too? Grace had said the bishop sent them here. He would have to be notified and a new minister chosen—she didn't know how Protestant churches worked. Grace had also mentioned the sexton. Would he notify the bishop?

"We couldna find a trail from the church, so Gibson led a group down the banks of the Jewel and along the bay. Sent another over to Eagle River." The town sat above the bay that joined the Jewel River to the big Eagle Lake, not far from the outlet of the larger Eagle River. "I joined up with Ivan Gregory and Thaddeus London and another Scot, and we scoured the lakeshore. Came across a camp of Piegan, smoking their fish this side of the big river."

"The Piegan. One of the Blackfeet tribes?" She'd seen Indian families a few times since her arrival, first from the train, then when they'd taken the Model T and camped in the brand-new Glacier National Park, christened this past May. Some people feared the Indians, called them savages or worse, but she saw no reason for that kind of talk or distrust. A band of Menominee had lived near her grandparents' farm and her grandfather had often traded with them, and let them hunt in the woods down by the creek.

"That's right. London wanted to roust 'em, but they were no more than a couple of families doing no harm." Paddy cradled the thick white mug. "This does a body good, Kate, your fine tea and your cake. The air's beginning to take on a chill, and tramping around like that, never sure what we'd find . . ."

He pressed his lips together and shook his head, and she was grateful she'd been able to give him some comfort, slim as it might be.

"Will you join the search again tomorrow? In the daylight?" she asked. *Daylight.* The word kept pestering her.

"Not me. The shop won't run itself. I'm good for identifying who's been in and out, who's new in town, but I'm not so good at reading signs and trails of men on the run."

She didn't believe that for a minute. Far as she could see, Paddy Murphy could do anything he put his mind to.

"They're long gone by now, I expect," he continued. "Spending the night in a camp deep in the woods, or in an old homesteader's shack."

She thought of the two loggers who'd been in the Mercantile today. Not that she suspected either of them. But there were plenty of men on their own in these parts, working for themselves, living alone or in pairs, some quite rough. They came into Jewel Bay or Somers, the mill town across the lake, to sell their labor and pick up supplies, and otherwise went unaccounted for, except by a sharp-eyed shopkeeper. Not like life back in Baraboo.

"Paddy, about Grace."

She felt his blue eyes on her.

"We have to keep her, Paddy, until it can be decided what's to be done. She has no family to speak of. Her father's people are all gone. Her mother died three years ago, and the only relative she knows of is her grandmother, who blamed Reverend Haugen for her daughter's death and wanted nothing to do with him or Grace. I'll write to her, of course, if we can find an address, but it could be weeks before we hear. I know quarters are tight, and it's another mouth to feed, but we've got to do right by her. I can't let the sheriff send her to some orphanage in Helena or God knows where. She's just a girl, Paddy, a smart, sweet girl alone in the world."

Paddy set his mug on the table, stood, and wrapped his arms around her. "Darling Kate. Your heart is bigger than you are. We'll keep her as long as need be. And don't worry about feeding her. You married a grocer."

"And the dog?" Buster had raised his head at the disturbance, then lowered it again.

"And the dog."

Kate felt her body soften, her heart open, tears flow as she embraced this man. *Her husband.* Who grew up with so little and was so determined to make a life for her, for them, to make their shop the beating heart of this rough diamond of a town.

∞

Kate sat up. What was that sound? Was someone lurking outside?

She ran a hand over her forehead, brushing back the fine hair that had escaped her braid. Yesterday's events came back to her, a rush of tangled memories. The thieves. Reverend Haugen, dead on the altar of his church.

The girl. *Grace.*

The dog.

That's what she was hearing. Kate slipped out of bed, careful not to disturb Paddy, and pulled on her dressing gown. She found their guests in the kitchen. At some point during the night, Grace had wakened, no doubt surprised to find herself asleep on the Murphys' sofa, fully dressed except for her shoes. She'd changed into her nightgown, visible under her coat, her feet bare inside her shoes, as she attempted to work the pump over the iron sink to refill Buster's water after his predawn trip outside.

"Let me help you," Kate said. "It sticks sometimes." It was a long reach for a short woman like her, and naturally, this was the moment that the handle decided to get good and stuck. Finally, using all four hands, the two managed to raise the handle and set the water flowing. Grace filled Buster's bowl and Kate filled the kettle, and between them, they managed to get the handle down, then traded looks, stifling giggles.

That's where they were when Paddy walked into the kitchen, in pants and undershirt, his mustache damp.

"And what female shenanigans do we have going on here?"

Grace's brow wrinkled and she bit her lip, but Kate could see Paddy's eyes were twinkling.

"Sit, you two," she said. "Out of my way while I get breakfast on."

At the word "sit," Buster sat. So did Grace, still wrapped in her coat, in Paddy's chair. Paddy disappeared and Kate began cracking eggs and frying ham. She enjoyed cooking, though the kitchen was small and cramped, and the cookstove temperamental. Memories of mornings in her mother's kitchen came unbidden, the chaos of four girls, her big-bellied father grinning as they teased and poked each other. What did Grace remember of mornings with her mother? What would she remember of her father, and of this painful time?

Paddy returned with a wooden crate, which he placed at the side of the table with a gesture that made clear that would be his seat, and Kate gave him a grateful look. At her direction, he chopped leftover roast and potato for the dog. The collies at her grandparents' farm had eaten table scraps and chewed on bones not meant for the soup pot. They'd have plenty for the sturdy brown critter. Then Paddy poured Grace a glass of milk—they didn't keep a cow but bartered with a neighbor, and the pitcher was running low, so she'd have to take care of that.

The water boiled.

"When I was a lad," Paddy said to Grace as he made the coffee, "my ma and pa eked three, sometimes four days of brew out of one pot of grounds. That's how poor we were. By the fourth day, the stuff was so weak you could see right through it."

Kate glanced over her shoulder and saw Grace smile.

"And I told myself," he went on, his brogue growing thicker as the tale grew taller, "that when I was a man, I'd make my coffee so strong you could walk across it."

Grace's smile widened.

Kate set plates of fried eggs and ham on the table and took her seat. Paddy perched on the crate and reached for her hand, then Grace's. The girl hesitated, then took it.

"Bless us, Lord God," Paddy said, "and this food we are about to eat, thy gift. Thank you, Lord, for keeping young Grace safe from the evil that took her father from her. From us. He was a good man, and we know you are welcoming him to your flock. We ask you to guide Deputy Gibson and his men as they continue their search, so we may have justice in this world as well as the next. Amen."

"Amen," Kate repeated, and heard Grace echo the word in a small voice.

Breakfast over, Paddy finished dressing and left for the Mercantile. Kate let Grace wash and dress in their bedroom, no bigger than it needed to be but more private than the front room, then took her own turn, putting on a dark burgundy skirt Alice had made for her and a white blouse. When she came out, Grace was sitting in the kitchen, Buster at her side, her book open on the table. She'd washed the plates and forks and left them to dry on a towel on top of the cabinet beside the sink.

"I didn't know where you keep the dishes."

"That's just fine, Grace." Kate poured herself the last of the coffee and added a splash of milk. It wasn't as strong as Paddy liked to claim, but close.

But the moment she sat across from the girl, a wave of despair struck her. As the third of four, Kate had not spent her own childhood looking after younger ones. She'd watched Alice's children many times, but they were small. Not eleven like Grace, her mind and body changing by the day, orphaned in shocking circumstances. Kate and Paddy wanted children, naturally, but she expected—her mother and Alice had assured her of this— that she'd learn by doing when they came along.

So that's what she'd have to do now.

First task, baking. Three pies—one for Miss Lang, and at Grace's suggestion, another for Mr. Gregory and his nephew. The boy lived with his uncle during the week so he could attend school—he was a year ahead of Grace—and went home to his parents' farm on weekends. Grace chatted easily as they peeled and sliced the apples, but after Kate placed the last top crust and slid the pies into the oven, she saw that the girl's eyes were moist, her skin pale.

"Do you want to tell me about your father?" she asked. "He seemed like a good man."

"Oh, he was, Mrs. Murphy. He was the best father in the world," Grace blurted. "I don't care what my horrid old grandmother says about him. He loved my mother and he loved me, and everything he did, he did for us. And for God, but for us first. Is that a terrible thing to say?"

"No, not at all." She led the girl to the table, where she sprinkled two bowls of sliced apples with sugar and poured in the last of the milk. "I think taking care of the people closest to us is the best way to serve God. We can't help others until we do that, can we?"

Arval Haugen, she learned, had been orphaned as a small boy and farmed out to distant relatives, good godly people by his daughter's account, who had never met the couple, now long gone, except through her father's stories. He'd been cared for, loved even. It was a common enough story, but her heart ached to think of the cycle repeating itself with Grace.

"What happened to the farm?" she asked. Perhaps it had remained in the family, a family who would welcome his only child.

"It was lost in the Panic."

The Panic of 1893, which had changed so much for so many. Kate had been small herself then, but she'd heard talk.

"And he met your mother in church, playing the piano?"

"In Chicago, during his theology training. His classmate was engaged to her best friend, and invited him to go along to her church for services. They stood up for each other at their weddings."

Might this couple take her, if the grandmother didn't come through?

"They're missionaries in Africa," Grace continued. "They write to us about the people they meet and the strange plants and animals. I got to tell their stories to the other kids when we studied Africa in geography class."

So they could not take the girl. But she should write to them as well.

They finished their fruit, and Kate asked the question she'd been dreading. Better that she know the answer before Deputy Gibson questioned the girl.

"Grace, did anyone dislike your father? Except for your grandmother. What is her name?"

"Agnete Swensen. My mother was Freya, and I'm Freya Grace."

"A lovely name. Can you think of anyone who might have wanted to harm him? Anyone he argued with, or who threatened him?"

"He didn't argue with anyone, Mrs. Murphy." Grace clasped her hands in front of her. "No one."

But clearly, someone had taken their rage out on the reverend. It was good that the girl had been protected from that evil. But if she didn't know, who did? Kate did not believe that any thieves smart enough to know the value of two silver candlesticks would carry out their bold burglary when they were likely to be seen. When the presence of the dog and bicycle suggested that someone might be in the church, even if they didn't know it was the reverend himself.

"Did he seem worried?"

Not that Grace knew. There had been no unusual visitors. Mr. Peterman had come by to discuss church finances, and Miss Lang had dropped in to ask if there were any funds to pay her brother for doing odd jobs. Grace thought the answer was no; most church work was done by volunteers. If any volunteers had seen anything suspicious, they would tell the deputy. Whom Kate prayed would find the killer soon.

While the pies cooled, they tidied up. Then they packed Paddy's lunch and the pie and headed for the school. It was impossible not to pass by the church. Grace walked very close to Kate, who took her hand and squeezed it.

They found Anne Lang seated at the desk in her empty classroom, her pupils playing in the yard between school and church. Smells of chalk and woodsmoke mingled in the air. At the sight of them, she rose.

"Mrs. Murphy. Grace. I didn't expect to see you today."

"We brought you a pie," Grace said and held out the basket with the warm pie, wrapped in a white tea towel. A plain towel. Kate dare not share her ragged embroidery with this accomplished woman, beside whom she felt young and awkward.

"Thank you." The teacher took the basket. "Frank will be particularly pleased. I manage a decent Sunday roast, but pie is beyond my meager kitchen skills."

Kate had seen Frank Lang in the post office across the street from the Mercantile. One shoulder was lower than the other and he dragged one foot behind him as he walked. She guessed him a few years younger than Anne, but it was hard to tell.

"We were also hoping to pick up some schoolwork for Grace," Kate said. "So she doesn't fall behind."

"Little chance of that. She's one of my best pupils. But I'd be happy to find a book or two. Grace, why don't you fetch your slate, so you can practice your sums? You can take a fresh piece of chalk from the cupboard." The girl obeyed and the two women moved toward a bookcase on the far wall.

"How is she doing?"

"Well, I think. She's talked about him, and her mother, and cried a little, which I think is good. Less than I would have, but she seems a stoic child. If that's the right word."

Anne Lang nodded. "It's good that she's with you. You're kind, but no-nonsense."

Kate wasn't entirely sure that was a compliment.

"Not that I would expect any nonsense from Grace. She's eleven," the teacher continued. "Almost a young lady. I am not of the opinion that children should be protected from unpleasant truths that affect them. They simply need to be spoken with in a way they can understand. Grace is intelligent and imaginative. Her mind will fill in what she doesn't know, and what she imagines may well be worse than the truth."

Kate shuddered. Anne Lang had not seen the body. She had.

She took the books. "Grace told me that you came to see her father a few days ago. Possibly to ask about employment for your brother—she wasn't sure."

Anne's jaw tightened and her shoulders stiffened.

"Did he seem worried to you?" Kate continued. "Did he mention any— oh, disagreements?"

"You're asking if I know who might have wanted to kill him."

Kate felt herself flush.

"And no." The teacher's tone softened. "As I told Daniel Gibson, I don't know who could possibly have done such a wretched thing."

At the sound of footsteps, they turned to see Grace, holding her slate against her chest, her gaze darting from one woman to the other.

"Mrs. Murphy, I'll take your students for the rest of the week," Anne Lang said, then smiled at Grace. "We'll give your star pupil a few days off."

Kate handed Grace the books and the girl sat at the nearest desk, turning pages.

"I'd like to keep her out of school another day, if you think that's advisable. She can make a fresh start on Monday. You're sure she has no family other than the grandmother?"

"I'm sure. Have you spoken with her about the funeral?"

Kate had barely thought about that. Anne touched her arm. "Don't give it another thought. The sexton and church members will take care of everything."

But as Kate gathered up her young charge and started off for the Mercantile, she thought of little else.

Woman and girl made their way to the town's growing business district. At the north end stood the Jewel Bay Inn, built earlier in the year, a two-story white frame structure with a high false front and a porch that spanned the width of the hotel.

On the west side of Front Street stood the Jewel Bay State Bank, as impressive as any back home. A man on his way out tipped his hat and offered his condolences, as did others they met. Word of the reverend's death had spread like the fires of last August.

An empty wagon parked in front of the Mercantile reminded Kate that Paddy might need to make deliveries this afternoon, requiring her to keep shop for a few hours. Even when he hired a delivery man, he was counting on her to work by his side. The prospect was both exciting and frightening.

"There's my bride," Paddy cried when she pushed open one of the double doors. "There's my Mrs. Murphy."

A cheer went up from the men clustered in front of the hardware display and Kate knew her skin was betraying her.

Then Paddy caught sight of the girl. "Hush now," he said. "It's Reverend Arval's girl she's got with her and we want to show the man our respect."

The hubbub stilled. One of the men stepped forward and stood in front of Grace. "Aye, lass," he said in a thick Scottish brogue. "Your father was a good man, doing good work. Never a harsh word, never a quarrel."

There was a general murmur of agreement. But had that been true, Kate asked herself, one hand on Grace's thin back. Had the man been killed for a reason, a quarrel, none of them suspected?

The place was busy. Kate set the basket with Paddy's lunch on the steps to the tiny office under the eaves. Showed Grace where they hung their coats, then plucked her apron off another hook.

"What a beautiful day," she said to the girl. "The season will be changing soon. You might sit on the bench out back and read one of the books Miss Lang gave you. Keep the mule company."

"Can't I help you? And Mr. Murphy?"

"I suppose you could."

For the next half hour, Kate took orders and packed up groceries, while Paddy tended to men at the hardware counter. Grace stayed close to Kate, fetching items she pointed out, loading bags and baskets.

"I'll be off making deliveries, lass," Paddy said. The shop was empty but for the three of them. He pulled his apron over his head and handed it to Grace. "Way too big for yeh, child, but yeh might as well put it on."

She did, looking pleased, though Kate had to knot the neck strap to hold the apron up and wrap the ties twice around her middle.

"Don't forget your lunch," Kate said.

"My stomach would never let me." Paddy kissed her cheek. "I'll be back before dusk. If there's anything you can't find, or orders you aren't sure about, we'll figure it out later."

He grabbed his lunch basket off the steps. Then the back door closed and they were alone. *I'm only ten years older than she is,* Kate thought. *Ten short years.*

Though the customers when she arrived had all been men, the female side of town streamed through in the afternoon. Women from the church, or mothers of Grace's classmates, who offered her a quiet word or a quick embrace. Kate blinked back tears at their thoughtfulness, a reflection of their esteem for the reverend and their understanding of the girl's loss.

"So good of you to take her in," a woman said while Grace's attention was elsewhere. "It must have been dreadful, finding him the way you did."

Dreadful, sadly, did not begin to describe it. Twice during the night, Kate had cried out at the memory and sat up, pressing the heels of her hands into her eyes while Paddy wrapped his arms around her.

What else could she have done? It might have been her Christian duty, as another woman had said, before recalling that Kate was Irish and a Catholic, but Kate hadn't acted out of duty. She hadn't intended to take the girl at all until it became clear that Anne Lang could not keep her, but in that moment, her mind had been made up.

"It's no trouble," she said. "Grace is a lovely child. Your total is one dollar and seventeen cents."

She gathered up the bits of advice the women gave her, and gratefully accepted their offerings of bread and a few extra eggs. Yes, the Murphys sold groceries, among other things, but Kate understood that bringing food to the house of the bereaved—for that's what they had become, with the addition of Grace—was a way to extend condolences. A way that people instinctively took care of those around them in times of sorrow. From her customers, she learned that the reverend had not just prayed with those in need, but organized members of his flock to provide food and firewood for the family of an injured man, given an impoverished widow train fare to return to her parents' home, and performed other good deeds both expected and unexpected of a man of the cloth. She heard no hint of animosity in the talk, but fear edged in when two women mentioned that their husbands had joined another search party today. Until the thieves were captured and brought to justice, children would walk home from school in groups, or their mothers would come to walk with them. These women would keep their families home after dark, and bar their doors.

She learned, too, that the sexton and other male volunteers had scrubbed the blood off the wood floor. A group of women were busily airing out the church and cleaning it from top to bottom, washing the windows and floors and polishing the pews with bees' wax to make them gleam. Cleaning, too, was an instinctive response to loss, especially one so harsh and abrupt.

But like her, they had not touched the reverend's office. They'd leave that to the minister from Pondera, when he came on Sunday to preside over the funeral and burial.

That seemed too soon, but it wasn't. Yesterday, the day of the murder, had been Wednesday. What made it seem rushed, Kate realized, was that the death had been so unexpected. She had not yet had time to notify Agnete Swensen, though if Grace were right, that would make no difference. And even if she had, where else would Arval Haugen be buried but here in Jewel Bay, the site of his church as well as his death? He had no family to welcome his body home. His wife had been buried with her people, and it seemed unlikely that Mrs. Swensen would spare room in the plot for her murdered son-in-law. The farm was gone, the town a part of his past. He had no home ground but this. How strange it would be for Grace, if she did return to Chicago, to leave her father behind.

But despite the women's kindness, Kate fretted. She had known life here would be nothing like life in Baraboo, in the cocoon of the Flannery family home dominated by her mother's strong presence and her father's steady hand. She had known this was the frontier at the edge of the untamed wilderness. Front Street lacked a boardwalk, although some businesses, like the inn and the bank and the Mercantile, had built their own. Volunteers had regraded the street this past summer on "Good Roads Day." But despite the residents' efforts and ambitions, Jewel Bay was raw and unfinished.

Could she be the helpmate Paddy needed, a trusted figure behind the counter that townspeople would rely on, as they did him?

Never mind all that. Today, she had to figure out where the extra canned peaches were, how to adjust the scale, how to deal with the leering faces of the lumberjacks who came in for beans and potatoes and salt pork and the prying eyes of the society women, such as they were, wondering what sort of wife and woman this slip of a girl so new to this great big roaring state of Montana might turn out to be.

She straightened her shoulders and got to work.

Midafternoon, Grace was deep in conversation with a stout woman of about sixty, no taller than she. A member of the church, Kate guessed from the woman's comforting tone and gestures. Grace looked more at ease than Kate had ever seen her, except at the piano.

The door opened and Laura Peterman entered. She glanced around the shop, spotting Grace, and her lips curved.

"I see you've put the child to work."

Kate cursed her fair skin, flushing again. Would she ever learn to control it?

"I mean no judgment," the elegant woman said as she pulled off her gloves. Today's dress was a pale peach, almost too pale for the season, but not quite. Again, a hint of lavender surrounded her. "Only that it's good to keep children busy. Not that anything will keep her mind off what happened. Or yours."

So she knew that Kate had found the body.

"What can I get for you today?" she asked, eager to steer the conversation away from the tragedy and her handling of it.

"Not a thing. My husband is in important meetings all day, so I decided to drive the buggy in and gather the children from school. And I wanted to let you know Elizabeth will not be able to attend her piano lesson today. I'll pay you—"

"No, no," Kate said. "Miss Lang is giving the lessons today, and I am certain she won't mind."

"Good. And how is Grace? That's the doctor's mother-in-law speaking with her, by the way. A very good soul."

"Ah, thank you. As for Grace, she's a brave child. Sweet, and very helpful. She has no family other than a distant grandmother. I'll write to her, but I am not sure what the future holds."

"As none of us is," came the reply, and Kate wondered what unexpected hardships she'd endured. After a long moment, Laura Peterman spoke again. "I understand Deputy Gibson led a search party last night, but they didn't find the killer. Or killers. Have you heard any news today?"

"Only that another search is underway. Deputy Gibson seems competent. Paddy—Mr. Murphy—is certain he'll find the killer."

"Oh, I am sure he will," Laura Peterman replied. She was a genuinely pretty woman, with light brown hair and eyes of a golden brown. Kate's younger sister, so skilled in portraiture, would very much enjoy painting her. She was about to say so when Laura reached across the counter and touched Kate's arm with her ungloved hand. "Do let me know, Mrs. Murphy—Kate—what I can do to help you and Grace."

She called out a greeting to the doctor's mother-in-law, drew on her gloves, and left.

Paddy returned earlier than expected, freeing Kate and Grace to head home on foot to start supper. Grace was silent on the walk, and Kate wondered if she'd heard something she shouldn't have, in the conversations that had swirled around the shop that afternoon.

"We'll stop and pick up a few more things for you. I imagine your father kept an address book, so we can write to your grandmother." They were nearing the parsonage now.

"Buster!" Grace called and crouched to embrace the muddy dog racing to her.

"Good heavens. What is he doing here?" But it was obvious. The dog had seen no reason to stay at the Murphys' when Grace wasn't there. How much the dog understood about his master's death, Kate had no idea. But clearly, the dog knew Grace needed him. He licked her cheek, then laid his big head on her shoulder, one muddy paw on her skirt.

It will wash, Kate reminded herself. It was good for the girl to have a companion.

Kate had not taken a good look around the parsonage yesterday, and now she saw that it was sparsely furnished, the pieces mismatched, serviceable but well-worn. Donated, no doubt, by members of his congregation. Arval Haugen and his daughter had been in Jewel Bay nearly three years, but clearly, he had not been the sort of man who paid attention to homely details like whether the furniture matched or paintings hung on the walls. His mind had been on higher things. Her gaze fell on a small secretary, cherry with a glass-front upper cabinet, the mullions in an elegant diamond pattern.

"That was my mother's," Grace said. "It's the only piece of furniture we brought west."

Kate's breath caught in her throat. The upper shelf held hand-painted porcelain cups and saucers. Freya's work? She tilted her head to read the titles of the books on the lower shelves. Theology texts. She rummaged quickly through the notes and pamphlets tucked in the cubbyholes, but found no address book. Grace had no idea where he'd kept it, and Kate could see nowhere else to search in the tight quarters.

"Why don't you pack up your school clothes and a nice dress, dark if you have one, while I go see if I can find the address book in the church office?" A dark dress for the funeral, which they had not yet discussed. "And bring your piano music. We'll start our lessons again next week."

Grace agreed, and Kate went outside. The air was warm, though the birch and aspen leaves had changed color and begun to drop, and the afternoon would have been quite lovely had it not been for her difficult errand. As she neared the church, she wondered if she should have waited for Paddy to go with her.

Don't be a silly girl, she told herself. *You're a grown woman. Now act like one.* But it was nice to have the dog walking with her.

She decided to try the side door rather than go in the front, so she could duck into the office without passing by the altar. Despite the thorough scrubbing, she knew she'd never enter the church again without seeing the blood, the dead man, his beseeching eyes.

Without warning, the dog darted past her out of sight. "Buster. Come back here."

She followed him to the rear of the building, to a woodpile large enough to serve both church and school. The dog was digging furiously at the base of the pile, dirt flying from his paws.

"Buster, stop that! You'll bring the whole pile down." He'd already dislodged several smaller pieces. But that wasn't what momentarily stopped her heart.

In the opening he'd created, where a chunk of firewood should have been, was a gleaming silver candlestick.

After the discovery, Kate hesitated to dare enter the church. Did the school even have a telephone? The lines were new, the school location temporary. Besides, classes had ended, and with the Peterman girl not taking a lesson today, the building would be empty.

In the tidy homes up and down the street, children were doing chores and schoolwork. Fathers were returning from their work and mothers getting supper ready. She could not bring herself to disturb them.

"Kate Murphy, don't be foolish." She took a deep breath and straightened her filthy skirt, not bothering to brush it off. "Stay here, Buster."

First, she went back to the woodpile. Retrieved the candlestick and tucked it into her bag, then returned to the church. Marched in, pushed open the office door, and placed the call to Deputy Gibson.

"Fetch Ivan Gregory," the deputy told her. "Ask him to keep watch until I get there. Then take Grace home."

Why did he not simply call the man himself? Because he wanted her out of the way. Was that a harsh judgment? She'd had the impression the deputy didn't think a young woman, barely more than a girl even though she was married, had any business mucking about in murder. But she hadn't chosen to become involved. She'd found the body, and that gave her a responsibility.

Maybe she was misjudging him. Maybe he simply wanted to keep her safe.

Her, and Grace.

But she held her tongue. The muddy dog had waited for her outside. No one was in sight. She crossed the wide, dirt street and hurried to Gregory's house.

No lights in the windows and her knocking went unanswered. What should she do? Deputy Gibson had wanted the woodpile guarded. But she had left Grace alone.

At the sound of footsteps, Kate turned to see a man walking toward her. Though his dark cap was pulled low, she was sure she'd seen him before. In the shop, she supposed. A laborer. What was his name?

"Hello," she called, and the man stopped, raising his head in surprise.

"Why, if it isn't the new Mrs. Murphy," he exclaimed, sweeping off his cap and bowing in a theatrical gesture. It was quite silly, given his dirty work clothes and scuffed boots, and all that weighed on her mind, but even so, she found herself smiling, almost charmed. "Thaddeus London, at your service."

London. That was it. She'd heard the name from Paddy, though what he'd said about the man escaped her.

"I've come to see Mr. Gregory, but he doesn't appear to be at home."

"Noo. No, he's not. Fine place like this, but it belongs to the power company. I hear he's got his eye on building himself an orchard, on the edge of town," London said, jerking a thumb over his shoulder. "Might there be something I could help you with? A fine lady like you."

"I wanted—no. It's nothing that can't wait." Deputy Gibson had told her to summon Ivan Gregory. Yesterday in the church, she had detected a carefulness between the men, but no distrust. This London, though, seemed a different kettle of fish. Jewel Bay might be a young town, but it was like any other town that way, full of all kinds of men, and women, too, here for their own reasons. "But I thank you."

That should have been enough for the man, a dismissal, an indication to go his own way. But he did not. He kept his gaze on her a moment too long, and then another moment, and she had to remind herself not to show her discomfort. She had as much right to walk these streets as he did, as anyone did.

Then London flashed her a toothy grin. "Good day to you then, Kate Murphy."

She watched him saunter down the street and round the corner. "Go find Grace," she told the dog.

Buster cocked his head. "Go," she repeated. "Go find Grace." And off he trotted.

She followed at a distance, keeping an eye on London. As the man neared the church, he turned and waved, then kept on going down the hill. Aiming for one of the taverns, she guessed, or the boardinghouse. She watched until he was out of sight. She checked the woodpile, but it had not been disturbed any further. Then she scurried to the parsonage.

Grace was sitting on the front step, a book in her lap, a valise at her feet.

A valise, and the dog.

Kate blinked back her tears, put on a smile, and marched toward them.

∞

She might almost have been back in the house in Baraboo with her sisters, laughing, as she and Grace sponged the mud off their skirts, then started supper. Was it right to laugh, in a time of loss and fear? Or wrong not to enjoy the moment? What, Kate thought, did God want of us in such times?

At the sound of the automobile, she patted her hair. No need to pinch color into her cheeks, already pink from the heat. Paddy came in the kitchen door, as he usually did, and after hanging his coat on the hook, he took Kate in his arms and held her as tight as ever he had held her. He smelled of work, and leather, and the hay he'd fed the mule.

"Will you give us a minute, child?" he asked Grace.

The girl nodded and went into the front room, closing the door behind her.

"You're all right, then, lass?" He held Kate's shoulders and searched her face. "You and the girl?"

"We are. How did you hear? What did you hear?" She laid her hands on his and searched his face, her eyes hungry for news.

"All news passes through the doors of a general store, in any small town." He led her to the table and sat, then bent to unlace his boots. "Aye, and it's what I wanted my shop to be, but I do wish the news were better."

"Have they found anyone? Or anything?"

"The other candlestick? No. And what have you done with the one you found? What have you told the girl?"

"You tease me for carrying a big cloth bag instead of a lady's purse, but it came in handy. I didn't dare leave the candlestick behind. If the thief returned, no one would ever believe I'd actually found it." Kate sat across from her husband. "All I told Grace was that I hadn't been able to find her father's address book, that we'd have to search for it later. Truth is, I never got a chance to look. I went inside long enough to use the telephone and left. It was Buster who got the scent, good dog."

The dog lifted his head and sighed as Paddy rubbed one floppy ear.

This time, Grace insisted on sitting on the box as they ate, and Paddy said he'd stop by the parsonage and borrow a chair. "For now," he said lightly, acknowledging all they did not know. How long Grace would stay with them, where she would go when the time was right, and when another minister might be sent to Jewel Bay.

Kate had just put the wash water on to heat when a knock on the front door startled them. Paddy left the kitchen, still in his stocking feet, and a moment later, Kate heard Daniel Gibson's voice. She wiped her hands on her apron, then stood in the doorway, an arm around Grace's shoulders.

Deputy Gibson's dark eyes settled on her, his jaw tightening.

"If you've got any news, Daniel," Paddy said, "speak it plainly. No need to spare my wife. She found the reverend, you'll recall, and she found the candlestick today."

"Well, the dog found it," Kate said. Grace's thin body quivered and she tightened her grip. "And Grace is nearly twelve. She deserves to hear everything you know about her father's death."

But bad news—or good, for that matter—always goes better with a cup of something hot, so it was a few minutes before they sat, Grace on the sofa between Kate and Paddy, Daniel Gibson in the matching armchair, the bone china cup small and fragile in his hands. The candlestick Kate and Buster had rescued sat, partially wrapped in Kate's white handkerchief, on the mahogany coffee table her parents had given them as a wedding present.

"We tore that woodpile apart," Gibson said. "Searched every inch of church and school that we hadn't searched before. No sign of the mate, or anything else where it shouldn't have been. Tell me again, Mrs. Murphy, why you went looking for trouble in the woodpile."

"She's told you, Daniel," Paddy said. "It was the dog."

Gibson gestured with one hand. "And what on earth set the dog off? How did he know to dig there?"

His narrowed eyes made Kate wonder if he suspected she knew more than she should. That she'd been involved, somehow. Because it was strange that the same person—a woman, and a newcomer—had found both the body and the missing silver. People would stare. They'd talk. They liked her well enough, but they didn't know her yet, and they would talk. That's how small towns were.

"Buster sat at my father's feet every night," Grace said, speaking for the first time since Deputy Gibson's arrival. She glanced at Paddy. "Like he sits at yours, Mr. Murphy."

"Go on, lass," Paddy said.

Grace swallowed, then raised her eyes to Gibson's. "Buster went everywhere with my father. If he had a call to make, and it was close enough to walk, Buster walked with him. If he took his bicycle, when he went down to the lakeshore to visit the encampment or out to see Mrs. Peterman, Buster trotted along beside him. He waited by the front door to the church and barked to let Papa know someone was there to see him."

The Indian encampment. Kate had heard of it, but had not seen it. "I spoke with Mrs. Peterman this afternoon. She didn't mention a visit with the reverend. Did he go out there often?"

"No. Well, I don't know. Once, about two weeks ago? And Mr. Peterman came to see him at the parsonage."

Perhaps Laura Peterman was active in the churchwomen's guild. Churches depended on donors and volunteers, from those who paid for the candles and lights to those who scrubbed the floors and chopped the wood. And those who kept the records, a task for a banker like James Peterman.

"You're saying the dog might have seen what happened to your father," Deputy Gibson said gently.

"No one cares what a dog sees," Grace said, "because they can't talk. As long as he wasn't barking, the killer would have ignored him while he struck my father and left him there to die, then hid the candlestick in the woodpile. But Buster knew. And when Mrs. Murphy went to the side door, near the woodpile, he made sure she saw him digging and found the candlestick."

Kate squeezed the girl's hand, and Grace squeezed back.

Gibson sipped his coffee. Kate thought of the man she'd met in the street. No point mentioning him, though he had unsettled her.

"Deputy," she said, "no thief would leave behind the most valuable thing in that church. Nor would he have taken the time to hide it, once he'd killed a man."

"Why hide the one, though, and take the other?" Gibson said. "He has to have known it would be found. And one's not worth half what the pair would fetch."

True enough. Besides, if the thief tried to sell the single silver piece within a hundred miles, word would reach the sheriff.

"Might be it's hidden nearby, somewhere your men didn't search. Tossed down the hillside or into the water," Paddy suggested.

"Surely, though, the hiding means something." Kate leaned forward. "The candlestick wasn't simply dropped in the rush to get away. A killer bold enough to strike in broad daylight and then take the time to hide the candlestick in the woodpile wasn't a thief who got caught in the act and killed to cover his tracks."

The killer had known how to slip out one or two pieces of wood, hide the silver, then slip the wood back in. The killer knew how to stack wood. But then, almost every man did. Did the killer also know how much wood the church and school might use through the winter, and when the candlestick might be found?

"Mrs. Murphy, you've got a good head on your shoulders and I dare say there's a chance you're right. But the sheriff thinks the good reverend's mur—death the work of no-good drifters, and unless we find good reason to persuade him otherwise, that's the approach we'll be taking."

He was telling her to leave it be. To take care of Grace, and Paddy, and the things that a woman, a wife, should care about.

But it was clear to Kate that the discovery of the candlestick disproved the theory of killer thieves. It was equally clear that if Reverend Arval Haugen had been killed for some reason other than the missing silver, his killer might still be in Jewel Bay. And Grace could be in danger, too.

Deputy Gibson drained his coffee and set the cup on the table. Stood, patted his pocket, and withdrew a slim black leather book. "Reverend Haugen's address book. Found it in his desk drawer, right where you'd expect."

Kate felt Grace's gaze, almost heard the girl realize Kate had lied to her about not finding it. A white lie, meant to hold off the moment when she had to tell the girl what she'd found. She vowed to tell no more such lies. They bought time, but caused pain in the process.

"Thank you," she said. "Grace, please fetch the deputy's hat and coat." While the girl did as she asked, Kate unwrapped the handkerchief around the base of the candlestick and pointed, wordlessly, at a dark red spot on the silver. Beside her, Paddy stifled a gasp and even the deputy grew more somber. She rewrapped the candlestick, then wrapped it carefully in a soft shawl. When he'd donned his coat and hat, the big man took the bundle from her as though it were a newborn baby, and headed out into the dark night.

∞

The night was quiet, the only sounds an odd sigh or snort from the dog asleep on the kitchen floor. Dreaming of running beside his master, as the reverend pedaled out along the lakeshore to the Petermans' grand home?

The dog snorted and shuddered, and Kate wondered if he truly had seen the killer, had watched his master die.

With the door between the kitchen and front room closed, she could not even hear the faint ticking of the clock. Paddy was asleep in their bedroom, Grace on the sofa. Late as it was, though, Kate had no thoughts of sleep, certain that the moment she lay down, all that she'd seen in the past two days would play itself out against the darkness.

She cradled the cup of tea, its scent reminding her of home and the day she'd left to come west. She pictured her mother's fine dark eyes—Mrs. Flannery was a handsome woman—filling with love and tears of longing and excitement, all that had flooded through Kate herself. But of all the things she had imagined in her new life, she had not imagined finding a man murdered, or taking temporary custody of his daughter. She had not imagined listening to the deputy sit in her own home and tell her the sheriff believed the tragedy a theft gone wrong, though the evidence said otherwise.

"Lass, yeh may be right," Paddy had said to her after Gibson had gone. "But leave it be. Leave it to Daniel."

If there was a killer walking around Jewel Bay, were any of them safe? Could this be the haven Paddy and Ivan Gregory and James Peterman and so many others had worked so hard to create if a killer walked free because the sheriff had made up his mind?

She took a long sip, letting the toasty aroma and smooth, slightly sweet flavor soothe her. Then she set the cup in the saucer and opened her writing box. She threw two sheets of the creamy linen paper her sister Alice had given her as a wedding gift into the cookstove firebox before managing to complete a note she could bear to send to the formidable Agnete Swenson. Then she opened Reverend Arval Haugen's black book and copied out Mrs.

Swenson's address, folded the letter, and slipped it inside the envelope. She'd forgotten to ask Grace the names of the missionary couple, and didn't want to flip through the book, searching for an address somewhere in Africa. Too much like prying.

So she poured another cup of tea and started a letter to Alice.

She was late. Since arriving in Jewel Bay, she'd written her mother every Sunday and her sister every Wednesday. But she could not have written last night, not with all that had happened. They shared her letters, although Kate trusted Alice to hold back any doubts or fears she expressed that might worry their mother. This letter was nothing but doubt and fear, and she wasn't sure she would send it. Alice didn't need to hear about the gash on Reverend Arval Haugen's forehead or the look in his sightless eyes.

Was it fanciful to even think she'd seen a look in them? A plea to protect his daughter and find his killer?

She'd always been too sensitive, Kate knew. Everyone had said so. Except Alice, who had held her and let her cry when they were at the farm and saw the colt break its leg. Alice had rushed her inside and held her hands over young Kate's ears but it hadn't been enough; she'd heard the gunshot anyway, heard the mare whinny long and loud. She could almost hear it now. Could almost hear Alice utter soothing sounds, hear her father tell her mother they couldn't baby her, she had to grow out of it. "Hush, Michael," her mother had replied. "Let her be. It's her big heart that makes her our Kate." If she tried to hold back her emotion, to say anything less than what she felt, Alice would know.

A tear splashed onto the paper and spattered the damp ink.

The door to the front room opened. Kate raised her head. Grace stood in the doorway, in her white nightgown, a wool shawl around her shoulders.

"Can't sleep?" Kate asked. "Sit. I'll warm some milk for you."

As she poured milk into a saucepan, the dog woke, stretched, and padded over to the table. Grace buried her face in his neck.

Kate set the mug of warm milk on the table. The girl took a long drink, then raised her swollen eyes to Kate's. "Thank you, Kate. For everything."

Kate nodded, not trusting herself to speak. Her tea would be cold now, too bitter for comfort, but she didn't want to busy herself heating more water, cleaning the pot, making a new cup. Sometimes it was better to stay put.

She touched the envelope on the table. "I've written to your grand-mother. Would you like to add a note to her? I haven't sealed the envelope yet."

"What would I say?"

"What would you like her to know?"

Grace's fingers tightened on the mug, her knuckles almost as white as the milk itself. "That my father was a good man. That he loved my mother and me, and that he made a good life for us here in Jewel Bay." The shawl slipped off one shoulder and she tugged it into place.

Kate waited.

"That he never hated her," Grace continued, "even when she said hateful things about him. He believed everything he preached, about forgiving those who harm us. About praying for those who do wrong in the world."

Someone had hated Arval Haugen. Had done him wrong. Who? There could be no forgiveness until they knew who had killed him, could there?

How could she send this earnest, wounded little bird back to the woman who had sent her and her father away? Too lost, Kate presumed, in her own grief to stand the sight of the man who had loved her daughter.

"I've told her you're safe with us, for now," Kate said. "We can write her again in a day or two, when you're ready."

"Who else are you writing? I have no other family."

"My sister, Alice."

"Oh, the one with two children who lives near your parents in Bear—Bear what?"

"Baraboo. On the Baraboo River." The girl heard and saw everything, forgot nothing, just as in her piano lessons. They would have to be very careful. "Funny name, isn't it? I've heard half a dozen different theories about its origin. Most likely it came from a French fur trader who settled on the riverbank."

"What's it like, having three sisters?" Grace asked. "I wish I had a sister. Or even a brother. Miss Lang's brother lives with her."

You have me, Kate wanted to tell her, but held her tongue. Grace belonged with family. Perhaps there was an aunt or a cousin she didn't know about, someone who would open their arms and welcome her.

What if her ideas about her grandmother were wrong? Even a bright, perceptive child like Grace would not understand everything. Kate was counting on that, though the girl was so certain of the old lady's judgment that it would be difficult to persuade her otherwise, even if the woman wrote back immediately and extended every possible welcome. Even if she got on a train and came to fetch Grace herself.

And if the girl was right, and the grandmother did begrudge her existence but sent for her anyway? Should she be sent to a house where she would surely be alone, and lonely, even if warm and well-fed and educated? Sometimes children were better off in other situations, weren't they?

Don't be fanciful, Kate. You know nothing about raising children yet, let alone girls Grace's age. Although she had once been a girl Grace's age, interested in many of the same things. Not as drawn to books, but Grace had grown up alone with a bookish father.

"Come with me," Kate said, and led her back to the front room. On top of the side table sat several framed photographs, one of Kate and Paddy on their wedding day a month ago. Hard to believe so little time had passed—so much had happened. At the same time, her wedding day seemed like yesterday, so vivid. So happy. "My parents," she said, indicating a woman with strong features under a glorious sweep of dark hair and a man with a round head and a mustache, his railroad watch chain straining across the ample belly under his dark suit coat. "And this was taken last summer, just before Margaret left for art school, underneath the beech tree out back."

Grace held the photo of the four girls in both hands. Kate pointed at a woman who strongly resembled their mother. "That's Alice. Then me, and Margaret. And Mary, who's three years older than I. She's a teacher."

"Like Miss Lang."

"Teaching is an excellent occupation for a woman. You might consider it yourself."

Grace studied the photo for a long time, then returned it to the table and ducked behind the sofa. Opened her canvas bag and drew out a framed photo. Held it for Kate to see, but kept a firm grip. Kate did not try to take it from her hands.

"Oh, Grace. She was lovely." Freya Swensen Haugen had been a beauty, with wavy blond hair pulled into a loose chignon, a firm jaw and nose, and an enchanting smile. Kate glanced at Grace. Her face was still a child's, but if the maternal influence won, she too would catch eyes and hearts.

And in that moment, Kate understood how difficult the resemblance might be for Mrs. Swensen, and in her heart, she asked the good Lord to show them all the way.

∞

The next two days, the threesome, and Buster, fell into a rhythm. Grace proved enormously helpful, having been something of a housekeeper for her father as well as cook and daughter. Paddy left after breakfast Friday morning, Kate's letters in his pocket. Buster settled into his guard post in the tiny front yard. Kate and Grace washed up and tidied the house, then readied a basket of fresh garden vegetables a churchwoman had brought by for a hearty soup.

Midday, Kate and Grace walked to the shop with Paddy's lunch, exchanging a few words with the shopkeepers and villagers they met on the streets. After he'd eaten, Paddy took the wagon out to make deliveries, and Kate kept shop with Grace as her assistant. Late that afternoon, Laura Peterman dropped in again, bringing her daughter, Elizabeth, and Kate readily agreed to Laura's suggestion that the girls walk down to the bay for a bit of fresh air. The two practically bounced as they headed out the door and down Front Street.

"Thank you," Kate said. "I'd hoped Grace would want to spend time with other girls her age, but she hadn't mentioned any friends and I'm too new in town to know all the adults, let alone their children."

"I'll confess, I wanted a moment with you," Laura said. "To ask how Grace is doing, and how you're holding up. But also to confirm a few things for the funeral service and the burial at Lone Pine."

Paddy had pointed out the cemetery, a few miles north of town, but she'd had no reason to visit yet. "It's a lovely spot, and the mountains are stunning, but—" Kate broke off, holding her hand to her heart. "Is it fanciful to think he might be lonely there, so far from the land where he was raised, and from his late wife's grave?"

"One is never alone, or lonely, when one accepts God's grace. As Reverend Haugen most surely did."

Kate sighed. "I only wish he'd designated someone to care for his daughter, if he died." Surely a man who frequently confronted human mortality would have thought about his daughter's future.

"I have the impression that there were family difficulties. As happens from time to time."

Would Kate's letter make those difficulties better or worse? Had she meddled where she ought not?

"The churchwomen will organize a picnic lunch after the burial," Laura continued. "Since the church hall is being used by the school right now, we can eat at the cemetery after the burial, if the weather holds, or plan to gather in the school, if you'd prefer."

She had no preference, no reason to have one. It was good of Laura Peterman to ask, out of courtesy for her temporary guardianship of the girl, but she had no idea what to do.

"Which would you choose?"

"I would choose a picnic on the cemetery lawn. It's the custom back East, and I've always enjoyed it."

"Where back East did you come from?" Kate wasn't good at identifying accents, probably because she'd been so few places herself.

"Pittsburgh," Laura said, after a brief hesitation. "Now, is there anything you need? Anything we can do for you?"

"Thank you, no. People have dropped by extra food, which I appreciate, though Grace doesn't eat much and we are grocers." Kate flashed a quick grin. "She'll be going back to school on Monday, and once we're in a routine . . ."

"Yes. Routines are good for children. But Sunday, after the service and lunch and all the excitement . . ." Laura's voice trailed off. "You should be prepared."

Kate took a deep breath and exhaled. Be prepared for tears, as the loss sunk in. "Thank you. You've been most kind."

Laura Peterman responded with a sweet, slightly sad smile, and bought a few sticks of candy before collecting the girls. Grace returned with a healthy flush on her cheeks and a lightness that gave Kate hope.

The rest of the day went smoothly, the whoosh of wheels and clack of hooves outside mingling with conversation and the jangle of the cash register inside. Saturday followed much the same pattern. There was no word of the thieves, or the second candlestick. Kate did not see Thaddeus London again, and she didn't mind. At home, in the evenings, she attempted to sew while Grace read to them, but she was not a good seamstress at the best of times, and her nerves were too jangled for delicate work right now. Later. There would be plenty of time later, in the long winter ahead.

In the front pew, Grace sitting straight-backed between her and Paddy, Kate tried to focus on the visiting minister's words. Tried to forget that he stood on the very spot where she had found Reverend Haugen on what the minister called "that unholy day." But how could she, the way the man went on about his dear, departed friend's faith and his love of Christ and his constant prayers for the soul of the community, and finally, a word about his love for his only child.

She could not, would not, forget that Arval Haugen had been a man first, and a father, and then a minister. His failure to consider Grace, should anything happen to him, was troubling. He had lost his wife; he knew better than most the dangers. He and his daughter had been cast out, if Grace had the story right, from the only family remaining. As Laura Peterman had said the other day in the shop, these things happen.

But she could not blame Reverend Haugen for not wanting to believe he might die early. Surely he had expected there would be time to repair the relationship with his mother-in-law. For Grace's sake, and the love of his late wife.

After the service, a procession of automobiles, buggies, and wagons headed for the cemetery. Laura's recommendation had been a good one. The view of the mountains was magnificent and the minister's words mercifully brief before the six strong men, Paddy among them in a nod to his role in the community and to having taken in young Grace, even though he was a Catholic, lowered the casket into the grave.

Grace stood silently. After she had tossed a handful of rich, dark dirt onto the casket, she'd tucked her bare hand into Kate's gloved one and kept it there as the mourners filed by, paying their last respects. Grace accepted their condolences in a manner that suited her name, convincing Kate that Arval and Freya Haugen had been good parents, despite their feud with Mrs. Swensen.

And then Kate and Paddy were alone by the grave with Grace, the minister and sexton a few feet away.

"Shall we leave you here with your father for a bit?" Kate asked.

"No," Grace replied quickly. Then she knelt, the skirt of her dark brown dress just missing the fresh dirt around the edge of the grave. Folded her hands and bowed her head. Kate took Paddy's hand, and they waited.

Then the threesome picked their way down the slope to the sprawling lawn where the churchwomen had spread out quilts and opened their baskets. Kate hadn't brought a basket, having been told it wasn't necessary, but she wasn't immediately sure where to go. Anne Lang beckoned them, rising and giving her pupil a quick but firm embrace.

"Kate, I don't believe you've met my brother, Frank." Anne gestured to the young man who had pushed himself up with difficulty, his shoulders uneven, one leg several inches shorter than the other. "Frank, this is Mrs. Murphy."

"I've seen you in the post office," he said, holding out his hand. "Your husband owns the Mercantile." Frank Lang's words were not easy to understand, and one side of his face drooped. But his grip was firm and his eyes were gentle.

"He does," she said. "Grace and I have been helping out this past week."

They settled on the yellow-and-white quilt, in the popular Flying Geese pattern. Paddy sat beside her a few minutes later, after the inevitable stops for a quick conversation. Anne passed around plates of ham and potato salad, and poured glasses of lemonade. Ivan Gregory joined them, telling stories of the small towns where he'd worked before settling here. He kept it light, though Kate had heard enough from Paddy and the men in the Mercantile to know that conditions were sometimes quite dangerous, pay low, and bosses hard. Ivan Gregory did not seem like a hard boss, and she hoped that was true, particularly when she saw the effort he made to amuse Anne Lang and the flush on the teacher's cheeks. It was almost like a carefree summer picnic, despite the reason for the gathering, and Grace ate more than Kate had ever seen.

"There's Daniel Gibson," Paddy said to Kate. He handed her his plate and pushed himself up. "I'll go have a word."

Kate watched him go. She recognized several families from the shop or piano lessons. The Petermans sat not far away, Laura and James and their three children, and Laura waved. When she turned back to her own group, Gregory was relaying a story about a stubborn mule that had Grace and Frank captivated, but Anne's attention was elsewhere. Kate followed the teacher's gaze to where Paddy stood with Gibson, beside a graceful birch. Then the two men shook hands and Paddy moved on. The teacher kept watching the deputy sheriff, and Kate could not read the expression on her face as the man looked toward their quintet.

"I should go say hello to a few people, if you don't mind," Kate said when Gregory finished his story. "Grace, would you like to say hello to Elizabeth?"

Grace quickly agreed. They thanked Anne, said their goodbyes, and joined the Petermans, where Grace accepted a slice of cake and settled in next to her friend. Laura stood and walked a few feet away with Kate.

"This was an excellent recommendation," Kate said. "Thank you. It's good for Grace to see the community's respect for her father."

"He was a good man. I only wish—" She broke off, catching her lower lip between her teeth and clutching her elbows.

Kate did not dare ask what she wished. Then Laura took her hand and spoke fervently.

"You're young, Kate. And it's clear that you have a good heart, if an innocent one. Please, don't judge people for their mistakes. We all make them, and some . . . well, some mistakes simply can't be undone."

And with that, Laura Peterman squeezed her hand and returned to the colorful log cabin quilt where her family sat, and began to pack up. Kate could not see her face. Perhaps, when Reverend Haugen had ridden his bicycle out to visit with the Petermans, he had told her about the rift with his late wife's mother. Yes, that was it—Laura had mentioned something of the family trouble when she'd been in the Mercantile.

Kate was relieved to know he'd found someone to confide in. How difficult it must be for men of the cloth to hear other people's concerns and not often have the chance to express their own.

"Mrs. Murphy," the mother of another piano student called. Kate greeted the woman and was introduced to her husband and other children. She wove her way through the gathering, hoping to remember new names and faces the next time they met. To her surprise, the atmosphere was quite pleasant, not maudlin at all. Perhaps that was because the town was too new for many graves. There would be more grief to come. Almost everyone shared a story about Reverend Haugen, and it seemed clear that he'd been well-liked, even loved. The doctor expressed his fervent wish that today's visiting minister would not be taking over the church in Jewel Bay, "or we'll all turn deaf, from him talking our ears off." Several women asked about Grace, and Kate had to acknowledge that she did not yet know what would happen to the girl.

But she had not grown up with three sisters without developing the ability to hear bits of conversation not meant for her. A shocking suggestion that Reverend Haugen might not have kept every secret as quiet as he should have. A comment that Ivan Gregory might now have the chance to buy the land he'd been coveting for his orchard, land some thought better for a new church and school. She needed a break from all the talk.

Pretend you're in Baraboo, she told herself. *Smile, say a few words, like Alice or your mother would do. And keep moving.*

When she reached the top of the cemetery, she paused to read the inscription beneath a stone lamb. An infant, dead at just three months.

"You there!" a rough male voice shouted, and Kate jerked her head up. Who could be yelling at her?

"What are you up to?" the man continued, his heavy forehead wrinkled, a thick hand waving. "He bothering you, miss?"

"Who?" Was he talking to her? She twisted her head and glimpsed Frank Lang, partially hidden by a large spruce, one of a row that marked the far edge of the cemetery. Frank was hurriedly buttoning his pants. "Oh, good heavens, no."

But the man ignored her protest and grabbed at Frank's arm. Frank tried to pull away, but with his poor balance, he stumbled and the man easily snared him.

"How do we know an imbecile like you didn't kill the reverend? We know he had a hankering to marry your sister. He'd have tossed you out on your ear," the man said. "Now here you are, making a pest of yourself with this young woman."

"I—I just came up—here to—to make water," Frank stammered.

"I don't know who you are," Kate said to the man, "but I'll thank you not to speak so rudely. Frank has done nothing wrong." A movement caught her eye and she spotted Daniel Gibson a short ways away.

"That's enough, Henry," Gibson said, stepping into the scene. "Mrs. Murphy says Frank wasn't bothering her, and we'll take her at her word."

"You should be looking at him for the murder," Henry said. "We all know it doesn't take much for a defect like him to turn violent."

"I know no such thing," Gibson replied as he led the man away.

Kate put her hand on her heart to slow it down. Frank had finished buttoning his pants and was watching her uncertainly.

"Are you all right, Frank? What a horrid man."

"He—he'd have hurt me if—if you hadn't stopped him. Thank you, Miss Ka—Kate."

"Shall we rejoin your sister?"

Frank nodded and they made their way down the hill. Frank walked slowly, planting one leg and swinging the other around, using his arms for balance. Kate stayed close, though she was too small to help much if he fell. It was plain that some folks had heard Henry's words and shared his distrust of Frank, while others had no idea what had happened.

How terrible that Frank, and Anne, had to endure such hatred. How widespread was it? Was Jewel Bay, despite its name, not as polished or genteel a town as its leading residents might want to think? Was Paddy right to believe in the town's promise? Could a town where thieves went uncaught and murder—in a church, no less—went unsolved prosper and thrive? Should they pull up stakes while they could?

If they could.

No. It was impossible. Paddy had sunk everything into this town—his money, his heart, and his hopes. And on a day so bright and clear, how could she not believe, too—even if they were gathered for the funeral of a well-loved man. Even if there were gossips and cruel tongues amid the offers of spare clothing for Grace, and a cot that could be folded up and tucked out of the way. This was the town they had chosen. The town where they had cast their lot and their luck.

They reached Anne's quilt and Frank thanked her again before settling himself next to his sister. Should she mention the incident? Then an arm slipped around her waist and the touch and scent of Paddy Murphy enveloped her. She buried her head in his shoulder. A silent sob wracked her and he held her close.

"Ah, lass," he whispered. "You're safe with me."

Was she safe? Was Grace? Oh, how she wanted to believe it.

"Paddy," she said when they were alone that night in their bedroom, "is it true that Reverend Haugen wanted to marry Anne Lang? What would have happened to Frank?"

Paddy's eyes went wide as he unbuttoned his shirt, the collar hanging loose around his neck.

"News to me, lass. Where's this coming from?"

She told him about the incident in the cemetery.

"Henry Clyde," Paddy said, his eyes darkening. "It's him you got to be watching out for."

"Was the reverend courting Anne?"

"Mighta been. I'd say if she's partial to anyone, it's Ivan Gregory."

That made sense. Anne had invited him to sit with them, after all, and they'd chatted easily. It had been Anne who suggested Ivan take the reverend's bicycle for his nephew, who ran errands for the power company, since it was too big for Grace.

Kate unpinned her hair and reached for her brush. "She is attractive, and there aren't many unmarried women of a suitable age in town."

Paddy tossed his collar on top of the dresser and wriggled out of his shirt. "Sounds to me like you did as much watching as you did listening."

"I could hardly help it, could I? Tell me about your conversation with the deputy. Does he think Frank Lang might have turned violent? I can't believe it. I sat with them for nearly an hour and Frank seems as gentle a man as there is."

"Oh, aye. And I don't mean to be sharp with you. Frank talks slow and moves poorly, but he's right enough in the head. Can't say the same for Henry Clyde."

"He didn't like me setting him straight, that's for sure. I expect that's one customer we've lost."

"And one we don't need," Paddy answered. "But you know how cruel people can be about those who look different."

They were both thinking, Kate knew, about a man back home who'd been kicked in the head by a horse, leaving him with one eye and a misshapen skull. He'd done no harm to anyone, but a group of older boys had been merciless, mistreating him to the point that town elders had intervened and put a stop to it.

"I think they're scared," he continued. "Because they don't understand, and they know it could happen to any of us."

Kate finished brushing her hair and began to braid it for the night. "Do you know what happened to Frank?"

"School board hired Anne on the recommendation of a woman in Pondera, and when she arrived with Frank in tow, it went about that he'd been injured in the same train wreck that killed their parents. I've never had any reason to doubt it. He would have been a boy, though I'd put him at twenty-one or -two by now. He does odd jobs around town—feeding stock, stacking wood. But it can't amount to much."

If he couldn't support himself, then he was a burden. If that limited Anne's marriage possibilities, did she mind? It was hard to imagine Ivan Gregory resenting a crippled brother, and as manager of the power plant, surely he could afford to support his wife's relative, especially one who could work around the house. If they were right about Ivan's interest, and if Anne returned it.

Stacking wood, Paddy had said. Gibson and his men had taken the woodpile apart but hadn't found the second candlestick. Where could it be?

"There must be something we can do," Kate said. "To stop the awful talk."

"Lass, what a heart you've got. But let the questions go." Paddy pulled back the bedcovers and held out an arm. His eyes danced in the lamplight and his lips curved. "Come to bed."

And she happily did.

Monday. A clean slate, full of promise, her mother always said. And this Monday was both. Kate decided to walk Grace to school, since it was her first day back, and on the way, they chatted about lessons and the books Miss Lang had lent her, already finished.

Children swarmed the school from all directions, alone or in clusters.

They shouted, laughed, and taunted each other, and Kate relished the sound.

"Grace!" Elizabeth Peterman called. Grace waved back, then glanced at Kate.

"Go on then," Kate said. "After school, wait for me outside and we'll walk home together."

Grace flashed her a smile and ran to her friend.

"Good to have her back," a woman said. Anne Lang. The two women watched the girls, Grace showing Elizabeth the borrowed books, the pair chatting happily. "She seems to be coping well."

"Most of the time," Kate said. "It's a big loss for a girl who's already suffered a serious blow."

"I was much older than Grace when our parents were killed. Almost twenty-one. But Frank was so young, and I left teachers' college to take care of him."

"A big responsibility to take on, at a hard time. How did you decide to come to Montana?"

"Not so much a decision," Anne said, "as the only option we had. The president of the college took a special interest in finding a placement for me, and wrote to an alumna who lives in Pondera. She arranged a position, even though I hadn't finished my training. But when we arrived, I discovered that there was no opening after all."

"Oh, my. That must have been devastating. What happened?"

"I never knew whether the woman I was to replace ended her engagement, or something happened to her intended. The school board allowed her to rescind her resignation, which was the right thing to do, but it left me at loose ends."

One generosity becoming another's hardship. It was unfair that a woman could not teach after she married, a subject of much debate among the females in the Flannery household, especially after Kate's sister, Mary, chose a teaching career, but it was almost universally true.

"We were fortunate," Anne continued, "that Jewel Bay needed a teacher and was willing to overlook the unusual circumstances."

Which no doubt included Frank. But Kate wasn't going to ask about him.

"I'd like to hear," Kate said, choosing her words with care, "your thoughts on a long-term situation for Grace. If no relatives step forward. I've written to her grandmother, though from what Grace has said, a welcome seems unlikely."

One of the older boys rang the bell, and the children began to form lines by grade, girls in front, boys in back.

"No, not a happy tale, I'm afraid," Anne replied. "I'm sure you'll hear, if you haven't already, rumors about Arval Haugen and me. About marriage."

"I—" Kate raised her hands in protest.

"No. I want you to know. We did take a few walks together, down along the bay. Ate a picnic supper by the ferry landing. Arval was a good man. I would have married him, if he'd asked."

If.

"But he never did. He was burdened by the sense that marrying again would betray his late wife."

Better, Kate supposed, than treating marriage as a transaction or convenience. But given the risks of the world, a view that condemned one to loneliness, and denied the heart a second chance.

"I'm sure you'll have other opportunities," Kate said. "An attractive single woman, in a town with a lot of single men . . . I'd say Ivan Gregory has his eye on you. And maybe Daniel Gibson, too."

"What is it that makes every married woman think every single woman desires the same state?" Anne Lang said in a tone that could be joking or serious. The bell rang again and she bustled off.

Kate watched her usher the children into the school and wondered what bucket of mire she had stepped into.

On her way down to the Mercantile late that morning, she again saw Thaddeus London walking near Ivan Gregory's two-story yellow house. The man said nothing, though he tipped his head and lifted his cap. She'd ask Paddy about him later. She asked a lot of questions, but that was the best way to get to know the townspeople, and as Paddy often said, he knew everyone because everyone needed potatoes and nails.

On Mondays, Paddy did not make deliveries, but there was plenty of custom, so Kate stayed until it was time for piano lessons.

"You're a quick learner, lass," Paddy said, and his compliment made her warm inside.

The week grew long. No sign of the suspected thieves was reported and no arrests were made. A thin fog of fear had settled over the town, which Kate hated. She did not want to live like that, but nor did she want Grace to go on without knowing the truth about her father's death. Even if it was harsh, more than an eleven-year-old ought to have to bear. It did no good to hide the truth from children and claim you were protecting them.

One evening, Grace took the embroidery hoop from Kate's hands.

"Let me show you." She made a length of backstitches then a graceful sweep of stem stitches, making sure Kate watched closely. "Now you try."

"How did you learn to embroider so beautifully?" Kate asked as she took the linen and loop.

"My mother taught me."

Every night, Paddy helped Grace set up the cot behind the sofa. It was a good solution, but a temporary one—a growing girl could not sleep forever on a borrowed cot in the front room. More than once, Kate heard her crying quietly. Sometimes she steeled herself against the tears and let her be, but other times, she put a hand on the quivering back and the girl threw her thin arms around Kate and sobbed.

One afternoon midweek, Kate finished her lesson with Elizabeth Peterman and went outside with the girl. Grace sat on a bench reading and keeping an eye on Elizabeth's younger brother and sister. A canvas satchel lay open on the ground, papers sliding out, and Kate picked them up. One was a drawing of a man in a cap, arm raised, mouth open, a woman close by. Behind them stood a large house with columns flanking the front door and a tall leafy tree.

A chill rippled up her spine. Did these bright, lively children with their beautiful mother, their prosperous father, and their elegant home, live in the shadow of violence?

"Oh, Mrs." Young James, seven or eight, ran up. "That's mine."

Kate handed him the satchel but held on to the picture. "Did you draw this?"

"Yes. We were supposed to draw a visitor. It's a man who came to see my mother last week."

"It's not your father? I mean, the man in the picture."

"Oh, no. He never gets angry. Not with our mother, anyway. He was angry when he heard about the man who came to visit, though."

"I should think so. Do you know who the man was, or what he and your mother were talking about?"

"No. I was in the tree, way high up. Too high to hear them. I am very good at climbing trees."

Kate handed back the drawing. "I can tell. What did your teacher say about your picture?"

"She never got to me. She only looks at the good drawings, and I'm not very good."

"I like to draw. Maybe we can draw together sometime."

"It's okay," he said. "I'd rather climb trees."

But his drawing had been good enough to convey the man's anger and the woman's fear, Kate thought. Then the children's father drove up and they ran to the Packard. The house was a long walk, even without concern about thieves, and it was no wonder Reverend Haugen had used his bicycle to visit the Petermans. But it was not Reverend Haugen in the drawing. The boy would have known him, and despite his lack of skill with the wax crayon, would have added the reverend's distinctive hat.

Who would assail the kind and gentle Mrs. Peterman? Why? And what had James Peterman done, when he heard the story from his wife?

"Grace," Kate said as the two walked home. "Has Elizabeth ever said anything to you about her parents arguing? Or about a man making threats?"

But Grace said no, and Kate let the matter drop.

On Friday, five days after Reverend Arval Haugen's burial, a letter arrived from Chicago. Paddy left it for Kate, propped on the brass cash register, and she took it up to his private office to read.

Mrs. Murphy,

Thank you for your letter with news of the misfortune that has struck Mr. Haugen. How distressing it must have been to find him. You will think me cold for lacking much sympathy for the man, and perhaps I am. I have not yet forgiven him, despite the passage of time, for putting my daughter into the impoverished condition that led to her death. By serving God, you will say. No. By his insistence on doing so despite knowing that she was fragile, that working in the slums amid filth and poverty would expose her to disease. By allowing his belief that God had destined him to bring the comfort of Christ to the poor and the immigrants to outweigh his responsibilities as a husband and father.

There it was, the barest acknowledgment of her granddaughter. But the woman went on, continuing her description of the vile conditions of those Reverend Haugen had ministered to, and her rage over her daughter's death. Her anger, Kate could understand. It was part of grief. Consumption was a horrible disease, but it could have struck Freya Haugen anywhere. Even in her mother's wealthy neighborhood. Even here, with all the fresh air one could breathe. And why blame him? It was clear that he had suffered deeply, even letting his loss keep him from the possibility of new happiness.

In conclusion, she wrote, *if there is no one else willing to take the girl, you may send her to me. I am sure there are those among my acquaintance who can make arrangements.*

"Arrangements?" Kate spat out the word. "We're talking about a child, not a garden party. Your flesh and blood, Mrs. Agnete Swensen of Chicago. And I am not sending an eleven-year-old girl halfway across the country on a train by herself."

Paddy would help her figure out what to do. She dried her eyes and started down the stairs, the gray linen envelope in hand. At the sound of a man speaking in the hallway, she stopped.

"It's this business about Arval Haugen, Paddy," the man said. "It's shaking things up. People are talking about leaving town, pulling up stakes."

"Not you, James," she heard Paddy say. James Peterman? "Not with all you've done to establish the bank. The investments you've made."

Among them, the loan that had financed the Mercantile.

"We'll have to see, Paddy. We'll have to see. But it would be better, don't you agree, if we all acknowledged that the murder occurred in the course of a theft, and left off asking questions?"

Kate froze, her hand over her mouth. He was talking about her. James Peterman must have heard from his son that she'd asked about the drawing, about who he'd seen and what he'd heard. James Peterman wanted her to stop asking questions and—he'd made this clear by his tone as well as his words—if she didn't, he would withdraw his support for the Mercantile. The shop that was Paddy's heart and dream.

She could not hear Paddy's reply over the thumping in her chest. Not until she heard two sets of footsteps heading back to the shop floor did she dare to breathe again. When she was sure they had gone and could not hear her move, she retreated to the office under the eaves.

Had the boy pretended that the man he'd drawn was a visitor, not wanting to admit it was a picture of his father shouting at his mother? Secure in the knowledge that the teacher would not inspect his drawing, had the boy drawn the violence he'd seen, knowing no one would ever guess the truth? Until she'd picked up the wrinkled paper, smoothed it out, and asked him about it.

Or the man, not much more than a stick figure, might have been Reverend Haugen after all, the boy unable to see him clearly from his leafy perch.

Or what if—and this sent a chill down her spine as cold as the Baraboo River in the dead of winter—what if James Peterman, by all accounts as good-natured as he was prosperous, had himself been involved in the reverend's murder?

She could not stay up here all afternoon, and she couldn't sneak out the back door. Paddy would worry, and troubled as she was, she would not add to her husband's burden. Besides, they truly did have to decide what to do about Mrs. Swensen's letter, and Grace.

Thank goodness Paddy was alone, polishing the perfectly clean counter with a thick white cloth. At the sound of her footsteps, he raised his head, his hand stopping mid-swirl. His face was pale, his hair mussed.

His Adam's apple bobbed. "There yeh are, lass. Bad news then?"

She gestured with the envelope. "How could a woman as horrid as Mrs. Swensen raise such a loving wife and mother as Freya Haugen?"

"Kate, you know she's acting out of her grief, first over her daughter's decision to marry against her wishes, and then over her death."

"It's been years, Paddy. Why can't she put her grief aside for the sake of her granddaughter? The granddaughter whose love and comfort she has denied herself, out of her own bitterness." Kate's own parents had not approved of every decision their daughters had made. They'd worried about

Alice's intended before their marriage because his father had been known to strike his wife and children. But he'd proven himself a good provider and a devoted husband and father. They'd worried that Mary's decision to teach doomed her to a life alone, though Kate suspected that was what Mary wanted. They'd only agreed to let Margaret go to art school in Chicago because the school kept a private boardinghouse for its female students and did not allow men and women to study together until they reached advanced levels.

And her own decision to marry a man who was building a future hundreds of miles away had not been easy to accept.

Chicago. She couldn't ask her younger sister to visit Mrs. Swensen—the old lady would not take a young unmarried woman seriously. But what about Alice or Mrs. Flannery? They were mature women, mothers themselves, though Alice wasn't thirty yet and her children small. But she had a persuasive manner, and if the two women took the train together, to visit Margaret, maybe they could pay a call.

"It isn't right," Paddy said, "though I can see how Freya would have wanted to get away from her mother."

She must have been torn, but she'd chosen her husband, as she should. She'd chosen to make her own future. As Kate had.

Kate felt a battle of her own right now, between her fear that she'd put their future in danger, and her conviction that Reverend Haugen was murdered not by thieves but by someone right here in Jewel Bay.

One of their neighbors. A hot, sour taste filled her throat.

What if she was right? What if she was wrong?

But she had to put those feelings aside and focus on young Grace. She was just about to ask Paddy what he thought about enlisting her mother and Alice when the door opened. Paddy tucked the corner of his towel into his apron pocket. Kate straightened her spine and readied her face to welcome their customer.

But their visitor was not there to order supplies.

"Paddy," Deputy Gibson said. "Mrs. Murphy."

"Aye, Daniel." Paddy put out his hand and the men shook. "What's bringing you into the Mercantile today?"

"Is there any news?" Kate asked. "About the murder?"

The deputy deflected her question. "Mrs. Murphy, might I ask you to tell me more about that altercation in the cemetery?"

She glanced at Paddy, who gave her an encouraging nod. She'd told him everything Sunday night, so he wasn't surprised by the details, or the language, but she could see the protective glower drop over his face.

"I know the man," Gibson said after she wrapped up her story. "Farms north of town, by the river bend. I suspect his wife dragged him to Sunday services."

"Why are you asking, Daniel?" Paddy said. "Has something happened?"

"Yes, but it doesn't involve Henry Clyde. We've found the second silver candlestick."

"Where?" Kate and Paddy spoke at the same time.

Daniel Gibson rubbed his unshaven cheek.

"In Ivan Gregory's woodpile." He trained his steady gaze on Kate. "A pile he hired Frank Lang to stack."

Kate was grateful to have no students that afternoon. She knew she ought to go see Anne Lang, but feared her presence would be unwelcome, even though she'd done her best to intervene when Henry Clyde confronted Frank. Though Gibson had questioned Frank, he had not arrested him. He'd told his boss that he couldn't spare the time from his other duties to haul him thirty miles to the jail in Pondera. The real reason, he'd told Kate and Paddy, was that Frank's stammer and limp and the accusation that he'd killed a man of the cloth would make him an easy target of the other prisoners.

How long he could keep Frank out of jail, Gibson hadn't wanted to guess. Most likely, the sheriff would overrule the decision, even though Frank's damaged leg meant he couldn't escape without help. Even so, the delay was a relief. Kate didn't know if Gibson possessed a tender side she had not seen until now, or was motivated by his admiration for Anne.

Did it matter why you did the right thing, as long as you did it?

She'd stayed in the shop the rest of the afternoon, helping Paddy, though both were subdued. A few customers had heard the news and offered their theories. Why, one wondered, had Gregory hired Frank to stack the wood, a job his nephew could have done? So the boy could focus on his schoolwork, Kate supposed, since that was the reason he spent the week in town. Plenty of work to do on weekends at his parents' homestead. She'd almost bitten her tongue half through when a man in a dirty coverall said, "That's the thanks you get for hiring an idiot." Paddy, bless him, had told the man to take his purchases and leave.

By unspoken agreement, Kate and Paddy said nothing when Grace arrived after school, smiling, with a new book a teacher had lent her. Not Miss Lang, who had been absent this afternoon. Kate offered the girl her choice from the penny candy jars, and she chose a long stick of hard candy, which turned her tongue purple.

Not until they were home did Kate tell her about the discovery of the candlestick and the fear that Frank Lang had killed her father.

"But that can't be," Grace protested. "Frank respected my father. He helped out at the church whenever he could, making small repairs or stacking wood."

"To some, that means Frank would have known exactly how and where to hide the candlesticks."

Grace's hands flew to her mouth. "But why? Why would he do that?"

"I don't believe it either. But people are ready to think the worst of him because of his condition." Kate paused, wanting to get the words right. "Some think Frank knew of your father's fondness for Anne and feared that if she married him, he, Frank, would be left on his own."

"Miss Lang would never have done that! Papa would never have wanted her to!"

Kate was surprised. "Did your father speak to you about Miss Lang?"

"Not in that way," Grace said, her pale cheeks pinking. "But he enjoyed her company, and I thought he might want to marry her. She would have been a wonderful mother, I think, as good as my real mother. And Papa was the kindest, gentlest soul, Kate. He would never have thrown Frank out."

Kate believed her. And she did not believe Frank Lang had killed Arval Haugen. Not over his sister, and not over a useless pair of silver candlesticks.

She stood and crossed to the stove, where she picked up a heavy wooden spoon and stirred the soup, its fragrance filling the tiny space. Besides, if Frank Lang had taken the candlesticks, wouldn't he have hidden them more carefully?

Had the killer wanted the single candlestick to be found? Why? And why leave the other in Ivan Gregory's woodpile? So it could be found, too?

She used the edge of the spoon to pry bits of ham off the bone.

One thing she knew for sure: something, and someone, in Jewel Bay was not as it appeared to be.

∞

"Ah, Kate. You know I love your big heart. But she belongs with her people," Paddy said as they sat at the kitchen table after supper. Grace had taken Buster outside, then settled down to read in the front room.

"Even if they don't want her? What will happen if that bitter old woman dies? Paddy, think about the dangers a young girl, a young woman on her own faces in this world. At best, she'd be farmed out as a servant and at worse . . . I'll find her a home myself before I commit her to that fate."

"We've got our own future to think about. Our own family."

"You always say that the Irish make room at the table, even if it means one less mouthful for those already there."

Paddy pressed his lips together. "Aye, lass, yeh got me there. But it's a big decision. Let's not rush it."

Maybe he was right. She wasn't sure anymore.

Not until after both Paddy and Grace had gone to bed was Kate able to sit with a cup of tea and the letter from Alice, nearly forgotten in the confusion created by Mrs. Swensen's screed and the conversation she'd overheard between Paddy and James Peterman.

My dearest Kate, Alice wrote in a strong, clear hand. *How wrenching to find that poor man.* After expressing her sympathy for his daughter and concern for Kate, she assured Kate that she would not reveal "the lurid details" to their mother.

> *Never hesitate, little sister, to unburden yourself to me. Even the heaviest load is lighter when shared, and you are wise to grasp that there will be matters you do not want to share with your husband, good man that he is, for fear of worrying him.*

Alice went on to talk about the family, including the latest antics of her children, five-year-old William and three-year-old Frances.

As for the girl and her grandmother, Alice wrote in closing, *that is a heartbreaking situation. No family is everything we want it to be. You must consider your decision long and hard, as I know you will, and be guided by your generous spirit.*

Easy to say, Kate thought as she folded the letter and slid it back into the ivory envelope, her sister's initials engraved on the back. Not so easy to do.

∞

The next morning, Kate knew what she needed to do.

"I can walk to school by myself," Grace said when Kate untied her apron.

"I know you can. But I need to speak with Miss Lang."

Anne Lang was at her post when Kate, Grace, and Buster arrived, and if the woman's shoulders stiffened at the sight of them, Kate could not blame her. Did she suspect Kate of pointing the finger, after the altercation in the cemetery? Kate wanted Anne to know that she had not accused Frank, and to assure her that Daniel Gibson was not her brother's only friend in Jewel Bay.

"Anne. May I have a word?" The other woman hesitated briefly before drawing Kate aside. "Deputy Gibson told us about the discovery of the second candlestick, and that there are those who believe it proves Frank killed Reverend Haugen. They are fools."

Anne gripped her elbows, tightened her lips, and waited.

"I've told him everything that happened in the cemetery. How the farmer accused Frank of following me, mocking and taunting him when he had trouble replying. I made clear then, and again yesterday to Deputy Gibson, that Frank was blameless. That it was I who had startled him, when I came around the big tree at the top of the cemetery and found him—" Kate willed herself not to blush like a schoolgirl. "Well, there is no outhouse and sometimes a man can't wait."

Anne's lips twitched.

"My mind's been spinning ever since the deputy's visit, and the more I've thought about it, the more convinced I am that Frank could not have killed Reverend Haugen."

"But how can we prove it? Henry Clyde is not the first man to spread rumors about my brother. Frank swears he was sitting by the river all afternoon the day Arval was killed, listening to the birds. He often does—birds have always fascinated him. But no one saw him," Anne said, her voice breaking.

"When we were walking down the hill in the cemetery," Kate said, "I noticed how Frank has to set one leg as a brace, when the ground is uneven, then swing the other leg around. He holds out his arms to steady himself." She demonstrated.

"Yes," Anne said. "The injury affected his balance. That's one reason he can't work a regular job, or a full shift."

And one reason why people feared him. His movements appeared menacing, but Kate had seen how they took every bit of his concentration.

"Ivan Gregory was being generous," Anne continued, "paying Frank to stack the wood. He and his nephew cut and split it—Frank can't swing an axe that long. But stacking is work he can do, even with his damaged leg and his twisted shoulders."

"The reverend was hit and killed on the altar," Kate said. The early bell rang. "Frank couldn't have stepped up onto the altar without grabbing the altar table to steady himself, could he?"

"No."

"And he couldn't have grabbed the candlestick and hit the reverend. He'd have lost his balance, even before taking a swing. The reverend wasn't old, and he was fit. He walked or bicycled everywhere. And he knew Frank's infirmities."

"He knew Frank was no threat to him," Anne said. "Have you told Daniel Gibson this? I am convinced he wants to believe Frank innocent, but it's difficult. So many people are willing to believe Frank guilty just because he's different."

"I'll tell him. Let's hope he's willing to believe a young woman." She hesitated, knowing they didn't have much time for the other topic on her mind. "Anne, I've heard from Grace's grandmother. As you predicted, her response bordered on the cruel. I wish I could ask you to take the girl—she admires you so. But I know you can't. It wouldn't be seemly, not with an unmarried man in the house. Especially not now, with all that's happened."

"The second bell's about to ring," Anne said, stretching out a hand, not quite touching Kate's arm. "My mentor in Pondera might be able to make a place for Grace, but I would hate to uproot her from her friends and school right now. Kate, are you sure you can't keep her?" Then, without waiting for an answer, the teacher swept toward the students, hands in the air, calling out greetings.

How could they keep her? They had no room in their tiny log refuge, and Kate was too young to mother a girl Grace's age. But family, it seemed, though the thought broke every rule in Kate's heart, was not always the best place for a child.

As the children processed into the building, she saw Grace pair up with Elizabeth. What about the Petermans? Laura appeared to be an excellent mother and had a daughter Grace's age, as well as a large house. But not if there were violence in the home.

Back at their own house, she was surprised to find a basket at the front door. It was lined with a linen towel, beautifully embroidered, and held jars of apple jelly and strawberry jam, a brown paper packet of tea, and a box of French milled soap studded with lavender. A small ivory envelope bore her name.

Inside, Kate refilled Buster's water dish and sat to read the note.

My dear Mrs. Murphy, it began. *Thank you for your kindness toward my son, James, Jr., outside the school on Wednesday afternoon. What he lacks in drawing skill, he makes up for in imagination. His head is so filled with tales that I think he might well be our next Mr. Twain or Mr. Baum.*

Mr. Twain had been a favorite in the Flannery household, and they had all been saddened by his death last spring. Mr. Baum's novels, they had not enjoyed so much.

> *It was good of you to tolerate his antics, and as he is only seven, I trust you will not take him too seriously.*
> *Yours most sincerely,*
> *Laura Peterman*

Kate sat back. The dog had finished his drink and sat beside her. She stroked his head and peered into his deep brown eyes.

"What do you think, Buster? She's telling me not to be concerned. But why me? We've just met. Which makes me more concerned."

Adding a person to the household made more work, and Kate was busy all morning. She again spent the afternoon helping customers while Paddy made his rounds. Talk had turned back to the murder and to Frank Lang, with half the town convinced he was the killer and that Daniel Gibson knew it; his failure to make the arrest clearly meant he was a victim of Anne Lang's charms; and what had Ivan Gregory been thinking, hiring a man like Frank, though some of the words used were far too unkind for Kate to repeat, even to herself. The other half would have sworn on a stack of Bibles that the poor soul was as innocent as a newborn lamb and thank goodness Daniel Gibson had a good heart as well as a good head. More than one wondered if Ivan Gregory himself didn't warrant a second look. Why a prosperous man would have stolen the candlesticks and hidden them in woodpiles, no one could explain, but it must have had something to do, the theory went, with Gregory coveting land meant for higher purposes for his orchard. Or his fear that the reverend would beat him to the altar with Anne Lang.

As if, Kate thought in disgust, that capable woman were a ball to be batted back and forth between men, her beloved brother nothing more than a hindrance.

A shopkeeper, Paddy had told her more than once, must not let on that he thinks his customers full of blarney. When they came into the Mercantile, they expected to have their say. Let any argument come from other customers, he'd said. Talk was their sport. Let them have it.

And so she did, keeping her head down and her tongue in her mouth, to use her mother's phrase.

Kate did not give lessons on Friday afternoons, so Grace was to walk down the hill with the postmaster's daughter, a year older, after school. When she didn't arrive, Kate took advantage of a quiet moment in the shop to dash across the street. The other girl had waited, then decided Grace must have left without her and walked down alone. It was perfectly safe, she said, casting her eyes sideways at her father. Busy with a customer, the man did not comment, but Kate understood the gesture. Until the killer was caught, or until Frank Lang was arrested, the opinion was that young girls were not safe on their own in this town.

And no town could prosper under that cloud.

But when Grace did not appear, Kate's own fears grew. Paddy returned and listened to her fret, then replied in his reassuring way, "We'll find her at the parsonage, as you did the other day, or back at the house, petting the dog, plumb forgetting she was meant to come to the shop."

But Grace was not a forgetful girl, or a disobedient one, and the knot in Kate's stomach did not loosen. They climbed in the Model T and motored up the hill. Grace was not at the parsonage. She was not at home, and the dog could not tell them if she had been there. Her school satchel was not where she usually left it, with her other things.

"Either she's run off, or somethin's happened to her," Paddy said.

That wise, practical Paddy would voice such fears made the knot tighten. If Grace had run off, she'd have come here first, knowing the house would be empty, to pack her little bag with clothing and her hairbrush and the photo of her mother, still on the side table where Kate had placed it.

"We'll take the automobile back down to the Mercantile and telephone Daniel Gibson."

"Let's check one more place," Kate pleaded.

But the surprise on Laura Peterman's face when she opened the door of the big white house overlooking the lake dashed Kate's hopes. Grace had not gone home with her friend.

Quickly, Kate explained their presence. Laura invited them in and called for her daughter. Elizabeth was tall for her age, taller than Kate, and though still girlish in build, promised to be both strong and elegant, like her mother. But she had not seen Grace since school let out. Had not seen what direction Grace had gone and had no idea where she might be. Kate sensed no deceit. Whatever Grace's plans, she had not confided them to her friend.

Kate sighed and glanced away from mother and daughter, wondering what to do next. The coin purse Kate had first seen in the Mercantile when Laura took it out to pay for the children's candy lay on the marble-topped hall table. The monogram reminded her of the basket and note.

"Forgive me," she said. "I nearly forgot to thank you for your gift. Did you embroider the towel yourself? I confess, the art has escaped me."

"I do enjoy needlework," Laura said. "Creating a bit of beauty from something plain."

Though the note had been intended to tamp down any concerns Kate might have of violence in the household, it had kindled them. But she could not ask the woman if she were safe, even obliquely, in the girl's presence, and not now, when more immediate matters pressed.

"Mama embroidered the altar cloths for the church," Elizabeth said. "Reverend Haugen called them the most beautiful handwork he'd seen, even better than his own wife's."

"Hush, child. We'll not boast in front of Mrs. Murphy," Laura said. But the compliment clearly pleased her.

Church work, then, had been one reason for the reverend's visits. Had Laura confided her situation to the minister? Had he known she was in danger in her home? Had he helped her form a plan to leave her husband and take her children to safety? Had James found out, become enraged, confronted Reverend Haugen and killed him?

Talk about imagination. And yet, it did happen, even in well-off families and gracious homes.

Her gaze settled on the monogrammed purse. *LLC*, though Laura's married name began with a *P*. Perhaps it had belonged to Laura's mother or another older relative, passed down after death. Kate's mother didn't carry one, but that didn't mean they weren't fashionable for that generation as well. Surely there was some explanation.

Her thoughts were disrupted by James Peterman, ushering Paddy through the front door. At the sound of their father's arrival, the two younger children emerged from elsewhere in the house, and they joined Elizabeth in greeting him. No mistaking their happiness.

Laura, too, had brightened. There was nothing fearful or guarded about the woman when she looked at her husband. No hesitation, only love and trust. Kate had been wrong. But that drawing, and the note . . .

She felt Laura's gaze on her and met it. It asked her—and she knew this; it was not imagination—to keep her secret. What was the secret? And why did it matter so much?

In the meantime, they had to find Grace.

"I'll telephone Gibson and we'll get up a search party," James Peterman was saying as Laura instructed Elizabeth to take the younger children to the kitchen and keep them occupied. "He must have some idea where that band of scoundrels is holed up."

He was voicing Kate's worst fear, that whoever had killed Reverend Haugen had come back for Grace. But who, and why?

"I think . . ." Kate said, hesitating.

"Out with it, lass," Paddy said.

"I think Grace may have heard us last night, talking about sending her to her grandmother. Then this morning, at the school, I talked with Anne Lang about finding a place for her. What if she overheard, or guessed that's what we were discussing, and that's why she's run off?" Too upset to gather up her few things first.

Laura gasped, and her husband slipped an arm around her.

It was quickly decided that while James summoned Deputy Gibson, Paddy and Kate would make another search of the familiar places. Perhaps there had been a misunderstanding. Perhaps Grace was fearful and hiding in the parsonage, or hungry, waiting in the Murphys' kitchen.

Not much of a plan. But what else could they do?

As they drove, a whirlwind of thoughts whipped through Kate's head. About Grace and her father. About James and Laura Peterman. Both husband and wife had consulted the reverend, who had also visited their home. Had Laura reached the same conclusion as Kate, after hearing him in the Mercantile with Paddy, that James had been involved in the reverend's death?

As they drove above the lakeshore, Kate frowned. "Paddy, that smoke down on the lakeshore. Is that the Indian encampment?" Grace had spoken more than once about visiting the Indians with her father.

"Aye, lass. Ohhh." He slowed and steered the Model T onto a trail so steep and rocky Kate found herself gripping the door as the wheels bounced and the automobile lurched from side to side.

At a wide spot, Paddy stopped. "We'll walk the rest of the way. Can you make it, lass, or should I be going down alone? It's ankle-spraining ground."

"Paddy Murphy, you are not leaving me here. If there's a chance Grace is with those Indians or they might know where she is, I don't care if I sprain my head!"

The trail narrowed, flattening as it reached the lakeshore. A man Paddy knew waited for them; no doubt he'd seen their headlamps. By the water's edge, a campfire blazed. Kate squinted in the last bit of daylight, searching, searching . . .

And there she was. A mix of relief and anger nearly overwhelmed Kate. She ran across the rocky shore and wrapped her arms around the girl.

"Grace! We were so frightened." Hands on the girl's shoulders, Kate searched her face in the firelight. Clearly, Grace had been frightened, too.

"Don't send me back," she pleaded. "Please. I'd rather be on my own, or be a servant, or anything but go where I'm not wanted."

"Oh, child." Kate pulled her close. "You're not going anywhere you don't want to go."

They thanked the families for tending to Grace for a few hours and the Indian man led them up the trail. Grace carried her satchel. Paddy guided the automobile up the hill, only cursing twice. Then he drove back to the Petermans to let them know the lost lamb had been found. They declined the offer of a hot drink by the fire, though when Laura suggested Grace spend Saturday with them, Kate readily agreed. With all the people who came into Jewel Bay to pick up groceries and tend to other errands, Saturday was Gossip Day, and with the discovery of the second candlestick and the focus on Frank Lang, tongues would be wagging. Grace did not need to hear the idle talk.

And Kate would find a moment, and a way, to speak with Laura alone. They had much to discuss.

∞

Back in the Murphy kitchen, the fire in the cookstove crackling and the kettle on, Kate wished she could ask her mother or Alice for advice. How could she keep her promise to Grace?

First things first. Keep her warm and feed her, though she had been well treated down at the lakeshore. Kate had made her remove her boots and stockings and change into a dry dress—her school dress had gotten dirty and damp as she'd made her way through the brambles and undergrowth to the lakeshore.

Now she sat on the floor, hugging the dog. In her clean dress.

But it was good to see her acting like a child, this young girl who'd been forced to grow up too soon. She needed a place where she could run and play with other children, and without fear.

Kate set a steaming mug of coffee in front of Paddy and filled her teapot with hot water. The way she was going through the tea, she'd have to speak to him about ordering a decent supply sooner rather than later. Thank goodness for the small packet Laura had given her.

As if knowing the time for play had ended and the time for talk begun, Grace rose and sat in the third chair, the one they had stopped at the parsonage to fetch on the drive home.

"Did you have a plan, girl?" Paddy asked gently. "Or were you so set on getting away?"

"No! No. You've both been so good to me. I—" Grace bit her lip. "I'm sorry. I heard what you two said last night, and then the way you were talking to Miss Lang, Kate—I knew I couldn't go back to Chicago, but I never meant to worry you."

Kate squeezed her hand. "We know that. But we need to talk about your future. Miss Lang has a friend in Pondera, the woman who arranged for her to teach here. She has a lovely home not far from the county high school, and a grand piano and—"

"Can't I stay here? With the two of you? I don't mind sleeping on the cot in the front room. I don't."

Kate and Paddy exchanged glances again. "We'll need some sort of legal permission, I expect," Paddy said. "From the courts, or your grandmother."

"She'd give it. She hates me."

"Oh, Grace. She doesn't hate you," Kate said. "You—you remind her too much of your mother. Losing a child is the hardest thing in the world for a parent and it feels, I think, like a failure. A failure to protect the most precious thing in the world."

Grace sat silently.

"I've seen it more times than I'd like," Paddy said, "back in Ireland and in this country. It breaks a soul, it does. It's not the natural order of things. The older generation wants to pass on first. I can't blame her for being angry, only for taking it out on your father and letting it keep her from knowing you." He smiled at her. "Because you're a grand girl."

"Oh, Paddy." Grace slipped out of her chair and threw her arms around him.

"I'll talk to Daniel Gibson," Paddy said over her shoulder. "See what we need to do to make it legal, at least for now."

"And you and I will write to your grandmother again," Kate said, though what they would say, she had no idea.

∞

But there was still the matter of who had killed Reverend Haugen. Kate spent much of the evening thinking about it, and much of the night, as she lay awake next to Paddy. The man could sleep through anything, a trait he attributed to growing up as the fourth of seven and then two weeks in steerage at twelve as he and his oldest brother crossed the stormy Atlantic.

By morning, she had worked out part of the puzzle. She worked out another piece while kneading bread dough. The tricky part would be to talk to Laura Peterman without terrifying her. Clearly, she was in a difficult situation and had confided in the reverend. Now that Kate had been in the Peterman home and seen how husband and wife treated each other, the obvious affection between them, and the health and happiness of their children, she no longer believed James Peterman a violent husband or father.

But the drawing nagged at her, as did her memory of the dismay on Laura's face when she saw Kate pondering the monogrammed coin purse.

They'd agreed that Laura would drive the buggy into town late morning to fetch Grace from the Mercantile. Kate and Paddy would drive out after closing to pick her up. Laura had promised Grace a chance to play the grand piano, a beautiful instrument that had struck a deep chord in Kate's soul.

Grace's letter to her grandmother lay on the table. Kate resisted the temptation to read it, instead slipping it into the envelope with a note saying simply that she and Mr. Murphy were pleased to keep the girl, who was excellent company and a good student, with a deft touch at the piano and with the needle, until plans could be finalized. What those plans might be, she did not elaborate. Could not say yet. Not until they'd gotten advice from more experienced minds.

When the baking was done, Kate wrapped up an extra loaf, tucked it in the basket Laura Peterman had given her alongside a jar of strawberry jam, and she and Grace set out.

"Where are we going?" Grace asked.

"To pay a call."

Anne Lang came to the door wearing a calico dress and an apron, her guarded expression easing at the sight of her visitors. Then her brow dipped.

"I'm not sure I should invite you in."

"We're not afraid of Frank," Kate said firmly. "Or of talk. But we can't stay. I wanted to bring you some fresh bread, and ask if there is any news." While she didn't want Grace to overhear idle gossip, she and Paddy had told her everything they knew about the search for her father's killer.

"None," Anne said. "Daniel's been able to keep the sheriff at bay, and I've been able to keep Frank busy. He's out back with his chickens right now. The way he clucks and flaps his arms like wings, they think he's one of them."

That put a smile on all their faces.

"It helps," Anne continued, "that Ivan believes Frank is innocent. But that doesn't explain the discovery in his woodpile."

"What if," Grace said, her voice tentative, "someone wanted us to blame Frank, or even Mr. Gregory, to distract attention from the real killer?"

The older women looked at her in astonishment.

"I read a book where that happened," she said.

"Not a book I gave you," Anne replied. "But I'll grant the possibility."

Who, though?

Kate and Grace said their goodbyes and continued on their way. Grace dashed across the street to slip the letter in the slot at the post office—always fun, even for a girl of eleven.

In the Mercantile, Kate set Grace to work dusting shelves. Not long after, Laura arrived, Elizabeth behind her.

"The younger two are home with their father," Laura said. Kate remembered James's comment to Paddy about leaving Jewel Bay. This family had the means to move, but would they? If the reason were compelling enough. Kate needed to probe carefully.

"This could be one of the last warm days," she said. "Maybe we could stroll down to the bridge. If my dear husband can spare me."

"Oh, go on with yeh, lass," Paddy called from behind the hardware counter, where he was weighing out nails.

The girls dashed ahead. "Grace seems no worse for the adventure," Laura said as they strolled down Front to Bridge Street. "Though she certainly made her feelings about returning to her grandmother's house clear. Have you decided what's to be done with her?"

How Grace's future had become Kate's decision, she wasn't sure. Merely because she'd found the reverend's body, or had fate had a hand in it?

"What would you do?" Kate asked. "Knowing what you know about the grandmother, and that there is no other family."

"I would keep her," Laura said, then held up a gloved hand. "And no, that's not an offer. I have my hands full with my three. But she seems genuinely happy with you and Paddy. And too much change at a time like this could be very difficult."

Anne Lang had said much the same thing.

They had reached the wooden bridge across the river, only a few years old, though there was already talk of replacing it with a new steel structure. In unspoken agreement, they stopped mid-span to watch the water coursing down the flume behind the power house, creating the invisible electricity that sparked so much growth and excitement.

The girls had crossed the bridge and were now down by the river, safely back from the water's edge.

"The power company, the bank—think of all that's happened here in such a short time," Kate said.

"And the Mercantile. We are lucky women, to have such forward-thinking husbands, who work hard and love us so, despite our faults."

"Laura." Kate faced her new friend, droplets of water splashing up from the river and misting the side of her face. "I can see you love James dearly, and your children, too. But—and forgive me the intrusion. We have not known each other long enough for me to speak so freely, and I wouldn't do it if it weren't for Grace."

Apprehension clouded Laura Peterman's lovely face.

"But," Kate went on, "I know you were speaking with Reverend Haugen regularly. Not about new altar cloths or cushions for the pews. About something deeply personal. And I wonder if it might in any way be connected to the tragedy that befell him."

It occurred to her in that moment that she might have chosen an unwise place for this conversation. Laura was several inches taller than Kate and a good deal stronger. If she had swung a silver candlestick at Reverend Haugen, what would stop her from pushing Kate over the side of the bridge and into the rushing river?

"Oh, Kate," Laura said. "I was so afraid that James had done something rash. But when the second candlestick surfaced, I knew I'd been mistaken. I thought—I feared that the reverend would feel compelled to reveal our secret and that James killed him to keep him quiet."

She paused, a hand to her chest, collecting herself.

"And he feared that's what you had done," Kate said, just loud enough to be heard above the river noise.

Laura's eyelids fluttered closed then opened again, her hand traveling from her chest to her mouth and back. "With James's prominence in the community, would any decent minister dare keep a secret like that? Even with children involved?"

What secret, Kate did not ask, but waited.

"James," Laura Peterman said, the single word rising and falling like the water from the flume as it struck the river, rose, and fell again, "is not my lawful husband."

Nothing this gracious, graceful woman could have said would have shocked Kate more. And yet, it explained the fear. And the monogram.

"I was married young, in Philadelphia, where I was reared. My late father's lawyer arranged the marriage, as I had no family but had come into a bit of money. He believed I needed a husband to manage it, even though the law allowed me to do so myself. The marriage was not a success. My husband was a gambler and the money was quickly gone. He drank to excess. He became violent at the drop of a hat."

Kate repressed a shudder. "And the law?"

"The law could not help me." Bitterness clung to Laura's words. "We no longer lived in the city. There are women in the cities who help women in need. I had no such recourse. But I did have a friend. She gave me shelter and bought me a railway ticket to Pittsburgh, where her family took me in."

"And that's where you met James."

"That's where I met James. My husband had made clear that divorce was out of the question. He would see me dead first, he vowed, and I believed him."

"That's why you and James came west, starting over as man and wife."

"Thirteen years ago. It's been everything a marriage ought to be. Then the children came, and James dotes on them. We have been so happy, and so intent on building our new life that I rarely gave the past any thought."

So what had caused the two of them to confide, separately, in their minister?

As if she heard Kate's musing, Laura answered the question. "Until my lawful husband tracked us down."

"The man in the drawing," Kate said, understanding now. "He threatened to reveal that you and James are not legally married and your children are illegitimate."

She could well believe it of the odious man Laura described. But she could not believe that Reverend Haugen would have revealed the truth. Nothing she had seen in his demeanor or heard since his death persuaded her that he would have acted so cruelly. He might have helped the distraught woman obtain a quiet divorce and remarry, if a few years late, but he bore his own scars from the past. He would have done nothing to put a family in danger.

"The truth would have ruined James's reputation. Everything he's worked for, all his business interests. The children would have been shamed. We would have had to leave Jewel Bay. Unless we paid him a monthly sum."

"Blackmail. That's vile."

"We were on the verge of agreeing to pay when he saw the candlesticks in the church. He became enraged. That's when he came to the house, when young James saw him from the tree. He no longer wanted money. He wanted blood."

Now Kate was confused. "The candlesticks?"

"They were a wedding gift," Laura explained. "From my father's lawyer, the scoundrel who arranged the marriage. No doubt bought with money siphoned from my inheritance. I had kept them all these years as my security, thinking I could sell them if I became truly desperate. But the church here was so plain, so unadorned, it needed a touch of beauty, and we were doing well. James was doing well—"

She was interrupted by a shout. Kate followed the sound and gasped. There was no mistaking the man in the drawing. The man she'd seen near Ivan Gregory's house. Thaddeus London. And he was standing amid the rocks at the water's edge, holding Elizabeth by one hand, Grace by the other.

"That's him, isn't it?"

Hands to her lips as if in prayer, Laura nodded. How foolish they had been, letting the girls go on ahead, caught up in their conversation, not noticing the man watching their every move. But what to do now? Even if they could get to the girls in time, they couldn't fight him off.

Think, Kate.

They needed to get help. But Laura would not budge. It was up to Kate. Suddenly the Mercantile seemed so far away.

A whizzing sound came from the bridge's wooden planks. Ivan Gregory's nephew, riding Reverend Haugen's bicycle. The boy grinned and raised a hand but Kate stepped into his path, forcing him to swerve to a stop. She grabbed the handlebars.

"Ride! Ride to the Mercantile as fast as you can. Tell Paddy there's trouble below the bridge and he must come. Hurry!"

The bicycle wobbled as the boy rode off, standing on the pedals to urge it forward. Would he be fast enough?

The scene on the riverbank had not changed, the girls tugging one way, London the other. He glanced up at Laura, the evil spreading across his face. And though she did not have the history Laura had with him, had never been his wife or his victim, Kate knew the terror Laura felt for Elizabeth, because she felt it herself for Grace. For both girls, of course, but Grace—Grace was *hers.*

"Stay here. Help is on the way. Distract him if you can, then send the men down when they come." And with that, Kate Flannery Murphy grabbed her skirt and ran as fast as she could, across the bridge and down the slope.

As she crept closer, she saw London look up at the bridge again. He threw a wicked laugh into the wind and dragged the girls closer to the water.

The cold, rushing water, the riverbed studded with hard, jagged rocks. If any of them went into the river, they'd be swept into its depths and smashed against the rocks. It was mid-October, the birches and vine maple changing color, the air warm enough that she hadn't even grabbed a shawl in her eagerness to talk with Laura Peterman. But the water was cold. It would batter and beat them and suck them out into the bay.

"I know who you are," she shouted. "I know why you're doing this."

"Do you?" Though the river was loud, his words were short and sharp.

"It doesn't have to be this way." She pushed closer. "Let them go. They're children. They've done nothing to you."

"They're nothing to me," he replied. "They are nothing."

They're everything to me.

"You don't have to do this." Could she get closer? Damn this heavy skirt. She put a hand on a rock and stepped around it, gasping as the cold water flooded into her boot.

The girls had seen her now and began to struggle, twisting London's arms this way and that. Grace's foot caught between two rocks and she fell. As London tried to regain his balance, he lost his grip on Elizabeth. He swung his free arm, striking her in the face. Kate watched in horror as she fell, hitting a large rock, slippery with mud, and slid out of sight.

It was only a moment, a moment that took forever, a moment Kate would never forget.

"*No!*" she screamed and rushed forward. London was lashing at her now as she stretched her hand toward Elizabeth. She heard him cry out, a cry of pain, and then Grace was beside her in the water, fighting to grab hold of Elizabeth. Where was London? She couldn't see him. She had to get the girls out of the water, but she couldn't let that evil man get them first.

Where was he?

Then strong arms reached past her and grabbed Elizabeth. She could no longer see Grace. Other arms, arms she knew, pulled Kate out of the water, picked her up, and carried her to safety.

"Grace! Where's Grace?" Kate cried.

"She's safe, lass," the sweetest voice in the world answered. "She's safe. Yeh're all safe now. Thanks to you, my brave wife, yeh're all safe."

Later that day, Thaddeus London's body washed up on the lakeshore near the Indian encampment. Though Kate spared not one whit of grief for the man who had caused so much pain, she was deeply sorry that the Indians had to be the ones who found him. They had treated Grace well, and all the white men did, Kate thought, was rain down sorrow and sadness on them.

It turned out that Daniel Gibson had been in the Mercantile with more questions for her when the Gregory boy arrived, breathless. He and Paddy had rushed down Front on foot. They'd raced across the bridge, barely pausing to size up the situation below. It was obvious that London intended to drag both girls into the water and that Kate, determined as she was, could not stop him. She was too small, he too strong, the terrain too rough. But luck, or fate, or God, had intervened.

What Kate didn't understand was why Thaddeus London had killed Reverend Haugen. With both men gone, only Laura Culver London, the *LLC* of the monogrammed coin purse, could venture a plausible explanation.

"He understood what I'd been through," she'd said to the group that had gathered in the Mercantile after the girls were pulled from the river. Paddy had closed up shop for the day and stoked the woodstove to warm them. Kate had put on Paddy's old iron kettle—what he called his bachelor kettle—and they'd found enough cups for coffee and tea. The rough leaves Paddy sold the loggers weren't so bad after all, Kate decided, under the circumstances.

"He knew," Laura continued, "that women have few options when their husbands mistreat them, and he could not countenance that." James had arrived during the rescue and now he put a reassuring hand on his wife's shoulder. She laid hers on top of his. They were truly husband and wife, Kate thought, even if not before the law. "He could see that James and I cherished each other. It pained him that we were not legally married, but that troubled him less than the abuse I'd suffered and the threats Thaddeus was making. Nor could he tolerate blackmail, particularly when innocent children were involved."

"And," Paddy suggested, "when the fate of this community could well have been at stake. Including his own future and that of his daughter."

"When the reverend refused to promise silence, London struck him with the candlestick," Daniel Gibson said. He was leaning against the counter near the front door, his hands red with cold despite the hot mug in his hands. "Hid one behind the church and stashed the other in Ivan Gregory's woodpile. He was nursing a grudge against Ivan, too, for kicking him off the job at the power company."

"That must have been what he was doing when I saw him," Kate said. "After Buster and I found the first candlestick and I went to summon help. London was coming around the corner of the house. I wondered why he was there, but assumed he was working for Ivan. He headed back toward the church and I think if I hadn't been following him, he would have gone to the woodpile and retrieved the other candlestick, meaning to stash it somewhere else that would incriminate Ivan. But it was too late—I'd taken it. And I was watching him, so he changed course."

Paddy slid his arm around her and she leaned into his warmth, realizing for the first time how much danger she'd been in. It frightened her more now than it had then, when she'd been unaware, acting on instinct.

"I'll make sure word spreads quickly," Gibson said, "that Frank Lang had nothing to do with the murder or the theft. He's a good soul, despite the stammer and the bad leg, and it's not right that London sought to blame him for his own crimes. Mrs. Murphy, I owe you an apology. I underestimated you, and I promise not to do it again."

He'd smiled, and as she smiled back at him, an idea popped into her mind. But it could wait for a private moment with her husband. She'd gazed around the room, at the deputy, at the three Petermans, at young Grace and Paddy, her own true love. Paddy wanted the Mercantile—the Merc—to be the heart of Jewel Bay, and it was.

It was.

A week later, two letters arrived from Chicago, one for Kate and one for Grace. In the letter to Kate, Agnete Swensen apologized for the unkindness of her original letter and asked Kate's forgiveness. She was ill, she wrote, deathly ill, and did not expect to live out the year. It pained her to know that she was not likely to see her only grandchild again in this world and asked if Kate could perhaps send her a photograph or two.

I knew that Arval trusted me to come around and to love the child, the woman wrote, *and I would have, were I not ill.* The reverend, it seemed, had retained his faith in her, despite her behavior.

Mrs. Swensen had asked her lawyers to obtain references on Kate and Paddy, and instructed them that if all appeared in order, the Murphys should be given full legal custody of Grace, if they were willing. There would, she hinted, be a small legacy attached, though her lawyers would administer it. Kate thought briefly of the lawyer who had cheated Laura Peterman and forced her into an ugly marriage, but then remembered the kindhearted lawyer in Pondera whom she and Paddy had consulted about Grace, at James Peterman's suggestion. She decided she was willing to trust Mrs. Swensen's business judgment, even if her personal judgment had failed her.

Kate did not read the letter Mrs. Swensen's had written Grace, though it clearly touched the child deeply. Tucked inside were photographs of Freya through the years, and one of Freya with baby Grace, which Kate placed in a frame and set on the side table where Grace could see it every night from her cot.

The church in Jewel Bay was not expected to receive a new minister until spring, at the earliest, so the bishop made the trip to Pondera to preside over the lawful marriage of James and Laura. It was a quiet ceremony, except when Kate sniffed back tears, followed by coffee and cake at the Peterman home, where Kate finally set her hands on the grand piano.

Paddy readily agreed to Kate's suggestion that he hire Frank Lang to make deliveries and run errands at the Mercantile. Frank couldn't drive the Model T, but he could handle a wagon and the mule had instantly taken to him. Kate told Anne her suspicion that Daniel Gibson was sweet on her, but Anne replied he might have lost his chance to Ivan Gregory, and Kate considered that a good thing.

Grace and Elizabeth were becoming fast friends. While the girls chatted about books and lessons and classmates, Laura taught Kate a few embroidery skills. In the evenings, when Grace read to them, Kate worked on the monogrammed towels, no longer embarrassed by her stitches.

Paddy began to talk about adding a room onto the little log house in the spring. And when Kate wrote to her mother and Alice, Buster snoring on the floor between them, Grace wrote to her grandmother. Kate had ordered Grace her own stationery box and pen, and as the girl bent over the paper, Kate had to be careful not to let a tear of joy blot her own ink.

This, she knew, was where they all belonged.

Acknowledgments and Historical Notes

While Jewel Bay closely resembles Bigfork, Montana, my home, I've played with the geography and renamed a few places. It's easier to kill people that way, especially because I have no plans to move.

"Carried to the Grave" was inspired by a bit of family history, a few generations back. The late Ramona DeFelice Long edited the story with grace and insight. She taught me a great deal, as an editor and as a friend, and I'm grateful.

"The Christmas Stranger" was sparked by a real-life exchange I had with another customer in the local UPS store. When I mentioned it on Facebook, under the heading "Small Town Pleasures," reader Jane Meyer suggested it would make a good short story. She was right. The stamp given to Erin is fictitious, although temporary three-centers were issued in 1917 to raise war funds.

"A Death in Yelapa" originally appeared in *Malice Domestic 14: Mystery Most Edible*, edited by Verena Rose, Rita Owen, and Shawn Reilly Simmons (Wildside Press, 2019). Thanks to Shawn Reilly Simmons for her excellent edits.

The incidents in "Put on a Dying Face" come entirely from my imagination, and do not reflect on our local theater company in any way. Both building and company are true gems and a great asset to both the real and fictional villages.

I'm sure that when Donna Lawson bought a character name at a charity auction a few years ago, she did not expect to become a recurring character, but she epitomizes the spirit of the village, so here she is again. Similarly, when my sister-in-law, Kathy Jensen Budewitz, told me she would like to be a character, I knew she would fit in perfectly. Thank you both.

Several years ago, a trio of local heroes created a documentary film as both community history and a fundraiser for the Bigfork Art & Cultural Center. My husband, Dr. Don Beans, was asked to write and perform the score, giving me a chance to eavesdrop around the edges. As I wrote the historical novella for this collection, I pored over the accompanying book, *Bigfork: A Montana Story*, by Ed Gillenwater, Denny Kellog, and Tabby Ivy (2017). Both Ed and Denny helped me track down additional historical details, as did Laura Hodge at the BACC, home to the Bigfork History Network, a community history project spawned by the film. Though I've attempted to get the history right, this is fiction. Murphy's Mercantile draws from fact, but the building itself is a product of my imagination. In 1910, a year I chose long before I dreamed of adding historical fiction to the Food Lovers' Village series, the Bigfork elementary school was located in the Methodist church, which was then south of the current tennis courts, leased while plans were being made for a new school. For the novella, I added a church hall and turned it into a makeshift school. That and other historical fictions and inaccuracies are entirely my fault. The bell, by the way, was donated back to the school district a few years ago, and still rings on special occasions.

Thanks to my good friend, Peg Cochran, for reading the manuscript, to my agent, John Talbot, and to Bill Harris and his team at Beyond the Page.

Thanks, most of all, to the readers, especially the locals, who have embraced my books, particularly the Food Lovers' Village Mysteries.

Readers, it's a thrill to hear from you. Drop me a line at Leslie@LeslieBudewitz.com, connect with me on Facebook at LeslieBudewitzAuthor, or join my seasonal mailing list for book news and more. (Sign up on my website, www.LeslieBudewitz.com.) Reader reviews and recommendations are a big boost to authors; if you've enjoyed my books, please tell your friends. A book is but marks on paper until you read those pages and make the story yours.

Thank you.

About the Author

Leslie Budewitz is passionate about food, great mysteries, and her native Montana, the setting for her national-bestselling Food Lovers' Village Mysteries. She also writes the Spice Shop Mysteries, set in Seattle's Pike Place Market. As Alicia Beckman, she's the author of stand-alone suspense, beginning with *Bitterroot Lake* (2021). She's the proud owner of three Agatha Awards, for Best Nonfiction (2011), Best First Novel (2013), and Best Short Story (2018), and has won or been nominated for Derringer, Anthony, and Macavity awards. Also a practicing lawyer, Leslie is a board member of Mystery Writers of America and is a past president of Sisters in Crime.

Leslie loves to cook, eat, hike, travel, garden, and paint—not necessarily in that order. She lives in northwest Montana with her husband, Don Beans, a doctor of natural medicine and musician, and their cat, an avid bird-watcher.

Visit her online at www.LeslieBudewitz.com, where you can find maps of the village and surrounding area, recipes, and more.

www.ingramcontent.com/pod-product-compliance
Lightning Source LLC
Chambersburg PA
CBHW030632190726
48286CB00008B/2492